# SUPERNAL DAWN

*Transcendent Powers*
*Book One*

## J. A. Giunta
## &
## Sharon Skinner

Brick Cave Media
brickcavebooks.com
2018

Cover Illustration by Kyna Tek  www.kyteki.com
Interior Illustrations by Kyna Tek  www.kyteki.com

Brick Cave Media
brickcavebooks.com
2018

Also by J.A. Giunta
Available from brickcavebooks.com

The Ascension Trilogy:
    The Last Incarnation
    The Mists of Faeron
    Out of the Dark

Kinights of Virtue: The Guardians, Keepers of the Magic

Summoned: Caught by the Tale


Also by Sharon Skinner
Available from brickcavebooks.com

The Healer's Trilogy:
    The Healer's Legacy
    The Matriarch's Devise
    The Exile's Gift (Forthcoming)

The Nelig Stones

Mirabella and the Faded Phantom

Collars & Curses

In Case You Didn't Hear Me the First Time

# SUPERNAL DAWN

*Transcendent Powers*
*Book One*

J. A. Giunta
&
Sharon Skinner

Brick Cave Media
brickcavebooks.com

# One
Wed, Aug 24, 4:10pm

### - Lee -

It was the quiet that woke him.

The vibrations had stopped and left behind a lonely stillness. Everyday sounds filled the world, but it was just the clamor and shake of noise.

They had called it the Rumbling, though to Lee it had been more of a hum, a soothing inner melody, like a lullaby for his entire being. While people online had celebrated the existence of alien life, he'd become lost in the song of its embrace. It had made them want to drink, scream to the skies and dance together.

It had only made him want to sleep.

He rubbed his eyes and yawned, grabbed his phone off the nightstand, checked the time and groaned. He'd missed a day of school. He didn't know which was more annoying, that he'd been asleep for 23 hours or that no one had even bothered to try to wake him.

Lee sat up and stretched, yawned again. Aside from the stabs of hunger, he felt pretty good, better than he had in a long time. But he also felt disconnected, as if sensing the world from outside his body. It was like the hair of his arm standing on end in response to a static charge, but this response was in his brain, a fuzzy tingle from nape to forehead.

He wasn't sure how or why, for better or worse, but wondered if the Rumbling had somehow changed him. For all he knew, it'd changed everyone. It made sense, in a way. Why else would they have left technology on the planet, if not to guide or shape the civilization that came across and understood it?

Either that, or he was losing his mind.

The first Pillar had been discovered a hundred and twenty-eight days ago, on April 18th at Challenger Deep, the lowest point of the Mariana Trench. Only a foot of its top had stuck out from the ocean floor, and even though it was the length of a soccer field across, at that depth and shrouded in sediment, it had been easy to overlook. Once the Remotely Operated Vehicle had touched a symbol on the exposed side, the entire Pillar had lit up like a computer display, pulled free and rose up to its full height.

A thousand meters long, like smooth black glass, its top and bottom had remained clear, but the cylinder was covered with strange symbols, familiar basic shapes and dots all in rows. 1,618 of them, arranged like sentences or mathematic formulas, there was one for every Pillar that drove upward through the earth at the same exact time. Each one identical in every way and equidistant to one another, they covered the entire planet.

Governments had tried and failed to control them, to limit access, but there were too many to secure in such a short time. Within hours, pictures had appeared online of the Pillars and every one of their markings. It was impossible to hide, and despite misguided efforts at disinformation, countries relented one by one to work together at solving the puzzle.

In the end, after months of unparalleled cooperation, of discovery and realization, it was determined that the alien language was based on the mathematics of nature. The culmination of each row formed a pattern, an answer to a simple question: Are you ready? Once scientists had entered mankind's reply, the Pillars activated in unison, and the Rumbling began.

That was nearly twenty-seven hours ago.

When the resulting sounds and vibrations had first emanated from the Pillars, many across the globe thought it would never stop. Some had even hoped that it wouldn't. It had been like a drug, the happy warmth that came from knowing humanity was no longer alone. Lee wondered if he would've just kept on sleeping if it hadn't.

He pulled himself out of bed, changed clothes and headed for the bathroom to wash up. He sensed someone downstairs, like the way it felt when a person looked over a shoulder and got too close. It was a palpable presence, again like a static charge pressing against the edge of his mind. At this time of day, his mother would be working at the spice shop with aunts Gwen and Brianna.

*It's probably Ember,* he thought. *Bet I can convince her to take me to Finley's for a burger.*

He leaned forward on the sink and jerked back at the creaks of protest. The whole thing had sounded like it might break free of the wall. He chalked it up to the house being centuries old. It was a thing of pride with his relatives that they were one of the founding families to settle Sungrove, but he couldn't count how many times he'd wished they could just buy a new house.

Then it was the wiring acting up again. Either that or his electric toothbrush had finally died. No matter how much he pushed the button, it wouldn't turn on. A last push in frustration, and the whole thing snapped in half. He did his best to use just the brush half between two fingers, ignored the rest dangling from the break, but he squeezed way too much toothpaste onto the bristles.

He sighed and left it all in the sink.

The deodorant can broke next, the button smashed into place. It wouldn't stop spraying. He tried to fix it, but the bathroom quickly filled with the overwhelming aerosol fumes of mountain spring. He stuffed the can into a towel and buried it in the garbage.

He ran a brush through his hair and shrugged at the mirror. *Good enough.*

Once he was downstairs, he found his sister in the kitchen and came up short. The tingle became focused, like he'd gotten too close. It wasn't just that he could see she was agitated, the furrowed brows, fingers tapping against the counter, staring ahead at nothing in a deep concern. He could feel it. The increased heartrate and blood flow, the emotion coming off her, all felt like it was his own. It was strong. She was strong.

He blinked. *What the hell's wrong with me?*

Ember looked up, and agitation became annoyance.

"Hey," he said and cleared his throat, headed for the refrigerator for a soda. "What's for dinner? I'm starving."

She made a snarky comment but then nearly gagged.

"What's up with the cologne bath?"

Lee popped open a can of soda. The sensations were still there, nagging at his mind and trying to supersede his own, but talking made it easier to pull his attention away from the barrage. He thought to shoot back a snide remark but remembered he wanted something from her.

"Deodorant malfunction," he explained instead, with pursed lips and a bashful smile. "When's mom coming home?"

"How should I know," she said and crossed her arms,

gave her best big sister know-it-all look. "By the way, you might want to check voicemail." She nodded at the home phone. "School called. They wanted to know where you were. Not like you to skip so early in the year."

*Nervous?* he thought when the sensations struck. He'd been about to accuse her of not waking him when she left but saw the rumpled clothes from yesterday. He realized she hadn't gone to school either. *Is that why she's nervous?*

"I overslept," he said and nodded at her clothes. "What's your excuse?" He thought but didn't add, *Like you ever have a shortage of them.*

"Whatever."

She rolled her eyes and looked away. Her hair was a tangled mess, a serious case of bed-head. She tried to comb through it with her fingers.

Lee's stomach growled.

"Wonder why mom didn't wake us," he said and took in a deep breath then slowly let it out. He wanted to steer the conversation away from himself and put them on the same side.

"I don't know," she said offhandedly. "I'm not a mind reader." He nearly sighed when it didn't work, but then she added, "Maybe she thought we were sick."

"Maybe we were," he agreed and hoped it was enough. "Want to go grab a burger? You like Finley's, right?"

Ember struggled with a stubborn knot in her hair. "You just want to see Emma."

Emma was attractive enough, and he'd even thought he might like her, until she asked him for help with her computer science homework. He'd flat out told her no and wanted nothing else to do with her. Lee was done with girls who were only interested in what he could do for them.

"Like I have her schedule memorized or something," he said instead of giving away how he really felt about her. "Seriously, I'm hungry and there's nothing to eat here."

"There's plenty," she said and laughed, waved her arm

at the cupboards. One of them had a handle broken off. He would've pointed it out but didn't want to distract her. Besides, he'd probably get blamed for it, like everything else in the house. "You just have to make it."

"Well, that's not going to happen." Her emotions were all over the place. He needed a different approach. "Come on, first week of school. You just got mom's old car, and you're telling me you don't want to use it?"

"Maybe," she said with the irritating rise in tone that signified sarcasm, "I just don't want to be carpooling your ass over to see your girlfriend."

Lee ignored the jab. Emma was no more a girlfriend than Jen was, and he'd been friends with Jen ever since she'd moved in next door in the first grade.

"Call one of your friends," he suggested, tried putting the focus on his sister, "Allison or Sarah. Have them meet us there. I just want to eat."

Ember scratched at her scalp.

"Fine," she said and glanced over at the empty coffee pot in the sink. "I need caffeine, anyway."

Normally, Lee would've made a comment about her being too lazy to make it, but he'd put all that aside if it meant getting some decent food.

"I assume Jen's coming?" she asked.

"I haven't talked to her yet," Lee said and realized he hadn't checked mail or messages. He wondered how many Jen had left him. "But, probably."

"Give me a minute. I need to get dressed."

While she went upstairs to change, Lee tried to get a handle on what was happening to him. He leaned against the counter, closed his eyes and stopped fighting down these sensations invading his own, gave up holding back out of fear of what it could mean. There was a history of mental illness in his family. If he was losing his mind, he wouldn't be the first.

He knew exactly where Ember was. More than being

able to follow her every footstep or opening drawers by hearing alone, he could sense what she was doing. There was a vague outline of her body in his mind, as if she were encompassed by a million gnats flitting about her frame. The bulk buzzed and thrummed around her, but some went inside. It was from those that he felt the waves of emotion and physical activity threatening to overrun his own.

*So which is more likely,* he opened his eyes and considered, *that I've been changed by alien technology, or I'm going crazy like Aunt Kayley?*

His aunt had died in a psychiatric hospital three years earlier. Like him, she'd had no previous signs of a condition, but the sudden onset of psychosis and swift decline of her mental health seemed all too familiar.

He felt before he heard Ember coming downstairs.

"I don't know what happened in that bathroom," she said and fished keys from her purse, "but I won't be the one cleaning it."

Lee nodded. He was still coming to grips with the notion of whatever extrasensory ability had come over him. He could've just been imagining it.

*Maybe I am sick,* he thought. *I did sleep for a day.* He put the back of a hand to his forehead. *Kind of warm. Could be a fever.*

He followed Ember to the door leading out to the garage and was overcome by another set of sensations.

"Jen's here," he said more to himself than his sister.

He didn't know for sure it was her, but it was a logical conclusion. When the garage door lifted, he was both unsurprised and a little afraid to see her sitting against the wall. She looked up from her phone.

"Finally," Jen said. There were streaks of light blue in her blonde hair, a close match to her eyes. "Saw your light on. Figured you'd be coming out soon." She got up and dusted off her jeans. "Why'd you ditch without telling me? I would've stayed home too."

Ember said something under her breath and went to the driver side of the car.

"It wasn't on purpose," Lee said and opened the back passenger door. "We're going to Finley's. Want to come?"

"I could eat." Jen cocked her head to one side. "You do look a little pale." She pushed past him to get in. "Are you okay now?"

"Not really."

Jen spent most of the ride tapping away at her phone and talking to him about friends at school. Lee was in a bit of a daze but tried to follow along. Every car that went by was another assault on his senses, a brief barrage in passing that made it difficult to think. He tried to push it all from his mind, focus on the radio, but Ember kept changing the station.

In the end, she turned it off.

"Hey, Jen," Ember said, and her voice trailed off into the haze of people on the road and on the sidewalks.

He may have said something, tried to join in on the conversation, but it was like that part of his brain was disconnected from the rest. It only got worse when they pulled into the parking lot at Finley's.

There were two police cars with lights flashing, four officers on one side of a girl and a crowd of fourteen people on the other. Lee blinked and shook his head, could barely climb out from the car without losing his balance in the brewing storm of emotion.

"Careful with the door," Ember said, but her slight anger was quickly lost in the flow washing over him.

*What,* he thought and looked back to the door, *did I slam it or something?*

"Sorry," was all he could manage.

His attention was drawn to the girl at the center, at her rising panic and lonely fear, at the betrayal of her own body. From fingertips to elbow, her arms pulsed with a soft glow, as if sunlight shone through her skin and lit up her veins a dark crimson. Heat radiated off her, warped the air and kept the crowd back.

Lee recognized most of them from school, felt their outrage and unease. They were afraid for themselves, but that fear was momentarily overcome by concern for the girl. Some had their phones out and were recording. Two officers had tasers drawn, pointed at the girl who'd broken down into tears. Lee realized who it was, but Ember was already crossing the lot toward them.

"Is that Allison?" Jen asked.

There were scorch marks on the building, sidewalk and pavement. They formed a path that led to Allie. She grew more frantic as police continued to yell at her, to calm down, to keep her hands up, to stay still, not to move, to get down on her knees. Allie wiped away tears, which drew more shouting because she'd lowered her hands. She didn't know what to do, how to follow their mixed commands.

Wisps of smoke began to rise up from the pavement at her feet.

Lee and Jen followed, as Ember pushed through the crowd to reach her friend. An officer with his taser drawn spoke nervously into a radio at his shoulder, called for more backup. A second was pushing the crowd back, trying to keep everyone clear of Allie. The police were afraid, but the others didn't share the sentiment. Allie was their friend. In their eyes, something was happening to her, not the other way around.

"Allie!" Ember shouted and reached out a hand.

Lee didn't know why his sister thought she could be of any help in this situation, but he understood the need to comfort a friend who so desperately needed it.

Allie was visibly shaken, stared down at her hands, tear-strewn face framed by long dark curls. She'd been changed, like Lee, and felt helpless to stop it. When she caught sight of Ember, she ran for her friend. Their hands touched briefly, before the nearest officer shoved Ember back.

"Don't touch her!" he yelled and backed away from Allie with a hand fumbling for his gun.

Ember went down hard, taking two others with her who'd tried to catch her.

The glow had faded from Allie's hands. She looked at them, confused, then back to Ember with concern.

Lee stormed forward and shouted at the cop.

"Hey! That's my sister!"

The officer whirled around and glared at him, hand on his gun.

"Stay back," he warned, as if Lee was a genuine danger.

As Lee focused his sense on the four officers, he began to understand. They weren't afraid for the safety of those gathered. They only cared about themselves and protecting one another, from Allie and the crowd.

A mote of blue light appeared above of the man's head. Lee saw it and backed away in surprise. The officer mistook the reaction as justified fear and turned his attention back to the crowd.

The two officers tased Allie. She cried out in pain but otherwise seemed unaffected by the shocks. The third then tackled her like she was a physical threat, as if she were a fully grown man and not a teenage girl. He landed atop her, forced her onto her stomach and drove a knee into her back.

The two dropped their tasers and were on her in seconds. One grabbed her wrists and yanked them back, while the other grabbed her ankles. There was a crackle as he twisted one arm from its socket. She gasped, and people in the crowd started yelling. The officer ignored them and clasped handcuffs on her tight.

Allie pleaded with them to stop, said she couldn't breathe and tried to move beneath the three men to draw in air. The officer on her back drove his knee down even harder and put both hands around her neck.

*They're going to kill her,* Lee thought.

"What the hell!" a guy yelled and came toward them.

It was Rick, someone who used to be good friends with Lee when they were younger. The only cop still standing finally drew his gun and pointed it in Rick's face. His finger was on the trigger, not on the side like it should've been.

"Back off!" he shouted.

Rick flinched, looked scared, but didn't budge.

"Or what, you'll shoot me?"

The officer looked at the crowd, at all the phones recording him. He holstered his gun, took the mace from his belt and sprayed Rick without a warning. He ignored Rick's screams, grabbed him by the neck and left arm, tripped him and drove him down toward the pavement. Rick hit face first and lay still. Blood began to pool around his head, as the officer roughly cuffed him.

Another mote of blue light appeared over Rick. It faded quickly, as if it had entered his body. Others began to flash in and out of existence over the crowd. No one else seemed to notice it. They were preoccupied with Allie, who was being dragged unconscious toward a vehicle.

Ember had gotten to her feet. She had a few scrapes and the start of a nasty bruise on her elbow. She seemed otherwise unhurt but was still in shock at what just happened. She watched helpless as her friend was taken away.

An ambulance and two more police cars arrived. Once Allie and Rick were secured, officers began pushing everyone further back. One confiscated a phone, forcibly, which dispersed the crowd faster than any yelling. They threatened to arrest anyone who didn't leave. One's eyes fell pointedly on Lee and Jen.

Ember turned and joined them. The three went back toward the car, looking on as even more police arrived.

*What the hell just happened?*

Lee's mind was racing. It was like something out of a

movie or a comic book. Allie's hands had glowed, like she'd caused all those scorch marks. It had to be related to the Pillars and the Rumbling.

*I'm not going crazy,* he thought and looked back at the restaurant, *but I almost wish I was.*

Police were setting up yellow tape and making people leave. Had something happened inside too? Either way, they'd have to find somewhere else to eat.

# - Ember -

Ember trudged into the kitchen, feeling like crap. She curled her toes at the greasy feel of the tile on her bare feet. She opened the refrigerator, stared inside, then closed it again. The door slammed shut so hard the entire fridge shuddered like it had been hit by a linebacker. If she hadn't known better, she'd have said she was hungover, but it wasn't like she'd been out partying the night before. In fact, after that weird rumbling started, she just couldn't get her party vibe in gear. She stared at the clock for half a minute before the time actually penetrated her foggy brain. After 4:00 pm. She really had slept like the dead.

She opened a cupboard, stared inside, then closed it again with a loud bang and the metal handle came off in her hand. She clearly needed caffeine.

She tossed the handle into the trash and reached for the coffee pot. The sludge in the bottom of the carafe was cold. A layer of oily scum floated on top of the dark liquid that had once been coffee. She set the carafe down in the sink and heard an ugly cracking sound. Coffee syrup leaked out of the bottom of the pot.

Lee clattered into the room. "What's for dinner? I'm starving."

"Like that's anything new." She sniffed, and her hand went to her face. "Ugh. What's up with the cologne bath? You trying to cover up some new bad habit?"

"You should know. When's mom coming home?"

"When did it become my job to keep track of Mom?" She leaned back against the center Island and crossed her arms, in irritation. "By the way, you might want to erase the answering machine messages," she suggested. "School called. Skipping pretty early in the year. What's up with that?"

"I overslept. What's your excuse?" he nodded at her rumpled t-shirt and sleeping shorts. "Like you ever have a

13

shortage."

"Whatev." Her scalp itched. She tried to comb her fingers through her snarled hair.

"Why didn't Mom wake us up?"

"I don't know. Not like I'm a mind reader. Maybe she thought we were sick."

"Maybe. How about a run to Finley's?"

"Why? You have a date with Emma?" She would have made duck lips at him, but she was too tired to bother revving him up.

"Like I have her schedule memorized. I'm just hungry, and there's nothing to eat here."

His wheedling grated on her already raw nerves. She so wasn't in the mood for it. "There's plenty to eat here. You just have to make it." She waved at the cupboards.

"Yeah, no. C'mon, you just got mom's old car. Aren't you dying to use it?"

Ember snorted. She wanted to tell him that the car wasn't officially hers; it was more a communal car, but that would lead to questions about their extended family. Questions she couldn't answer. Just thinking about it made her mark flare and caused her to twitch. "Maybe, I just don't want to be chauffeuring your ass over to see your girlfriend."

"Come on. Have one of your friends meet us there. Allison or Somebody. I really need food."

She stared over at the broken carafe still leaking coffee into the sink. "Fine. I need coffee, anyway. I'm guessing Jen's going to be tagging along?"

"Probably."

She shrugged. "I gotta get dressed first."

***

She slipped into her cleanest pair of black jeans and laced up her boots. For some reason she felt the need for the security of ass-kickable footwear. When she strode back into the kitchen to grab her keys, Lee gave her the eyeball.

"You're not going to change your shirt?"

She looked down at herself and he laughed. "Man, you really are tired." He swung open the door and headed out. Jen was waiting for them outside the garage, face glued to her phone, as usual.

"Great. Now, I look like an Uber driver. I should start charging mileage." Ember adjusted the mirror as Lee and Jen hopped into the back seat.

The Lexus was old in years, almost as old as Lee, but mom had kept it pristine. Now, it smelled like the deodorizing cleaner Ember had used to try and get the spilled latte out of the carpet.

She glanced at them in the rearview mirror. Jen still had her head down, absorbed by her phone. Lee just looked back at Ember and shrugged.

She pressed the voice activation button on her phone to call Allison and felt the plastic crack. Damn! She must have dropped her crappy phone one too many times. She tossed it onto the seat and turned on the radio.

"Nice static." Lee rolled his eyes at her.

She turned off the radio. "Hey, Jen. Do me a favor and call Allie."

"Can't." Jen kept playing her stupid game. "Don't have her number."

"Oh yeah. I forgot. She had to get a new phone plan when her parents split and her dad's new girlfriend kept harassing them." Ember turned her attention to the road.

"Not sure trying to communicate with them counts as harassment," Lee said.

"This is me, rolling my eyes." Ember pulled into the crowded parking lot beside Finley's. "Must be the night for bad burgers. Place looks extra busy."

"Looks like cops." Lee opened the door and got out, slamming it shut behind him. Even Jen looked up from her phone at the sudden noise.

"Watch the door," Ember groused. "Last thing I need is a lecture from Mom on taking care of things."

"It was an accident." He held up his hands.

Ember shot him a dirty look and shut her own door gently, careful not to break anything.

"Isn't that Allison?" Jen asked as they crossed the parking lot.

"Where?" Ember scanned the crowd of people holding up cell phones, apparently recording something near the entrance to the burger joint.

"Over there," Jen pointed. "In the middle of the bunch of cops."

That stopped her in her tracks. "What the hell?" Allie stood on the sidewalk, sobbing. Four uniformed officers surrounded her, tasers at the ready. They looked twitchy. One had his hand on the gun at his hip. The front of Finley's looked like there'd been a fire. Scorch marks streaked the sidewalk and parking lot. In addition to the normal stench of frying meat, there was a scent of ozone in the air. And singed hair. Allie's hair. It looked like they had already tased her. *Why would they do that?* Ember wondered, confusion and anger battling to overcome her.

The cops were yelling, shouting about hands, giving Allie commands. Why were they yelling at her?

Ember shoved her way forward as Allie wiped at her eyes. The cops all started yelling at her over each other. Ember only caught a few of the words. "Hands!" "On your knees." "Subject not complying." One of the cops was talking into his shoulder radio.

Allie stared at her hands in confusion. Tears wended their way down her face to drop from her chin. Sunlight seemed to gather around her fingertips.

The weird light made Ember blink. Why were all these cops hurting Allison? They needed to stop! There wasn't time to think, she just suddenly knew she had to try to help her friend. "Allie!" Ember called and barreled through the crowd. She managed to slip past the cops and reach out to Allie before anyone could stop her.

Allie looked up and reached for Ember's hand. Their fingers touched and a shock zapped through Ember. She jerked back her hand and felt like crap at the look of hurt on Allie's face.

"Don't touch her," yelled one of the cops. He shoved her away from Allie before she could apologize to her. Ember fell back into the crowd and went down hard, her knee slamming into the pavement with a resounding smack.

Ember pushed herself up off the pavement. Lee was shouting at someone.

"Lee. Don't!" Despite the way they bickered, Lee had hit sibling protection mode on more than one occasion. Normally, Ember would have let him help her out, and given him crap about it later. But cops. Lee could get hurt taking on the cops.

She rubbed at her knee in surprise. She'd expected it to be totally screwed after that fall, scraped and bruised at the very least. Before she could really examine it, tasers zapped, and Allie screamed. Gut churning, Ember tried to push through the crowd again.

"Don't." Jen grabbed for her arm. "I don't know what's going on, but you can't help her now."

Rick Grainger came barreling across the lot, yelling for them to stop. One of the cops pulled his gun, pointing it at Rick's face. Rick pulled up short. An officer stepped up behind him, shoved him to the ground, pulled his hands behind his back and cuffed him. Ember stared at the chaos, stunned, heart pounding.

Lights flared. People screamed. Sirens blared as more cops arrived, along with an ambulance.

The cops cuffed Allie and dragged her to one of the police cars and shoved her into the back seat. Rick was taken to a separate car. Then the cops started grabbing cell phones and yelling at people to leave.

Jen stuck her cell phone into the back pocket of her jeans and backed away, trying to pull Ember with her. "We need to get out of here."

# Two
Wed, Aug 24, 5:23pm

### - Lee -

They got in the car and drove to Hotspot, a pizza place on Melody and Fifth known for its free Wi-Fi. It was a popular hangout for people from Middleton High. Ember borrowed Lee's phone, while Jen was typing away at hers.

"It's not just here," Jen said, or something to that effect. It was hard enough to focus on where they were going without all the extrasensory information clamoring for his attention. She kept reading and then typing more with both thumbs. "It's happening everywhere, all over the world."

Lee only nodded.

He wanted to know what was happening to him. He wanted to know what had happened to Allison. Not just with the police, but what had made her skin glow like that? How did she cause those scorch marks? It had to be from the Pillars. The Rumbling had only just ended 73 minutes ago. It couldn't have been a coincidence.

More unnerving than seeing that effect in someone else, he thought about the blue bits of light, like tiny fireflies in the air. They were alive, smaller parts of a greater whole and moved with purpose. They didn't seem to be a part of what had happened to Allison, and he had a sinking feeling he knew where they'd come from. Like the swarm of miniscule insects he sensed in his mind, outlining bodies outside his vision...

They were him.

Ember hung up and called someone else, but Lee was too distracted to listen in.

"Come on," Jen said and prodded him with an elbow, her eyes still on her phone. "Aren't you the least bit excited? It's like a comic book come to life! People are getting superpowers!"

Lee shook his head. "Sure, what isn't great about that? I'm sure Allison is loving it."

Jen's enthusiasm waned at that.

"Everyone thinks it's the Pillars," she said. "That the Rumbling somehow changed people. Not a big surprise, really." She looked away from her phone long enough to gesture with her hands. "I mean, we find this alien artifact buried in the ocean and think, 'Hey! Let's turn it on! What could go wrong?'"

Ember hung up as they pulled into the parking lot. It was busy but not overcrowded. She handed him his phone back.

He was already dealing with the rush of sensations from the forty-seven people eating and working inside, their individual heartbeats, the flow of blood and other fluids and the spark of every neuron that fueled their emotions. The longer he was exposed to them, or more accurately, the longer they were exposed to him, the more he knew about their health and state of mind.

*I'll never be the same,* he thought, and it scared him a little. A small part of him wished he was like Allison instead.

"Everything's about to change," Lee said to himself, quiet enough that he didn't think anyone else had heard.

"Some things don't," Ember said.

She was trying to comfort him, despite being scared herself, but Lee felt beyond the help of words. He didn't know what would help. It was only a matter of time before police came to take him the same way they had taken Allison.

The sense of envy and spite directed toward him caught his attention. Lee looked up and recognized other sophomores through the big glass windows, seated in large groups and laughing like nothing was wrong. He locked eyes with one and inwardly groaned.

Derek had made a point of picking on Lee whenever he could, no matter how much Lee tried to ignore him. Derek ran for the front doors as they got close, laughed and waved through the glass before walking back to his seat.

"He seriously needs to get laid," Jen said, though she never seemed to take her eyes from her phone.

"What's with him?" Ember asked.

Lee shrugged. "A lack of oxygen at birth?"

He was first to the door, took hold of the handle and pulled. There was a loud clank, and two metal pieces fell to the ground. It didn't help that his mind was in a haze from all the sensory input crowding in. He fought past it and managed to focus on the bits of metal.

*What the hell just happened?*

His thoughts matched Ember's expression. She put a hand to his arm, and he jerked away at the sudden silence. For the briefest of moments, he felt like he had when the Rumbling had ended.

Lee blinked and pieced it all together, just as Derek's eyes went wide with realization. The knowing look he gave Lee seemed to say, *You're one of them.*

The ass had locked the doors, and Lee just tore them open. He could feel Derek's resentment turn to panic. Lee quickly slid the metal pieces aside with his foot before anyone could see.

It felt like everyone was staring, as they walked to an empty table. They weren't, though. It was just the sense of each one of them flooding his mind, threatening to drown out any thoughts of his own. As usual, everyone else was wrapped up in their little worlds, talking and laughing together like nothing and no one else mattered, heads buried in social media. Only Derek seemed to follow them with his eyes.

Lee and Jen sat down, while Ember continued on to the counter to place an order.

"You should see some of these videos," Jen said from across the booth. "There's people flying, crushing rocks with their bare hands, blowing things up with their eyes. It's crazy!"

She shook her head and no longer looked as excited as she had in the car.

Lee knew why, could feel it himself.

"Not everyone can control it," he said. "Like Allison."

Jen nodded. "Some people are getting hurt. Police are trying to stop them, but they're just making it worse." The low sounds of gunfire and screaming came from her phone. She said, "They're like bulletproof or something."

Lee was surprised at that. "Who?"

"The Supers," she replied, "Like Allison. Bullets just bounce off them. This one ricocheted off a guy and hit a little girl."

She showed him the phone, but Lee didn't want to see it. Images like that never leave. He kept glancing over at Derek, who tried to look anywhere but back at him. The sense of panic in him had changed to something else, a quiet fear and a smug sense of satisfaction? Lee couldn't be sure. The sensations were still too new, and he only had his own experiences to compare with.

Ember came back with drinks, and Jen was first to make room for her. The video went quiet, and Jen frowned down at her phone.

"Everyone's talking about it," Ember said. "They all think Allison is a freak, or I don't even know. Tina's over there wishing for laser eyes."

Jen growled in frustration. "They took it down!"

Lee asked Ember, "Any idea if she's okay? They were pretty rough with her. I thought for sure they were going to kill her."

"I don't think they can," Jen said. "Ugh. They're all down now! What the hell? It's like they were never even there. The videos are just gone!"

"I wasn't able to get a hold of anybody," Ember said.

Jen said, "Rick was taken to the hospital. He's in critical condition. No word at all on Allison."

Lee sensed him arrive in the parking lot, the bottled fear and determination. He knew who he was there for the moment the bell jingled over the door.

A police officer entered. Middle-aged, in good shape but with an odd rhythm to his heart, he took a moment to scan the room and headed straight for their table. Lee looked over at Derek, certain it was him who'd called.

"What's up?" Ember asked.

Lee let out a deep breath. He wanted to tell her, but he couldn't, like saying it out loud might make it true. He didn't have powers the way Allison did, but something in him had changed. He could feel it from the moment he'd woken.

This time, everyone actually did stop what they were doing and stared. All their eyes fell upon him, and the not-so hushed whispers began.

"Lee Macconal?" the officer asked, forced confidence underlined with fear.

Jen touched a foot to Lee's. She knew.

*Of course, she knows,* he almost laughed. *Nothing gets past Jen.*

Her nod told him she was recording.

Ember had opened her napkin, folded it in half but still had the fork in her hand.

"What do you want with my brother?" she asked, both suspicious and protective. "Is this about Finley's? Do you know if Allison, the girl in the parking lot, is she okay?"

"We received a complaint about the destruction of private property," he said and nodded to the glass doors.

Lee said, "Sorry. It wasn't on purpose." He wanted to diffuse the situation but knew it was too late. The officer didn't care about the door. "We can pay to replace the lock."

"I'm going to need you to come with me," he said, "down to the station. We have some questions we need you to answer."

Jen risked angling her phone directly at him.

"Not without a parent you don't," she said. "He's a minor. Are you arresting him? Do you have a warrant?"

Ember's grip on the fork tightened. Lee saw it bend, and his heart sank.

*She's one, too.*

He kicked her under the table. When she looked back at him in shock, he slowly shook his head. If she wasn't careful, they'd both be going to jail.

"I don't need a warrant, young lady," the officer said. His fear was building to something more, as if readying his body for an action he didn't want to take. To Lee, he added, "Your mother is on her way to the station. She'll meet you there."

Ember hid the fork in her napkin but not before the officer noticed. She slipped out from the table.

"You're not taking him anywhere without me."

The officer swallowed hard. Lee hadn't noticed until then, but the man's holster was unsnapped. He hadn't taken his hand off his gun the whole time.

"Maybe that's for the best. Let's go."

Lee slipped out from the table and started walking to the door. The officer waited for Ember. She held out her keys to Jen.

"Can you take the car home?" she asked.

Jen nodded and reached for them, still recording the three leave.

"And," Ember called back, "see if you can get hold of my mom." She glared at the officer. "Just in case."

It was quiet as they left and stepped out into the parking lot. Lee's stomach felt anxious the entire way to the police car.

The officer opened a back door for them. Lee and Ember got inside. Lee couldn't help but notice there were no handles on the door to get back out. A metal grate separated the back and front seats. At that moment, he felt like a criminal. It didn't matter he hadn't done anything.

He was still going to jail.

# - Ember -

They got to the car and she froze. Panic struck her brain as she tried to process what had just happened. Her fingers still tingled with the shock of touching Allie. They were taking her away. "Wait. Where are they taking her?"

"Not the time or the place." Jen jerked her chin in the direction of the cops, grabbed her keys and shoved them at Lee. "You drive. We need to figure out what's up." She shoved Ember into the backseat and climbed in next to Lee.

"Lee, I need your phone." Ember reached her hand over the back of the seat.

"What's wrong with yours?" He put the car in reverse and backed out of the drive real slow, the way Great Gran Britta used to drive.

"Broke." She waggled her useless piece of crap phone in his face.

He pulled out his cell, unlocked it by placing his thumb on the print reader, and handed it over, as if he thought it was made of fine china, like one of Aunt Brianna's antique teacups.

She eyed it for a sec, then took it from him, treating it just as gently. It wouldn't do to wreck one more thing, and she was feeling the same way Lee was acting, like a gorilla handling fine crystal. She tried to call Allie, but the call went straight to voicemail, and after what had happened, she wasn't sure she should leave a message. "Where are we headed?" she asked.

"Hotspot. I'm freaked, but I'm still hungry." Lee signaled a lane change and steered the car, using just the tips of his fingers, like he thought it was going to break under his grip.

She tried to call their mom, but no answer there either, and she had no idea what to tell her, except that they were out grabbing food. What else was there to say?

She tried to search the web for the incident at Finley's,

but Jen was faster. She had always been a texting fiend, but now her thumbs moved like lightning over the buttons. She started calling out stuff that was happening. "Hey, listen to this, people are doing all sorts of crazy shit. The stuff at Finley's? That was nothing compared to what's been going on all over town." She kept typing and watching. Lee leaned closer to see what she was so focused on.

"Watch the road," Ember ordered as someone honked at them.

By the time they reached Hotspot, Jen'd filled them in. Super powers, cops out in force, people being arrested. Like Allie. Ember was still trying to wrap her brain around it all as Lee slipped the car into an open spot and got out, her mind spiraling around everything that had happened.

He opened the back door and looked at her, one eyebrow quirked up. "What?" She handed him his phone as she got out.

He just shook his head. "Everything's about to change."

"Some things don't," she told him, watching Derek wave at Lee, then run over to do something with the doors before giving them one of his dumbass smiles. "What's with your biggest fan?"

Jen didn't even look up from her phone as they headed for the front door.

Lee took hold of the door and pulled. Pieces of metal fell to the ground with a loud clang.

Ember started. "What was that about?" She put her hand on his arm, but he shrugged it off and let out his breath, trying to slide the metal bits aside with his foot, like nothing had happened. He mumbled something about the door being stuck and led the way to an empty booth.

She let it go and went up to the counter to order. "Medium veggie and one extra-large carnivore happy meal." She jerked her thumb in Lee's direction.

"So, the usual." Tina gave Ember a half smile. "You want three root beers, too?"

27

"Yes, thanks. Make mine—"

"Light ice," she finished over her shoulder, already filling the cups." She put the drinks on the counter and rang up the total. "You seen the craziness going on out there?" she asked as she took Ember's debit card and slid it through the machine. "And that Allison girl? What a freak. Zapping things and causing fires." Tina handed back her card. "Though, it would be nice to be able to shoot lasers out of my eyes. What I'd do to that cheating jerk, Todd. Right?" She opened her eyes really wide and bugged them out at Ember.

"Allison is not a freak," Ember said, yanking her card out of Tina's hand.

Tina narrowed her eyes at her. "Pizza will be out in a few."

Ember headed over to the booth with their drinks. Derek's pig-like eyes watched her the whole time. "He's acting creepier than usual." She set the sodas down onto the table and slid in beside Jen.

"It's all over the web. Everyone's talking about it." Ember glanced over at Tina. "They all think Allison is either a freak or...don't even know. Cripes. Tina over there is wishing she could shoot lasers from her eyes." She stuck a straw in her drink and sucked up a mouthful of root beer. It was kind of flat, but she didn't care. The sugar tasted so good, she almost finished half the glass in one go. She hadn't realized how thirsty she was.

"Grrrrrr." Jen tapped at her phone wildly. "Where'd it all go? All the video. It's gone."

Lee blinked. He seemed twitchy, nervous. "Any idea how Allison's doing?"

Jen kept tapping at her phone. "I can't find any of the footage, at all. They're all down! What the hell? Now, it's like they were never even there. The videos are just gone."

Ember shook her head. "Her phone went straight to voicemail, and I couldn't get hold of...anybody else. And now that I'm sans phone..."

The front door opened, a cop sauntered in, scanned the room, and made a beeline for their table. Lee threw Derek a dirty look and got a classic idiot grin and the finger in return.

"What's up?" She stirred her root beer around with her straw.

Lee just huffed out his breath, then froze when the cop addressed him by name.

She took the flatware out of the rolled napkin and slipped her fingers around the handle of the fork. "What do you want with my brother? Is this about Finley's? Do you know if Alli—the girl in the parking lot—is she okay?"

"Actually," the cop said, taking a half step back and placing his hand on the butt of his handgun, "this is about destruction of private property." He jerked his head toward the door. "A complaint was called in."

The people at the next table stared at them, apparently surprised by the officer's defensive posture.

Lee looked pained. "Sorry. It was an accident. We can pay to fix it."

The officer backed up another step. "I'm going to need you to come down to the station. We have some questions that need answering."

Jen looked up from her phone, nonchalantly tilting it so the camera lens was pointing up at the officer. "Not without a parent. Are you arresting him? Do you have a warrant?"

Lee kicked Ember under the table and shook his head. She looked down at the fork in her hand. It was bent out of shape. Her heart thumped like it was going to break through her chest. Ember stared up at the officer and quickly slipped the fork under the napkin, hoping he hadn't noticed the misshapen metal.

"I don't need a warrant," the cop said, his fingers tapping the butt of his gun. "Mrs. Macconal is on her way to the station. She'll meet you there."

"You're not taking him anywhere without me." Ember slid out of the booth and stood up before Lee could. "Jen, can you drive the beast home?" She held out her keys to Jen. "And try to get hold of our mom. Let her know what's happening." She flicked her eyes at the cop. "Just in case he's lying."

Jen nodded as she took the keys.

A few minutes later, Ember slid into the back seat of the cop car. The stink of piney disinfectant didn't quite cover up the reek of puke and homeless that clung to the plastic seat and floorboard. Lee looked just like she had felt her first time in the back of a cop car. She patted his shoulder. "One more thing you can cross off your bucket list." She laughed, but it came out high-pitched and forced. Lee's somber expression didn't budge.

She took her hand off his arm and leaned her head back. This entire day had already sucked. And now, against all odds, it was getting even worse. As the cop pulled out of the driveway, Lee's stomach rumbled. She stared back at Hotspot. They'd never even had a chance to eat the damn pizza.

# Three
Wed, Aug 24, 6:02pm

### - Lee -

He was growing more agitated as they drove. People in cars all around them went in and out of his sensory range, like perforating the bubble of his mind. They crashed over him with their emotions until his own were washed away. His heart thumped louder with each new impression, until even his body felt strange, unfamiliar and very different from those who passed through the bubble. His breathing became ragged, until his vision began to blur at the edges.

Ember noticed and touched his arm.

"We'll be fine," she said, or so he thought. He'd been getting words confused with the feelings he interpreted. "Mom won't let anything happen to us."

And just like that it was all gone. Every emotion not his own, every external heartbeat and flow of blood, it all vanished into quiet. It was almost uncomfortable, as if the silence left him lonely. It was the same way he'd felt when the Rumbling had stopped.

*Is this her power?* he thought. *To interrupt or cancel out others'?*

She gave him a pat and withdrew her hand.

"Don't worry," she said. "They can't hold us, since we didn't do anything wrong."

The sensations returned in a rush, his sister's first. She was scared. She believed what she was saying, but he felt fear inside her all the same. Lee took her hand, despite the quiet it caused. His mind needed the short break, and he could endure a little loneliness if it made her feel better.

The station was busy, with patrol cars and people moving through the lot. Lee had braced himself before he let go of Ember's hand, but it didn't help him in the least. The flood of sensations from so many people nearly caused him to collapse.

He blinked away the dizziness, used the car to steady himself. The officer asked if he was all right but didn't offer any help. He was too afraid to touch Lee. Ember came over to give a hand, but Lee waved her off. He'd have to let go again at some point. It was better to adjust now then to suffer another sudden stop and influx.

Inside the station was even worse. The sheer number of people and noise caused a commotion in his mind so loud he couldn't think. It felt as if his body had betrayed him, as the emotions and physical maladies of those around him overlaid his own. Their panic and pain, anger and anxiety, frustration and fear, it all roiled within him, from the tingles in his brain to thrumming aches throughout his body.

"This way," the officer said and took Lee by the arm.

Pain in his shoulder made him wince, but the injury wasn't his. Lee looked up at the man's arm. The noise seemed to fall away as he focused his attention. It was as if he could almost see inside the officer with his mind, sensed the torn ligaments and poorly formed scar tissue. The more he focused, the clearer the injury became, the jagged half-mending and bits of bone debris.

"Stay here," the officer said to Ember.

They left her seated in a waiting area, outside a pen of cubicles. As Lee was led toward the back, purposefully ignoring the sensory push of fifty-seven people, he came to realize he could do more than merely sense the damage in the officer's shoulder. He could force it to heal right, like fixing pieces poorly placed in a puzzle.

It wouldn't even take that much effort, though Lee imagined it might hurt. The idea of it left him stunned, that he could somehow heal a person.

"In here," the officer said and opened a door.

Lee stepped in to find an attractive woman seated at a table already waiting for him. The door closed behind him. There was a large mirror on the right side wall. It took barely a moment to sense the three people on the other side. Two men and a woman, adults, though the woman was much older. She had so many aches in her dangerously thinned bones it made him twinge.

"Please," the seated woman said and indicated the opposite chair. "Lee, right? I'm Emily."

She'd been reading and organizing files on a tablet. She'd set it aside and sat waiting with fingers interlaced on the table. Her nails were manicured but not painted. Her blonde hair was straight, cut at the shoulder, with a few platinum highlights. Green eyes, delicate cheeks and the firm jawline of someone in peak fitness, her beauty was more than a little distracting.

*Looks like late twenties,* he thought and glanced at the slight tan line on her ring finger. *And married.*

"You're not in any kind of trouble," Emily said. Her voice was pleasant, the tone friendly. "I just need to ask a few questions."

Even her smile was disarming.

She wore nice clothes, professional looking, with shiny black shoes and a suit jacket. She didn't seem like a police officer or a detective.

*A government agent, most likely.*

Lee sat in the metal folding chair and sensed relief pass through her. She'd been afraid but was less so now, as if they'd passed some sort of hurdle together. If she'd expected any resistance, he supposed, from a dangerous person with superpowers, it would have happened right away. But Lee had remained calm, shown reason and a willingness to listen.

He put his hands on the table, so she could see them. He didn't want to give her a reason to pull the holstered gun he could see outlined beneath her jacket.

"Do you know why you're here?" she asked. "What's happening out there? And not just here, in Sungrove, but all over the world?"

There were slight pauses in her speech. He could've attributed it to careful thinking, but when he looked for it, he caught sight of the earbud. She was being given information as they spoke, not necessarily coached but definitely guided. Lee didn't have to look at the mirror to know who was on the other end of that connection.

Emily was about to say more.

"Tell me," Lee said.

"People are manifesting powers," she explained. He stayed quiet, reading their emotions, trying to learn as much from them as she was from him. "Our analysts believe the soundwaves from the Pillars affected physical changes in some people. It's still too early to tell for sure, but it looks like only a small percentage of the population is showing signs of any change."

Lee nodded. He could sense the growing frustration from the three behind the mirror, particularly from the man in the middle.

Emily leaned forward and placed both her hands on his. He felt a shock go through his system, like a jolt of electricity up both arms and down to his privates. It wasn't that he'd never been touched by a girl before, but any contact from a pretty woman had an immediate response.

Unfortunately, her feelings didn't match her actions. He sensed no passion in her, no actual longing for his gangly body, only determination and...duty?

*Great. She's flirting because it's her job.*

"You seem like a good guy," Emily said. "No one's going to hurt you. Have you noticed any changes in yourself?"

Lee sighed. It would've been so much easier if he could believe she was attracted to him. He began to dread all the relationships his new power was going to ruin. He pulled his hands away.

"Sorry," he said. "That's not going to work on me. Ever since I woke this afternoon, I've been able to sense what people are feeling."

She sat back, genuinely intrigued. "Really? So you're an empath?"

Lee scrunched up half his face.

"Not exactly," he said. "I think it's more like a side-effect, a part of diagnosing injuries. I haven't tried it yet, but I think I can heal people."

She nodded and gave an appraising smile, obviously listening to the voices in her ear.

"That could save a lot of lives," she said. "You know, we have specialists who could help you, offer training and guidance, give you the time and resources to hone your ability. Think of all the lives you could save, how proud your," Emily paused, as she realized her mistake, and finished with, "you'd be."

She'd been about to mention his mother.

Lee guessed they wanted some kind of commitment before making any mention of his legal guardian. He let it slide. It was in his best interest to keep her relaxed, so she'd continue to make mistakes.

"Sounds like you're offering me a job," he said. "I haven't even finished high school. What kind of salary does a superpower get me?"

"A lot better than mine," she joked.

He wanted to smile, to laugh lightly along with her, but nothing she said or did stemmed from a concern for his wellbeing.

"More than just a great paying job," she went on, "we could offer you security, for your family and friends. It would be very dangerous if the wrong people knew what you could do. They'd want to exploit you, control you, and they'd use those you care about to do it."

*First persuasion and then bribery,* he thought, *now coercion.* She'd just threatened his family and friends in the guise of offering protection. *Isn't that how the mob worked?*

Lee supposed she would've tried blackmail, if he'd had any secrets worth exploiting. Though exposing his power to the world would've worked just as well. There was no denying dangerous organizations, lawful or otherwise, were going to try to take advantage of anyone with powers.

Lee groaned inwardly. She'd shown him the carrot, but a part of him just had to see the stick.

He said, "What if I don't want any part of that? I just want to be normal."

"That's not always up to us," she replied. "Sometimes we just have to make the best of what we're given. What we're offering is as close to normal as you're going to get. We can keep you and your family safe, despite what goes on at your mom's spice shop. We just want you working with us."

*What about the spice shop?*

Lee did his best not to show any surprise at the mention of it, though he didn't think he did a very good job. It didn't matter. Whatever she'd alluded to, she knew he was unaware. It was just another ploy meant to keep him off balance, to make him question the wrong things.

"Where's my mother?" he asked. "She was supposed to meet me here."

"She's already here," Emily said and showed him a live feed on the tablet. His mom was seated at a table, just like he was, talking to a different agent. "We're explaining the situation to her. If you're still undecided, we can go join them."

*They've already convinced her,* Lee thought. *They wouldn't risk putting us together, if they thought she'd say no.*

Lee said, "All right, let's—"

Gunshots rang out from somewhere in the building, followed by shouting and abrupt screams. The entire room began to vibrate, shaking dust loose from the ceiling panels. Shots continued in fast succession, loud pops from multiple guns.

Lee immediately thought of Ember and jumped to his feet. Emily had a hand to her earbud.

"What's happening?" he asked. "My sister's still out there."

Emily stood, reached toward her holster, though she didn't draw the gun.

"Everything's all right," she said. "I just need you to remain calm. Other agents are responding."

"I need to get to my sister."

Lee could feel the panic and pain in a dozen bodies but had no way of knowing who they were. He could tell where they were going, though, either running to or from something. He needed to get closer for a better look at the bigger picture.

"It's too dangerous," she said when he began to move. "You'd only be in the way."

The metal door buckled inward and flew across the room, crashed against the opposite wall with enough force to crack the concrete. It fell to the ground loudly, with hinges and pieces of the doorway still attached. A guy a little older than Lee stepped into the room. He was taller, more muscular, with short dark hair and a wide grin. He looked like a football player who'd just scored a touchdown.

"Mr. Tompkins," Emily warned, "you're making a mistake."

"Let's go, buddy," he said to Lee. "I'm busting us out of this place."

Tompkins wore jeans and a black tee. The shirt had several holes in it large enough to see skin, but there was no blood anywhere on him.

*Didn't Jen say the Supers were bulletproof? If I'm one of them, does that mean I'm bulletproof too?*

He focused his ability on the guy, felt the rush of adrenaline coursing through him and the high of being truly powerful. There were numerous things off about him, however, very noticeable differences in his anatomy.

*Is his skin altered in some way?*

It was, Lee realized, the deeper he probed. It wasn't just thicker. It was denser, stronger, infused with a foreign substance. His whole body was, every muscle and bone, every soft tissue and tendon. Each organ had been condensed and duplicated in a different spot. There were even new ones he didn't recognize, though he wasn't a doctor by any stretch. It just seemed too odd, made him wonder in what other ways he'd been changed himself.

There were still weak spots, of course, like the eyes and mouth, the ears, places where the brain could be penetrated. He may have been bulletproof, but he wasn't completely invulnerable.

"Come on, dude," he said. "I ain't got all day."

Emily drew on him.

"Place your hands behind your head," she said with forced calm, "and don't make any sudden moves."

Lee knew she screwed up the moment she pulled her

gun. He sensed the thrill inside this guy at the prospect of violence, at any opportunity to use his power.

"You're not buying their bullshit, are you?" Tompkins asked and pointed at her. Emily fired at the same instant, struck him in the chest. The bullet made a new hole in his shirt but didn't break the skin. "Ow, bitch! You know, this was one of my favorite shirts before today."

He thrust his hand out, and she fired again. The air between them wavered in rings, like visible shockwaves racing toward her. They struck the bullet, sent it wide into a wall, and then the vibrations rammed full force into her. Lee felt and heard bones break, as she was crushed against the concrete wall. She slumped to the ground, unconscious and bleeding from her nose and ears.

"So," Tompkins asked, "what's it going to be?"

Lee thought through every possible outcome of a life on the run, being a fugitive from the law, being thought a criminal from the very start, taking on the crimes of others by association, putting family and friends in danger for being close to him. There was no happy end to that road.

"Sorry," Lee said, "but running isn't the answer."

"And what is, working with them?" Tompkins shook his head and laughed. "They'll turn on you first chance they get. Or worse, they'll make you one of them. And you know what they say. 'If you're not with us...'"

Lee didn't flinch. He had the benefit of knowing what Tompkins was feeling at that very moment, the fear and uncertainty of what Lee's power might be.

"I've studied you," Lee said, "seen your power already and how it works. I know how to kill you. You really want to risk it?"

Tompkins narrowed his eyes. "Fine, be a dick."

He turned and left the room.

Lee rushed over to Emily and put a hand to the center of her chest, where the most damage had been done. He felt bits of him leave his body and enter hers, like the tiny blue fireflies he'd seen in the parking lot at Finley's.

Once inside, they began to multiply exponentially and spread throughout her body. He set them to the task of mending her bones and ruptured organs, then ran from the room for his sister. He could still feel the bits working, could direct them from afar, though he knew they'd stop healing if he left the range of his sensory bubble.

"Ember!" he shouted, when he caught sight of her past the hallway.

There were people slumped over, blood splattered over the cubicles and on the walls. Lee sensed eight unmoving bodies in the immediate area and could do nothing to bring them back.

"Are you all right?" he asked her when he got close, unable to get a sense. He assumed her power was blocking his. "Are you hurt?"

She reached out to take his arms, glad to see him as well but struggling with the situation. He quickly pulled back.

"Don't touch me," he told her.

If she interrupted his power, Emily might die.

They both instinctively ducked, as more gunshots rang out in nearby rooms. An officer was thrown from one room into the hallway wall and fell to the ground unmoving. A teenage girl walked out after him, looked toward Lee and Ember then headed the opposite way.

"This is crazy," Ember said, as Tompkins strode in from another corridor. He was holding a cop by the neck, had him lifted off the ground as he walked and tossed him like a toy across the room. "We have to find mom and Allie and get the hell out of here!"

Lee felt the officer die, as the man's body hit and went through a cubicle, a computer monitor and into the concrete wall on the other side. His neck had snapped upon impact, a shower of sparks in his wake.

"We have to stop them," Lee said. "We can't just let

them keep killing people."

"Isn't that what the police are for?" she asked, trying to stay hidden. "That's their job, right? Protect and serve?"

She grabbed his arm to pull him away, as if she already knew where to find their mom and her friend. Lee lost all sense of those around him. He'd only been halfway finished healing Emily.

"Damn it!" he snapped and snatched his arm away. "I told you not to touch me!"

"We don't have time for this," she said. Lee was busy trying to reestablish his control over the bits inside Emily. "We need to find mom. She can do more here than either of us."

*Like what,* he couldn't help think, *yell them to death?*

"Wait," Lee said, once Emily was healing again. "I need your help to stop this Tompkins guy. He's killed people here, and he's not going to stop once he leaves."

"You don't know that," she said.

She kept talking, but Lee was focused on Tompkins and the surroundings. He looked for something he could use, anything that could stop him. His eyes fell upon a gun under one of the desks.

"Trust me," he said. "I know. I can feel it. Besides, Allie can take of herself. You saw her at Finley's. She has powers. But this one," Lee nodded toward Tompkins. He had grabbed hold of another officer, held him up with one hand and was poking him in the chest with the other while taunting him. "We can't let him kill anyone else."

"Look at him!" Ember snarled. "How are we going to stop him?"

His plan would still work without her, but Lee didn't want to risk getting hit by those vibrations. It would be much easier to take him down if Ember blocked his power.

"We rush him," Lee said, already choosing a path. "Just grab hold of him, anywhere, but make sure you touch his skin. Don't just grab onto his clothes. All right?"

"Seriously," she said more than asked. "And while I'm trying to grope him, what the hell are you going to do?"

"I'm going to take care of him," Lee said with a grim determination.

There were no half measures here. Tompkins wasn't going to stop killing people, until someone put an end to him. He was too dangerous for a jail cell, if one even existed that could hold him.

Lee felt Tompkins plunge his hand inside the officer's chest, experienced the horror and pain of fingers wriggle through, wrap around the heart and begin to squeeze.

"I can feel your heartbeat," he teased and laughed.

"Now," Lee told her, "while his hands are full."

He charged forward and to the right, sensed her follow half a step behind. Ember lunged straight for Tompkins, took hold of one arm in both hands and began to squeeze with all her might. Had he been a normal person, she would've crushed every bone. As it was, he only managed to look annoyed.

"Get the hell off me," he said to her. "I'm a little busy playing here."

Lee had snatched the gun up from under the desk as he ran, walked up to Tompkins and put it to his eye. He pulled the trigger three times without delay. Ember shrieked and let go. The officer slid down and off the bloodied arm into a heap. A final gurgle, and he was dead. Bullets didn't come out the other side of Tompkins' skull but had managed to break through the thin bone behind his ruined eye. They shredded his brain. It took a moment for him to fall, much longer than Lee expected.

"You killed him!" Ember said, shocked and staring down at the corpse. "What is wrong with you?"

Her words and sentiment swept through his mind, a single gust in the storm of emotion raging all around him. So much of it was relief, he wasn't sure it was his own.

"It was the only way," Lee said quietly and put the

gun down. Men and women who'd been hiding began to come out from under desks. "He would've gone on to kill hundreds, even thousands, and no one would've been able to stop him." He raised his eyes to hers, wanted her to understand. "But I knew how. Every person he killed, if I'd allowed him to leave, would've been on me."

"Who are you to decide that?" she asked, hurt and afraid—not for what he'd done but for what was sure to follow.

Other Supers had come in, saw their savior on the floor and ran back the other way.

Ember shook her head at him, as if he was the one who didn't understand.

"If you knew what I knew," she said and swallowed, "you would never have killed him."

Lee's voice hardened.

"If you knew what I knew," he said and turned away, "we wouldn't be having this conversation."

# - Ember -

Ember stared out the window, watching cars pass them going in the other direction and wishing they were in them, instead of locked in the back of a patrol car.

Lee tapped his foot on the floor, his fingers twitching.

She started to ask what was wrong with him and remembered where they were. For all his faults, Lee was basically a good kid. She was the one who'd been in trouble before, who found the surroundings, if not quite familiar, at least not completely alien. Unlike him. She flexed her fingers, forcing herself to act relaxed. She was still worried, but she wasn't about to let a cop know she was afraid.

Lee's breathing got funny and she reached over to pat his arm. "It's all good," she said. "I told Jen to get hold of mom. She'll take care of it." He seemed calmer. Then he stared at her hand. It must have seemed kind of weird to him. Too big-sisterly a gesture. She pulled her hand back.

"Don't worry. They can't hold us. We didn't do anything wrong," Ember said, raising her voice on the last part so the officer in the front seat could hear. Her body buzzed with adrenaline, but she tried to keep the fear from her voice. No sense in getting Lee worked up again.

She stared at the back of the driver's head. Suddenly, she felt a zing of energy as warm fingers wrapped around her cool ones. She glanced over at her brother, but instead of pulling away like she normally would have, she gripped his hand in hers.

It didn't seem weird to be sitting in the back seat of a police car, holding hands with her annoying younger brother, until they reached the station and he let go, and an odd sense of emptiness washed over her.

Inside, the building was crowded. People talking. Phones ringing. Cops rushing around. Lee seemed distracted, his eyes darting around the room, like he was looking for something only he could see. She was about to reach for his hand when the officer stepped between them, pointed to a chair, and told her to sit.

She would have argued, but their mom had always told them to be polite with the cops. "We have friends on the force," she'd say, "but they won't be able to help if you go foul-mouthing the wrong people." Ember had learned the hard way the time they broke up the spring cut party at Pebble Cove. Teens cutting school wouldn't have been such a big deal, but they didn't much care for all the alcohol they'd busted them with. Not to mention a little herb. Mom hadn't found it at all amusing when Ember had gotten smart with the cop who'd hauled her butt in, and her Mom had let her spend most of the night in a rank-smelling cell.

So, she sat. She looked at Lee. He shrugged and followed the officer through the crowded room and disappeared into a hallway.

The room was filled with frightened people. Not the usual criminals, but ordinary looking people who, like Lee, probably hadn't ever been in real trouble before.

The cops were nervous, like they were afraid something bad was about to go down. They were doing a good job of covering, acting confident, solid, but there were signs. Mouths held too tight. Tiny muscles in their faces that twitched almost imperceptibly. The room and the noise drifted away, and Ember found herself honing in on the minute details of each officer. The tilt of a badge not exactly lined up with the pocket. A few stray white animal hairs dusting the lower edge of a pant leg.

Ember gasped and the details slipped away, the room coming back into full color and sound. How the hell had she seen that? The pet owning cop was all the way on the other side of the room from her.

*Craptastic. It wasn't just Allison and Lee.*

The kitchen, her phone, the fork at the diner. And now this? Worry ground into her nerves. Where had they taken Lee? What was taking so long?

She wondered if Jen had managed to get hold of their mom. Ember would have given just about anything right then for the ability to communicate with her mother over long distances, like Aunt Maureen could.

The small magics Ember had were mostly useless, except for entertainment value. Party tricks mostly. When they even worked. But even if she had been more adept, she would have had to keep hiding it from the world.

And from Lee.

Sometimes she thought Jen suspected, but she had never said anything. At least not to Ember.

She watched as they brought in an older woman with bandages over her eyes. They guided her to a chair beside an empty desk and left her sitting there. Ember tried not to focus in on the woman, but the room seemed to fall away again, and it was like she was suddenly right beside her.

The woman was crying, the bandages over her eyes damp, and she kept sobbing and repeating the same words over and over. "How could this happen? She's a good girl. She didn't mean it. She would never hurt anyone. I don't know how this could happen." Her bandages turned pink with blood and tears.

Ember forced her mind away from the woman, tried not to think of Allison and what she might have done, what the cops might be doing to her right now.

She needed to see Lee, make sure he was okay. She started to stand, but one of the suits across the way shook his head at her, so she slumped back into the stiff chair.

*Come on, mom,* she thought. *Where are you? I can only stand the rules for so long.*

Gunshots rang out and she jumped. Somebody screamed. People fell to the floor or ducked under desks. More gun shots. Ember dropped down and crouched in front of the flimsy chair. She was on the wrong side of the desk to crawl under it. Besides, the cheap metal didn't look bulletproof. She peeked around the edge of the desk, trying to see what was going on.

Uniformed cops rushed around shouting orders. Men and women in suits swarmed into the room. Noise. Screaming. The smell of gunpowder and blood.

*Crap!* Where were their so-called friends in blue now when they needed them? The building shook and walls cracked. Windows shattered, sending shards of glass into the room.

Ember felt the palms of her hands warming. No, not now. I won't be able to control it here. Not without help. She squeezed her fists into tight balls and willed herself to stay calm.

"Ember!" She peered up over the back of the chair. Lee barreled across the room, shouting her name.

"Lee! Get down!" She tried to signal him to hit the deck, but he just ran right at her. Beyond him she could see the wreckage of the room. Bullet holes. Blood.

"Ember! Are you all right?"

Ember kept her hands balled up as he came closer.

"Are you hurt?" His face was tight with worry.

The heat subsided from her hands and she reached out for him, but he jerked away. "Don't touch me."

She dropped her hands and stared at him. They both ducked as more gunshots rang out.

A uniformed body flew out of the hallway and slammed into the wall with a loud thud, then tumbled to the floor amid a shower of dust from the destroyed wallboard.

A girl, about the same age as Lee, maybe younger, her brown bangs dusting her eyes, walked out and glared at the cop on the floor. Her head snapped up and she glanced over at them, then dusted off her hands and quick-stepped away.

As soon as she was gone, some guy came out of another hallway, holding another man by the neck. "This is insane," Ember said, watching as the man's face turned red, his legs kicking at air as the guy holding him lifted him off his feet and tossed him across the room, like it was nothing. She heard a sickening crack and knew in her gut that it wasn't the furniture he'd landed on that had broken. "We need to find Mom and Allie. Get the hell out of here."

"No." Lee shook his head. "We need to stop this. We can't just do nothing while they kill people."

Ember looked at the big guy who'd just crushed and tossed the other man away like he was a disposable water bottle. The guy's shirt was filled with holes, like he'd taken a stroll through a shooting range, but there was no blood. She swallowed. She'd faced off with some pretty dark things, but never without her cousins for back-up. And nothing like this. "That's what the police are for. It's their job to protect people."

Lee was staring at the guy. Ember could see his mind working. No way was she going to let him go up against an annihilator like that. She grabbed his arm, but he yanked away from her.

"Damn it!" he yelped. "I told you not to touch me!"

"Geez, Lee. Stop being such an ass."

The guy was kicking over desks, swatting computers across the room like they were made of foam. They didn't bounce like foam, though. One slammed all the way through a window and landed on a car in the parking lot, setting off a howling alarm.

"We need to find Mom. She can do more here than we can." Ember started to creep toward the hallway.

"Wait," Lee said. "I need your help to stop this guy. He's killed a lot of people, and he'll kill more, if we don't stop him."

"You don't know that," she told him. "Besides, not my circus..." she eyed the big guy destroying the room and everything in it. "And that guy is sure as hell not my monkey. Plus, we need to find Allison before she gets hurt, too."

"Trust me," Lee said, "I know what he can do. I can feel

it. And, Allie can take of herself. You saw her at Finley's. She has powers. But this one..." he indicated the guy, who was still doing his best Godzilla versus Tokyo impersonation on the furniture.

An officer tried to sneak up on him, taser at the ready, but the guy spun around and grabbed him. He held the cop up with one hand and started poking him in the chest with the other, screaming obscenities at him. The cop tried to get his gun out of his holster.

"We can't let him kill anyone else." Lee sounded desperate.

"Look at him, Lee. How the hell do you propose we stop him?"

"We rush him," Lee said. "I just need you to grab hold of him, anywhere, but you have touch his skin. Don't just grab onto his clothes. Understand?"

"Seriously? And while I'm getting grabby with this deranged serial killer, what the hell are you going to do?"

"I'm gonna take care of him." Lee looked into her eyes the way he always did when he was dead serious.

There was an ugly ripping sound and a garbled scream.

"I can feel your heartbeat," Godzilla said. Then he let out a malicious laugh.

"Now," Lee said, "while both his hand are full."

"Wha—" Before she could stop him, Lee charged forward. Ember followed without thinking. No way was her little brother going up against this thing alone.

Once across the room, Ember managed to get her hands wrapped around one of the guy's forearms. She forced herself not to look where his hand was and squeezed with everything she had.

Ember swore. Why couldn't she summon the magic now? If she'd had any real control over her power, she'd have fried him, but by the look on his face, except for him lowering the cop's body, all she was doing was pissing him off.

"Get the hell away from me." He tried to shake her off. "You're killing my buzz." Blood spattered her face and arms, but she hung on.

Suddenly, Lee was there, shoving a gun in the guy's eye. He fired. Three rapid bangs. Right into the guy's eye.

Ember let go and shrieked like a little girl. Under normal circumstances, she'd have been embarrassed. But there was nothing normal about seeing her little brother shoot anyone. It wasn't like in the movies. Except maybe the ones by that Tarantino guy. This was real. And it was real ugly.

The officer slid off the guy's gore-covered arm in slow motion and landed in a heap on the floor. Godzilla collapsed beside him. Blood puddled around them.

"You killed him!" It sounded stupid, even to her. But at that moment, it was all she could think to say as she stared down at the body of the guy her brother had just murdered. "What is wrong with you, Lee? You just put a gun to the guy's head. And shot him. While I was holding onto to his freaking arm."

"It was the only way." Lee set the gun gently down on what was left of one of the desks.

People started moving. Men and women who'd been hiding crawled out from under desks.

Lee was still talking, his words tumbling out, like he was trying to convince himself. "He would've gone on to kill hundreds, even thousands, and no one would've been able to stop him. But I knew how. Every person he killed, if I'd allowed him to leave, would've been on me."

"Who are you to decide that?"

"It wasn't a decision." He glared at her, his eyes hard. "It was a necessity."

# Four
Wed, Aug 24, 7:28pm

## - Lee -

The entire area was a bloody mess. Cubicle walls were broken, scorched from smashed computers, torn down over splintered desks and crushed chairs. Files and papers littered the floor, where cabinets had been bent and forced open, one sticking out from a wall like a projectile. The painted concrete walls had been broken through by fists and thrown furniture. The ceiling was mottled with missing tiles, where blue and black cables let out occasional sparks.

The people looked even worse. Most were officers in blue uniform, detectives in business casual and agents in dark suits. The rest appeared to be civilians, probably there against their will. No one was left unmarked, with clothes ripped and dirtied, bloodstained from a wound—theirs or someone else's.

Lee felt seventeen unmoving bodies in the immediate area, either dead or soon would be. Another twenty-three were injured, with bruises, scrapes and fractured bones. Nine were badly hurt, with crushed and pierced organs, suffering severe blood loss. He didn't know if there was enough time to help them all or if he even had that kind of strength.

Ember was still angry and afraid, looked around as if searching for a way out. She was a bit frantic and rightly so. Still in shock from the gunfire, she caught sight of the blood spattered across her front and arms then turned her eyes on Lee like he was a stranger.

"We are so very screwed," she said and grabbed him by the shirt, started pulling toward the leftmost corridor. "You just made me a damn accessory to murder! We have to go. Now!

Lee looked down in surprise at Tompkins, the one who'd done most of the killing.

"He's not dead," Lee said, and it didn't relieve him the way it did his sister.

*Three bullets in the brain, and it didn't kill him. What the hell was it going to take?*

His mind began to race, reasoning out any other means.

The police chief entered with three agents, two men and an older woman. Lee recognized their sense as the ones from behind the glass.

"You two," the agent in charge said to Lee and Ember, "stay right there." Early forties, short dark hair and blue eyes, he had a commanding presence and a permanent frown that brooked no argument. "No one goes in or out. Thompson," he said to an agent with a hand over a side wound, "get this building secured. Isolate the Affected."

Their comms must've been damaged. Emily came in with a teenage girl Lee didn't recognize and motioned for her to take a seat on the bench. Emily caught sight of him and smiled, came over and touched his shoulder. Her injuries had been completely healed.

"I'm so glad you're all right," she said with a warm smile. Lee was confused by the genuine affection and concern. "When I woke up, I was worried you'd been taken."

*Mmkay,* he thought. *Something is very wrong here.*

He could tell she wanted to stand closer but was aware it would seem inappropriate to the other agents who were watching.

"Who the hell is this?" Ember asked Lee.

Emily was a bit terse but introduced herself as Agent Taylor without looking away. She only seemed interested in Lee.

"Uh-huh." Ember gave Lee a suspicious look then rolled her eyes. "Whatever." She asked the agent in charge, "So, what's going to happen to us now? Are we being arrested?"

When Lee focused on Emily, he realized all the bits he'd duplicated were still inside her. She was healed, but they hadn't left her like he'd expected. What were they exactly? He could feel that his body had been changed by the Rumbling, the same as Tompkins and Ember.

But the bits of himself that floated around him like an aura, his sensory bubble that glowed blue like fireflies when he was upset? Tompkins and Ember had them as well. They were part of a new, separate and stronger immune system. Lee's was much different, however. His extended outside his body, and he could control where they went, use them to sense others, feel what they felt. He could communicate with each cell, as if they were intelligent beings, and direct them into people, use them to heal.

"Detained," the lead agent replied to Ember, like a judge delivering a sentence. "You and the other Affected are considered threats to national security, a danger to yourselves and others, by direct order of the President. You'll be taken into protective custody and quarantine, until such time as the CDC can determine the extent of change in your bodies," he paused and looked as if he had a bad taste in his mouth, "and whether or not you're contagious."

Emily had moved closer to Lee, stood protectively beside him. Was this an effect of his cells within her? Was it gratitude or something else? Lee had a suspicion his cells were acting as a hive, and he'd inadvertently brought her into the fold. He could have withdrawn all the cells from her, used them to strengthen his sensory bubble or direct them into others, but he liked the idea of having her on his side. Lines were being drawn here, and he needed an advocate.

"We just saved you!" Ember said, a bit of growl in her voice.

It made him wonder, though. What would happen if he did the same to everyone else in the room? If he forced the cells already in them to replicate, could he influence their emotions? Turn them to his side as well?

*If I made them let us walk out of here,* he thought and inwardly sighed, *we'd be fugitives the second we stepped out of range.*

"It's true," an officer said nervously, forced himself to look away from the bloodied mess that may have once been a friend. He then glared down at Tompkins, looked as if he wanted to kick the unconscious killer. "They took him down when no one else could." To Ember and Lee, he said, "Thanks for that."

"We have our orders," the older woman said in a stern tone, "and protocols to follow." She had long, gray hair tied up in a bun in back, and she was so overweight she needed a cane just to walk. "Gratitude aside," she went on with a steely look to Ember, "every Affected goes to quarantine."

The lead agent finished speaking in private with the police chief and barked an order.

"Sanders, Ellison," he said, angry at whatever he'd just discussed, "escort them outside."

"No," a familiar woman's voice said from behind.

Lee turned to see his mother.

She'd always had an intimidating presence, but he'd never seen her quite like this. By the tone in her voice, the strength in her stance, the confidence and resolve he felt brimming within her, it was clear she felt like the one in charge. Others shrank away from her without realizing it, veteran officers with guns.

Blood smeared one of her cheeks, caused the scars on her hands and forearms to stand out in pale lines beneath the crimson slick. She may have stopped to help someone beyond saving, but for a terrifying moment, it looked entirely like something else.

"Mrs. Macconal," the older woman said in a careful, even tone. The sensations coming off her had changed in an instant, to fear and a begrudging respect. All of the agents' had. "It's an honor to finally meet you."

*Why are they so afraid of her?* Lee wondered and looked at his mom in a new light. *Just what the hell's going on at the spice shop?*

"Hello, Alice," his mother said with a withering gaze. Her eyes turned toward the lead agent. "Jim. You know better."

Aunts Gwen and Brianna entered the room and moved to stand behind her, followed by cousins Deidra, Rory and Steph. Grans Cara, Wynne, Dana and Abigail came in from the other side, just in front of aunts Kendra, Maureen and Rowena. More cousins trailed in after, all of them girls somewhat close to his age. Blair, Alanna, Genevieve, Cordelia, Arlene, Keara, Tara and Seanna, they filed in and filled the room with a threatening presence, like the charged promise of a brewing storm.

"You know who I am," his mother said, and it sent shivers across his skin. What he sensed in her wasn't anger. It was a warning. "What I am." Jim remained silent, but his jaw tightened in response. "You didn't really think you could take one of us without a fight?"

*One of us?*

Lee immediately looked to his sister. He'd always felt looked down upon by the older women in his family, all his grans and aunts. The only male Macconal since his father had died, he'd grown up feeling like he was to blame for everything, for his father's death, for being born a boy. He never understood why they'd held him in such disdain, barely tolerated his presence, made him feel like less of a person, unequal to the girls. His cousins didn't act that way. They loved him, and he loved them right back. But his grans and aunts? They could go rot for all he cared. There was no doubt in his mind that this show they were putting on was all for Ember.

"That I'd let you take my children?" his mother went on, and wires in the ceiling crackled with bright sparks.

Men and women were once more reaching for guns or backing away, like it was Tompkins all over again. The police chief ordered his officers to stand down.

To Lee's mother, the chief said, "Leslie, please. We didn't have a choice."

Jim had finally found his voice.

"Would you really risk it all right now," he said, and Lee sensed the duplicity in him, "with all that's going on out there? You'd expose yourselves like this?"

"For my children?" his mother asked, incredulous. She clenched both bloody fists. "You have no idea what I'd risk."

Cells had entered all of them as soon as they'd come into range. They were normal, just regular people, but there was something odd occurring as the moments drew on. There was a power building in them, especially his mother. He couldn't quite figure it out. It wasn't electric, surging through synapses or along the spine. It was...something else, an internal force growing at the center of their bodies and radiating outward, gathering in the air. It wasn't a visible energy, at least not yet, but Lee felt it filling the room with a static charge.

"You can take Ember," Alice offered, like she was trading gaming cards, "but we can't let you take both. It's already too late for Lee."

"That's fine," his aunt Gwen replied all too quickly, and he hated her for it.

His mother tightened her lips in a frown at her older sister. Gwen only stared back, her feelings on the matter clearly shown.

*Screw you, too, Aunt Gwen.*

He wanted nothing more than to reach out and hurt her. His anger at all her snide comments over the years, her poorly hidden disapproval, boiled up inside him. He wanted to yell at her, to walk over and slap her across the face, but all he managed was to clench a fist in frustration.

Motes of blue flared around her, and aunt Gwen lurched, grabbed at her stomach. She doubled over and threw up with a long and hard retching. Lee could feel how much it hurt her. It was all he could do to keep from laughing.

"Sorry," she said to his mother and glared at Lee. Did she know it was him? "Without a conduit..."

His mother nodded in understanding, helped her sister stand. She squared her shoulders and walked toward him. All the others moved in too, each placing a hand on the shoulder in front, until they closed around Lee and Ember and touched them as well.

"This isn't the way," Alice said in a weak warning, the way a victim might try to stop an armed robber. "Mrs. Macconal. We need each other."

"Leslie," Jim said, as if they'd worked together a long time, and she was throwing away all they'd built. "Don't."

*How the hell do they know each other?* Lee fumed.

His mother turned to Jim.

"If you come after them, after us," she said, and that power ran the edge of her tone, as if it strengthened the words, gave them weight and terrible consequence, "I'll make you regret it."

Everything turned white, and a ringing in his ears drowned out the sound of all else. When the brightness faded, they were standing in his basement. The others began to disperse, as if nothing strange had happened. He was still disoriented, trying to clear his vision, but everyone else carried on like they'd done it a hundred times.

*You knew,* he thought and scowled at Ember. Like the others, she wasn't the least bit surprised at what had just happened. *How could you not tell me?*

"Lee," his mother said, wiped her hands with a towel and sounded as if she were asking him to take out the garbage, "would you give us a moment? I need to talk to Ember."

He blinked and raised both brows.

"Are we seriously not going to say anything about how we just fucking teleported?"

"Language, mister!" His mother's voice was stern, but Lee refused to back down. She sighed and tried to give him a patronizing pat on the arm. He pulled away and gritted his teeth. "Please. You and I will talk later. But right now, I have something important to discuss with your sister."

"Fine," he said, beyond angry at the both of them, at everyone in his so-called family, "but this better be good."

He went upstairs confused and hurt. He had no idea what'd just happened, and no one would even look at him. Whatever secret they were keeping, it was clear he wouldn't find it out from anyone but his mother.

None but Ember had been changed, so they couldn't have powers. What then, magic? Lee stopped just outside the front door.

*Oh my god, they're all witches.*

"Hey," Jen said, without looking up from her phone. She was seated on the stoop, like she'd been waiting there a while. He sat down next to her, stunned by the realization that suddenly made sense of his shitty life. She leaned into him, both a nudge of relief that he was all right and to wake him from his stupor. "So," she said, "You're one of the Affected."

"The what?" Lee asked.

He looked over at her phone, saw messages in a chat room flying by.

"That's what they're calling them," she said, "people who were changed by the Rumbling. Seems some of them have powers. Most don't, but one thing's for sure, none of them are human anymore."

"Great," Lee said sarcastically. "Not only is everyone in my family a witch, but now I'm an alien. That's just awesome."

Jen almost laughed. It was easy to forget how pretty she was, especially when she smiled.

"That *totally* makes sense," she said. "Come on, you had to know something was up. The spice shop? All those grandmas and aunts and cousins getting together every week? I mean, your family is huge, and you're the only guy? I thought they were at least wiccans or maybe an all-female cult." She flicked imaginary dirt off her shoulder. "I was almost offended they didn't try to recruit me."

Lee could only shake his head at what his life was becoming. How could he trust any of them ever again? How could he keep living with them?

Jen slipped an arm around his.

"I didn't mean you were an alien. You still look and act the same. You're still the same guy I grew up with," she said and poked him in the ribs. "My best damn friend. You're just changed, on the inside. It's purely physical, you know?"

"You're not afraid?" Lee glanced at the texts going by, the pictures of chaos across the world. "They're afraid," he said, "and they should be."

"I am a little," she admitted, and he could feel the truth of it, "but not of you. I'm more scared for you than anything else. Take a look."

She showed him pictures of a giant yellow tent near the stadium. There were people in contamination suits directing a long line of Affected inside.

"They set up quarantine downtown," she said. "Every news station has been telling people to go to the hospital to get checked out if they think they're Affected. Then the CDC showed up with this tent. Now the hospitals and police are directing everyone there."

Lee saw military as well, for all the good those assault rifles would do them.

"It doesn't really look like a lot of people, though."

"It's not, when you think about it." She scrolled through more pictures. Most of the Affected were teens their age. She said, "Just a few hundred so far, and only a dozen or so with powers."

"That showed up on their own," Lee pointed out. "There's bound to be lots more out there. If any of them react like the guy I saw tonight..."

He let the idea fall away. It was too horrible to think about.

"What about you and Ember?" Jen asked. "Why'd the police let you two go?"

Surprised, he asked, "You know she's one too?" She made a face that clearly said nothing escaped her notice. "They didn't. Let us go, I mean."

Lee held his head against a rising ache.

"They're never going to let us go."

# - Ember -

Ember stared down at her hands. What the hell had happened? The room was a wreck. It reeked of blood. So did she. Blood spatter covered her arms. The front of her shirt. Her jeans. Sure, she had seen blood before. It wasn't unheard of in some of the meaner magics practiced by some of her even meaner relatives, but this was human. And it wasn't offered. For a moment, she thought she was going to throw up. Only there wasn't anything in her stomach to toss.

The shock began to fade. She swallowed the bile that had risen into her throat and focused on what had happened.

Then she made the mistake of looking down. Suddenly, she was staring down at the body of the man whose blood she wore. And once again reality struck her, hard.

Lee. Had. Shot. A. Man. Her baby brother, had killed.

"We are totally screwed." She grabbed him by the sleeve, pulling him away from the bloody mess.

"Let go." He yanked away from her, his shirt ripping.

"You—We killed someone, dammit!" She gripped the piece of fabric still in her hand. "We have to go. Now!"

"He's not dead," Lee said. He didn't sound happy about it.

"Are you serious?" She looked down at the body. Sure enough, the guy's chest rose and fell. Just barely, but he was still breathing. "Holy crap."

Before she could say anything else, the Police Chief marched through the door. He was trailed by two men and an older woman. All of them in dark suits. All of them with a look that said government agent so plain it might as well have been written on their foreheads in dayglow paint.

"You two," one of them ordered, "stay where you are." He turned to the suit beside him without fully taking his eyes off Ember and Lee. "No one in or out, Thompson.

Secure the building, and isolate the Affected."

The other man nodded and hopped to, pointing at able-bodied officers and directing them like a man who has been in charge of more than one ugly situation. Ember didn't like him. She didn't like any of them. And she especially didn't like it when the blond woman eased over to Lee and asked him how he was doing. The way she touched him was way too friendly.

Ember tried to move between them, but her brother brushed her aside.

"I'm so glad you're all right," the woman said. Her voice was husky, full of emotion. Who the hell was this wannabe cougar? "When I woke up, I was worried you'd been taken," she said, genuine concern showing in her face and her body language.

"Lee. You want to tell me something? Like who the hell this person is?" Ember asked.

"Agent Taylor," the woman said. "Your brother and I are..." for a moment her face grew confused. Then she shrugged. "We're good friends."

"Uh-huh." Ember raised an eyebrow at Lee. He just stared at her, like he was trying to figure something out. "Whatever." She glanced down at the undead guy Lee had shot, then looked away again, feeling sick. "What's going to happen to us now? Are we being arrested?"

"Not arrested. Detained," the man in charge replied. "You and the other Affected will be taken into custody, quarantined."

Agent Taylor sidled closer to Lee, like she was trying to shield him with her body.

Lee looked uncomfortable, but Ember was too busy ciphering the minimal difference between being arrested and detained to really care. "We just saved your asses!" She shouted. "How about taking that into consideration?"

"True," one of the uniforms said. "They seemed to know just how to take him down." He tapped his fingers to his forehead in a kind of salute. "Thanks."

"We have our orders," the older woman told her. "Protocol must be followed. There's no room for missteps. Gratitude aside, every Affected goes to quarantine."

"Sanders, Ellison, escort them outside." The lead agent waved a hand toward the door.

"No," said a familiar voice.

Ember never thought she would love hearing her mother say no. But right now it sounded better than anything she'd ever heard her say.

She watched as their mother, Matriarch of the Macconal clan, stalked across the room, people giving way before her as if they recognized her for the storm she could be.

Lee turned to face her. Even he seemed to wither beneath her imperial gaze.

The older woman was practically beside herself. "Mrs. Macconal," she simpered. "What an honor to finally meet you in person." It was clear she feared their mother, but she stood her ground and didn't give way like the others, even when their mom turned a sour eye on her.

"Alice." She gave the woman a curt nod, then turned to the suit in charge. "Jim, I thought you'd know better." She frowned, and her displeasure seemed palpable.

Quietly, but overtly, the room began to fill with aunties and cousins. If mom was a storm, the Macconal clan women were the apocalypse. Power rolled off them. Ember felt her magic being drawn, like an urgent need. Her hands itched, pricking with heat and energy. Only her stubborn anger and the knowledge that her mother didn't really need her untrained power held her rooted in place, instead of rushing to lock grid with them.

Cousin Seanna, her green eyes flashing, gave Ember the look. The one that told her she was being stupid. Again. But their mother acted like she didn't notice her reluctance. She ignored Ember completely. Instead, she addressed the agents, as if throwing down a gauntlet, one she expected them to leave where it lay. "You know who," her look raked over them, "and what I am; what we are."

The lead agent, Jim, kept his mouth shut. Ember had to give him credit in the smarts department. On the other hand, he totally lost cred in the guts department. Though, she didn't know anyone with half a brain who would stand up to her mother. Especially, not while she was backed by the force of the entire Macconal coven.

"You didn't really think you could take one of us without a fight?" Her question was obviously rhetorical and they knew it.

Lee glanced at Ember and she looked away, her face burning. She couldn't stand the hurt in his eyes. As much as they fought, she loved her brother, hated the thought of truly hurting him. She'd always known one day he'd learn about them, about the family business, all the lies she'd told him. All the things she had never said pricked at her conscience. The coven had chosen their own time and place for outing themselves. And some of them were so pleased, their gloating tingled in the air, riding the power that threatened to crest at any moment.

By now, the hum of power was so strong the room was all but vibrating. They truly had come for a fight. She threw a surprised glance in the direction of Aunt Gwen, but the older woman was lost in the rising power. For a second, Ember thought they were going to loose their magic on the agents with no concern for any of the other survivors in the room.

Their mother was still talking. Something about not letting anyone take her children. Ember would have laughed, but the room had turned into a powerful powder keg, primed to blow. The only thing holding the punishing power in check was the strength of the coven's lead witch. Their mother.

Stupidly, a few officers reached for their side arms. The smarter ones had backed away.

"Stand down." The police chief's words barely carried over the thrum of magic. "Leslie, please. We didn't have a choice."

"You'd really risk it all right now? Expose yourselves with all that's going on out there?" Jim asked.

"For my children?" Their mom actually sounded surprised by his question. "You have no idea what I'd risk."

"You can take Ember," the older female agent, Alice, said, "but we can't let you take both. It's too late for Lee. We have too much documented."

"That's fine with me," Aunt Gwen said, her thin lips turning up into a smug smile.

Their mother frowned at her.

Aunt Gwen stared back at her sister, her feelings on the matter obvious. Gwen was about the only one who dared to act that way toward her. She'd never liked either Ember or Lee. But Ember knew there was more to it than sibling rivalry, even more than Mom being the leader of their coven, but she couldn't reveal any of that to Lee.

Suddenly, Aunt Gwen lurched and grabbed her stomach. She retched, loud and long, the contents of her stomach spewing out onto the floor. It reeked of garlic and bitter herbs and tobacco. Ember had to cover her face to keep herself from joining her.

"Oh my," Gwen said, under her breath. "I think our conduit is maturing." She glanced up at Lee, a hungry look on her face.

Ember glared at her aunt.

Their mother nodded like she understood, like she'd actually even considered allowing them to use Lee like that. She moved toward him and put out her hand in a completely out of character, motherly gesture.

Ember felt the urge to jump between them. Only, she knew better. The coven had already shifted, making the elemental connection physical by the laying on of hands. They encircled Lee, and all she could do was to reach out and join in the raising of power before she got left behind.

"This isn't the way, Mrs. Macconal. We need each other," the older woman said.

"Leslie," Jim said, a hint of pleading in his voice. "Don't do this."

Mom's eyes turned hard. "If you come after them, after any of us, I will make certain you regret it."

Then, with the cone fully raised, the coven's power closed over them. The station faded away, shimmered, and became the familiar walls of their basement.

The look on Lee's face would have been priceless, except Ember knew how he would feel now, knowing how long she had been lying to him. Keeping secret their heritage. Who and what they were. Her stomach turned sour.

The others headed up the stairs, without comment. The trampling of their footsteps fading as they reached the upper floor and went about their normal activities. For them, Ember thought, this was business as usual. Lee stared after them, like they were aliens or something, which is exactly what they suddenly must have seemed.

All of them. Including her.

"Lee," Mom said, "I need to speak with Ember." She flicked her eyes toward the stairs.

"Are we seriously not going to talk about how we all just fucking teleported?" His voice was strained and, though he was talking to their mother, he glared at Ember.

"Language, mister!" Mom let out her breath and touched his arm. He pulled away. "Please. You and I will talk this out later. Right now, I have something important to discuss with your sister."

He folded his arms.

"In private," Mom said.

"I can hardly wait to hear you explain it." He stormed up the stairs.

They watched him go. Then, her mother walked over and sank down onto the worn leather sofa that had been hauled down into the basement when their dad had decided he needed a place to get away from all the Macconal clan 'women folk,' as he used to call them. Ember guessed it was better than saying witches out loud.

"Ember. Sit." She patted the couch beside her.

Ember shook her head. "What the hell, Mom? Did you see the look on his face? You should have let me tell him." She pushed the hair off her forehead and walked toward the stairs. "He's going to hate us, now. He's going to hate me."

"It couldn't be helped. You know full well we couldn't let them just whisk you away like that." She pinched the bridge of her nose between her thumb and forefinger. "Gwen is merely waiting for me to show any sign of weakness. And we can't have a schism in the coven. Especially, not now."

"What do you mean? What makes now any worse than any other time?"

"Don't be dense, Ember!" She shot up off the sofa. "Look around you. Things were hard enough for us before. We were just managing to hold it all together. Now. All this business with people gaining special abilities, developing powers that even we haven't seen before. We'll be fighting against more than just the powers that escape the Nexus." She smoothed her suit jacket. "I need you to stay close to him."

"A lot of good that's done us all these years." Ember felt the palms of her hands heat up and forced her anger back. The last thing she needed was to show her mother just how little control she'd managed to learn, despite Seanna's mentoring.

"He may not like it, but he's going to need you. Now, more than ever before."

The certainty in her voice made Ember shiver. "What has Granny foreseen?" she asked, her voice a low whisper.

Her mother shook her head and looked away.

"Tell me." She stepped around to lock eyes with her

mother. "I have a right to know."
   "Chaos and loss."

# Five
Wed, Aug 24, 8:16pm

### - Lee -

"So," Jen said, on the porch beside him, "you never said what your power is."

"I can heal people," he said, as if he'd already gotten used to the idea, and it was now somehow mundane. Of course, he was understating his new abilities. Something in him felt the need to keep the finer details to himself, even from Jen.

"Oh. Wow," she said, somewhat shocked and happy for him at the same time. "That's a good one. Guess you won't be flying me to school tomorrow, though, huh?"

"Guess not. That is, if I even go."

It hit him then, and he felt like an idiot. Jen's mom had stage two renal carcinoma and was scheduled for surgery in three weeks. She would've gone in sooner, but there'd been some sort of problem with her insurance that needed to be sorted. He was about to say something, when he heard voices coming toward the door.

"—activity at the park." It was Ember. "Said we should answer. I guess we're still on the same side. For now."

She opened the door and jumped a little in surprise when she saw Lee and Jen there. Tara and Seanna were with her. Lee sensed a bit of fear and anxiety in his sister, maybe at being overheard? Or possibly the lifetime of lies?

Ember said, "Hey. I thought you were upstairs."

"Nope," he said and refused to look at her.

Lee and Jen leaned outward to allow the three to pass. Seanna stopped to offer him a sandwich and an apologetic smile.

"Ember said you guys didn't eat dinner."

He took it from her, and their fingers touched. She was always warm, no matter the season. Lee knew it was wrong to be attracted to a cousin, but out of all of them, she was his favorite. Cute, funny and smart, Seanna always went out of her way to talk to him, to listen to what he had to say instead of only talking about herself. He wasn't as close to her as he was with Jen, but he enjoyed her company all the same. Besides, he had no reason to be angry with her, or any of his cousins for that matter.

If anyone deserved blame, it was his mother and sister. And his aunts. He didn't need new reasons to not like them, but he wasn't about to turn any away either.

"Yeah," he said and took a bite. He hadn't realized until then just how hungry he was. His words marred by chewing, he added, "Oh my god. Thank you so much."

Seanna giggled. "Relax. It's just plain peanut butter." He hated jelly and loved that she'd remembered. A little more seriously, she added, "Your mom's waiting for you in her office."

Lee nodded and took another bite. He seemed to struggle with swallowing it, when Seanna offered him a drink from her water bottle. He thanked her with a grunt and drank nearly half. With a shake of her head and smile, she left to join the other two.

"Where are you guys off to?" Jen asked and took a bite of the offered sandwich.

She seemed a bit annoyed at the whole exchange but didn't say anything about it. Jen was like that sometimes around his cousins. Or was it just around Seanna?

Ember said, "Errands to run," at the same time Tara said, "The park."

"Mmmkay," Jen said in a knowing tone. "Well, be careful."

The three girls exchanged looks, then headed for one of the four cars parked in the driveway.

"I gotta go," Lee said and plucked the last bite from Jen's hand. She slapped his arm playfully and laughed. "Time to find out just how much everyone's been lying to me."

"Hey." Jen reached out and took hold of his forearm, just long enough for him to stop and look her in the eyes. "It'll be fine. Text me later, okay?"

He gave a nod and headed inside.

The house was busy with all his cousins rushing about, carrying small boxes and candles, metal bowls and maps. It looked like they were getting ready for something in the dining room. His grans and aunts were already there, seated at the huge table, drinking coffee. The heady scent of incense filled the entryway, though he couldn't see where it was burning.

He went upstairs to wash the peanut butter from his hands and ran into aunt Gwen in the hallway outside the bathroom. She gave him a dirty look, as if she'd tasted something foul. The reek of cigarettes and alcohol coming off her was like a palpable aura.

"Are you staying the night or something?" he asked with contempt as he passed her. "Yay."

"Excuse me?" she asked and turned, looking as if he'd slapped her. "I don't care for the tone, young man."

Lee stopped and looked back. Normally he would've just let it go and kept walking, but he was still mad at her for what she'd said at the police station, at how she'd been first to abandon him.

"Get used to it," he told her flatly, brow furrowed and almost daring her to a confrontation.

"You just proved us all right," she said instead, with a smug smile. "A little bit of power, and it went straight to your head." Her eyes narrowed, and her voice took on a threatening tone. "A word of advice. It didn't help your father. It won't help you."

"Technically not a word," Lee said sarcastically, "but thanks all the same."

He wanted to ask about his father. She obviously knew something, but he refused to give her the satisfaction of denying him answers. That's what his mother was waiting downstairs for.

Lee left his aunt standing there in the hallway and went to clean up. When he came back out, she was gone.

*All for the best,* he thought. Who knows what he might've said to her if given the opportunity. He had years' worth of bile just waiting to be spewed.

He found his mother in the office, a downstairs room on the opposite side of the house from the kitchen and living room. She was sitting at her desk, poring through folders of paperwork. She had a laptop on the edge, not even plugged in. His mother didn't trust computers when it came to her work. There was a stack of giant leather books on the other end of the desk, and in the center was a brass bowl with smoke lilting up and out. It smelled like forest and dirt, like a kicked over campfire.

"So no one else can hear," she said and swatted away a wisp of smoke.

*I'm supposed to believe that's a spell?* He looked at the

incense with more than just disbelief. The sudden urge to slap it off her desk in a tantrum came over him. *Like I care who hears us!*

She closed the manila folder full of papers she'd been writing in, added it to a stack and dropped them heavily onto the laptop.

Lee reined in his emotions and sat in the wooden chair opposite her to quietly wait. He could sense her dread, the fear at how he might react. It was hard enough to get a handle on his own feelings, without having to constantly deal with everyone else's, but he didn't withdraw his cells from her. He wanted to know what she was feeling, if she was telling him the truth.

"You have a lot of questions," she began, "so how about if I try to explain everything at once, then you can ask me what you need to fill in all the blanks?"

"You can skip the part about being witches," he said, a little harder than he intended. "I figured that out on my own. I just want to know why you've kept it all a secret from me. Everyone in the house knows. Even people at the station knew. And if they didn't before, they sure as hell do now."

"Cerberus," she said. "The men and women in suits were from an agency that keeps the supernatural in check. Sungrove," she went on, searching for words, "the entire city, is built over a Super Nexus, a massive intersection of ley lines that generates a lot of magic. It sometimes causes unusual things to happen, portals to open, planes to cross over, realities to blend. And it all acts like a magnet for the supernatural. Our family, our coven, has been protecting the Nexus for generations, long before there was a California or United States. We work with Cerberus, and have for years, because our goals are aligned. They want the city safe. We want the Nexus safe."

Lee said, "So, what, monsters are real, and you use magic to track them down? Kill them?"

"No," she said with a small laugh. "I mean, yes, sometimes, we help track down the bigger problems, but that's what hunters are for. The rogue monsters that need to be put down are all dealt with by other families, people who've spent their entire lives training for nothing else. No, we help when magic is needed, to close a portal or sort realities, things beyond the physical. Demons and vampires are a bit beneath us."

Lee's eyes went wide.

"What the shit?" he said. "Those are real?"

"Language," she warned, but whatever authority she'd held over him as a mother was severely damaged. Lee didn't so much as flinch, just stared back at her in growing anger. "But yes, they're real. And you don't know about them, because there's a system in place. We all have jobs to do, and we do it well. Without Cerberus, keeping it all a secret would be much harder. It used to be much harder."

"That's it then?" he asked, voice rising. "You're all witches, and screw me because I'm not one of you?"

"What?" She was taken aback at that. "No, that's not it at all. I know your aunts can be hard on you, but it's not because of anything you did or who you're not." Again, she seemed to search for the right words. "They act the way they do out of fear, because of something your father and I did before you were born."

"Dad?" Aunt Gwen's words echoed in his mind. "So what did you do then?" He leaned forward in the chair. "And what's it got to do with me?"

"The women in our family," she tried to explain, as if still deciding how much truth she should share, "are almost always witches. Only once, maybe twice, in a generation is one born without magic, barren, like my cousin Riley. There was nothing wrong with her. She just didn't have any."

"I've never heard of her," Lee said and understood why. Magic was all his family cared about. If someone was born without it, they were probably treated the way he was.

"She was allowed to move away," his mother said, like it was some great concession, "to marry outside the family. All her children would've been barren, too."

*Which means they were useless,* Lee thought. *Wait, outside the family? What the hell does that mean?*

"And the men," she continued, "are almost always conduits. They're born without magic but can channel ley lines into other witches. They amplify our spells, make the coven more powerful."

"Let me guess," Lee said. "I'm supposed to be one, but I'm not. And since I can't contribute to the coven, I'm worthless, no better than the barren cousin you sent away. Oh, sorry, I mean the cousin you let leave."

He could tell his words had hurt her, could feel it in her chest.

"Lee," she said, on the verge of tears. Her voice and heart were full of sadness. "You're not worthless. And you are a conduit, but I'm forbidden to teach you how. It's part of my punishment."

"For what?" Lee demanded. "What did you do?"

"Your father," she said, fighting back tears from all the memories, "was what the others call an abomination. He was a warlock, a male witch and a conduit. He didn't have magic of his own, but he could channel ley lines into spells. He kept it a secret from everyone else, was too afraid to use it anyway, afraid of all the stories about how warlocks become corrupted. It's too much power for one person. No matter how good their intentions, they always end up doing harm."

Still, none of this explained what they'd done. As much as it hurt him to see his mother this way, that he even cared she was in pain, he wanted to know the truth. All of it.

"How many others have there been?"

"In our line? Just two," she replied, "and the number

of people they killed before they could be stopped?" She shook her head. "They were worse than any monsters our family's had to deal with."

"Again," Lee asked, "What did you do?"

She couldn't look him in the eyes.

"You weren't born yet," she said, "but we could tell you were barren. Your father kept having visions, of your sister in the future, facing a great darkness all alone. He was our last conduit. Channeling magic has a price. It burns you up from the inside. All the men in our family knew the risk, paid the price. Even using them sparingly, few conduits live past thirty. Your father was thirty-two, and there were no more like him."

"Wait," Lee said, as details began to click into place. "What do you mean I was barren? You said only girls could be born barren."

"Your father convinced me," she said and swallowed, wiped a tear from her nose, "that since you didn't have magic anyway, you could become a conduit. The family desperately needed one, and your father was running out of time. I agreed to do a spell."

Lee couldn't believe what he was hearing.

"You changed me." More than the notion that his body had been altered against his will, he was crushed by the thought of everything else that had been stolen from him. "I was supposed to be a witch, like everyone else. I would've been one of you, part of the family."

"No," she said, pleading. "Don't you see? You would have never...you wouldn't have been a witch. You had no magic." She shook her head, as if thinking it was too much to bear. "You would've been sent away. But as a conduit, you filled a void."

It was all too much, her words and jumble of emotion crowding his own, the realization of all that'd been taken from him and forced upon him.

"How could you do that to me?" he asked, betrayed

and disgusted. "Is that why you're being punished by the others? For stealing who I was?"

His mother wiped her eyes with both hands and shook her head.

"They found out about Ward's visions," she replied, "what your dad was. He would've been shunned, cast out of the family or worse, if he hadn't died shortly after the spell."

*Spell?* Lee thought, and it angered him even more. *You said he died in a car crash on the way to the hospital when I was born.*

She looked at him then, to let the words sink in, but all he heard were more lies.

"They were afraid we'd made you like him," she said, "that you'd become an abomination. I refused to give you up like they wanted. I just couldn't. But they wouldn't let me train you, either. They made me keep it all a secret. I've wanted to tell you so many times, but a witch's oath can't be broken. I swore I would never tell or teach you about magic. But today, at the station, they let me use magic to save Ember," she said and quickly added, "to save both of you. Doing so freed me from part of that oath. I could tell you everything I'd always wanted."

"But you still can't teach me."

Lee was beyond angry but tried not to let it cloud his judgement. He was struggling to comprehend it all, to be understanding and see things from her perspective, to see why she would do such a terrible thing to him. It was difficult to think straight with the influx of her emotions, the overwhelming regret and desperate need for his forgiveness.

"No," she admitted, "I can't. But now that you know the truth, maybe you and your sister can work it out. Your father's visions were never wrong. At some point, Ember's going to need you to be her conduit. But listen," she said, "if you're going to pursue this on your own, you have to resist. You can't give in to the urge to cast spells on your own. If I had access to the Nexus, unrestricted and unrestrained?" She shook her head with a single snort of nervous laughter. "Please. I know you're angry. You probably hate me, and you have every right to. But believe what I'm telling you. If you are like your father and you give in to those urges, you'll become the monster your aunts and everyone else are so deathly afraid of."

"Is that it then?" Lee asked and got up. "No more secrets I should know about? No more life changing news?"

"If Cerberus has taken charge," she said, "of dealing with the Affected...Without a conduit, I don't know what we can do to protect you and your sister. We have artifacts, spells we can cast in preparation..."

"But it might not be enough," Lee finished for her. She nodded. He could feel her desire to come around the desk and hug him. He wasn't there yet. She'd have to wait for his forgiveness, if he ever decided to give it to her. "I'll figure it out."

He turned to leave.

"Lee," she called after. "I love you."

He nodded and left the room.

There were yells coming from the front doorway. He hurried to see what the problem was, taking two steps at a time. Ember, Tara and Seanna had come back, and were struggling with a strange man he'd never seen. A bit dirty and more than crazy, he was shouting and kicking at the three, with both arms restrained behind him.

*Is this what they do when I'm not around?*

"Who the heck is this?" Lee asked and got too close. The guy kicked him in the upper thigh. A couple of inches to the left would have meant a whole new world of pain. "Jackass!"

Lee punched him across the jaw. By the sound of the crack and the way the head lolled, he was certain he'd broken something. What he sensed from the man was distorted, dual waves of pain and emotion, like it came from two different people.

"Hey!" Ember shouted at Lee. "You can't go around punching people like that. Not anymore."

The guy flailed all of a sudden and hit Seanna in the face with his forehead. She went tumbling back against a wall, as Tara caught a backward kick to the middle.

Something caught Lee's attention. He turned to the big mirror hanging in the hallways and saw in its reflection a pale vision of another person struggling to break free of the man's body. Dark chains wrapped around him kept the spirit trapped inside. The man saw Lee take notice and grinned at him with a wicked stare. The same pale light seemed to shine in his eyes.

Ember snapped open her right hand, and purple fire erupted from her palm. She smashed it against the side of the man's head and held it there while he screamed.

"Try it again," she told him and let the flames die out. "I dare you."

All Lee could think was that all this time his sister had magic. She knew about everything and kept it from him. They all did. Seanna climbed to her feet, and just the sight of her caused a knot in his stomach.

He was a stranger in his own family.

Ember dragged the man off to the basement. Tara took a deep breath and followed after. Seanna had a nasty cut on her cheekbone, and blood had begun to run down her jawline.

"Come here," he said.

He put a hand to her cheek when she drew close. It took a few moments for enough cells to form inside her before he could direct them to heal the wound. She must have felt the gash close, walked over to the mirror for a better look.

"Nice," she said in admiration and checked her jaw for a scar. "You're even better than Aunt Bri." She gave him a sideways look then leaned in and kissed him on the cheek. "You just became my new best friend," she said and left with a smile.

Lee slowly frowned after her, his affection for her deflated. He knew she was only joking, but her words instantly soured his mood. It just brought back all the time he'd wasted in junior high, spent trying to please girls who were only interested in what he could do for them.

Jen wasn't like that. She understood him, never asked or wanted more than to hang out. That's why she was his best friend and had been his entire life. Even with her mother dying of cancer, she didn't ask for his help, try to use him for what he could do.

Of course, he would heal her mother. It wasn't even a consideration. But she knew not to ask. That's what made him love her. That's why she was his best friend and why he'd always be there for her.

He went outside and headed next door.

# - Ember -

After dropping her chaos and death bomb, her mother glanced at her cell phone, stuck out her hand to ward off any questions and took an incoming call.

"Fine, but only because of our working relationship," she said. "If anything goes wrong, we will have more than words." She hung up, her face tight.

Ember had a few choice words for her mother, but she kept her mouth shut. Her mother was still the head of their coven, and when she talked business, nobody in their right mind smarted off to her. Not even Ember.

When she told Ember to round up her cousins and head to the park to pick up some rogue Cerberus informant, Ember spun on her heel, deciding she should leave before she said something that would get her warded in an attic room for the duration.

She found Tara in the herb room. Her long black hair, streaked with magenta, was pulled back into a ponytail to keep it from falling into whatever she was brewing. "Where's Seanna?"

"Kitchen," Tara mumbled without looking up from the concoction she was grinding.

"Ugh. Why are you grinding Jimson and wait...what is that?"

Tara glanced up at her distractedly and a puff of foul smoke whiffed out of the mortar. "Dammit, Ember! That was the last of the dried musk ox bladder."

"What the hell were you using musk ox bladder for? No. Never mind. I don't want to know." Ember stepped back from the table and bumped into a supply shelf, jostling a multitude of vessels and containers. She froze, waiting for everything to settle before sidling away. "Whoa. That was close. Last thing I need is to have to come up with replacements of whatever freaky ingredients the Greenies are experimenting with," she said.

Tara gave her a dirty look. "You know I hate when you call us that."

"Sorry." Ember tried to say it like she meant it, but Tara had always been a better empath than Ember was a liar. "Earth witch just doesn't have the same ring. And Hedgers? That's just cruel."

Her cousin frowned.

"Anyway, we have a gig."

"Something special?" Tara started scooping up her tools.

"Doesn't sound like it." Ember headed for the kitchen. "I'll grab Seanna and meet you in the front room."

Seanna was making lunch. At least, that's what some people called it. Personally, Ember hated peanut butter and white bread. "There's no accounting for taste," she said. *Especially in a family that likes mixing herbs and dried animal guts together.*

"Want some?" Seanna finished slathering the gooey spread on her bread and pressed another slice on top, then popped the sticky spoon in her mouth.

"Ugh, no thanks. Even without having lunch, you know I wouldn't touch that stuff. Especially not after the reek Tara just made in the la-bor-a-tory." She drew out the word like in a creepy old horror movie.

"Ha ha." Seanna gave her an annoyed look.

"Tough crowd." Ember gestured to the sandwich on the counter. "Grab your lunch, we gotta go."

She explained the plan as they headed out the door. "Mom got a call about some activity at the park. Said we should answer. I guess we're still on the same side. For now." She opened the door and clamped her mouth shut, almost biting her tongue.

Lee and Jen were sitting on the porch steps. He couldn't have set a better ambush if he'd planned it. No matter. The cat was out of the bag, now. The swear-spell Ember had taken at seven still seemed to have some effect. Or maybe she'd just been lying to him and keeping secrets so long, she couldn't break the habit. At any rate, it felt like her jaw had been slammed shut by an especially powerful charm, and it took a moment to get it working again. "Hey. I thought you were upstairs."

"Nope." He glared up at her. Then he and Jen leaned apart, meaningfully.

Ember took the hint and clomped down the steps. She knew it was childish to stomp, but the sound of her grungy ass-kicker boots on the wooden steps gave her a cathartic release. For about ten seconds. Till Seanna handed Lee that damn sandwich. It irked Ember how her cousin always managed to out-nice her with her own brother.

She didn't wait to watch the love-fest and tromped down the sidewalk, jingling the car keys at Seanna.

"Where are you guys off to?" Jen called over. She was clearly annoyed at the whole Seanna-Lee exchange. Good. That made two of them.

"The park," Tara blurted.

"Errands to run," Ember said at the same time and gave her cousin a look that their Grans would have called an evil-eye.

Jen rolled her eyes. "Uh-huh. Well, be careful."

It was obvious Jen could tell they were lying, but Ember was hoping Lee was so focused on his sandwich, he hadn't noticed. Ember raised her eyebrows at Seanna, who finally got the message.

Ember was in the driver's seat, revving the engine by the time Seanna hopped in the back. She barely had the door closed before Ember backed out onto the street.

"What the hell?" Seanna asked.

"Just buckle-up so I don't get a ticket," Ember growled as she put the car in drive.

"So, is Lee really that pissed at you?" Seanna buckled her seatbelt.

Ember glanced at Seanna's reflection in the rearview

mirror. Green eyes stared back at her, as if the answer really mattered to her.

Shit! With her eighteenth birthday coming up, it probably did. "Naw." Ember tried to sound convincing, but Tara stopped tapping at her cell phone and gave her a disbelieving look.

"How would you feel, if you suddenly found out your whole family had been lying to you your entire life?" Tara asked. "Especially something on the scale of this?" She waved a hand at the three of them. "I know I'd be whipping up something pretty lethal."

"He'll get over it." Ember stepped on the gas to get through the yellow light at the intersection.

"You better hope so," Tara turned back to her phone.

Seanna kept quiet. Her pensive aura seemed to permeate the space inside the car.

A deep itch formed at the back of Ember's neck as they pulled into the parking lot at Hillside Park. "Seanna. Knock it off." She slammed the car into park and rubbed at the back of her neck.

"It's not me," Seanna said at the same time as Tara whispered, "It's not her." She'd dropped her cell onto the car seat and was staring intently out the passenger side window.

"Damn!"

"Language, young lady," they both chimed, mimicking Ember's mother.

Ember purposely ignored them.

Slowly, the three of them opened their doors and slid out of the car. Ember went around to the passenger side and assumed the point position of their standard triad posture. She felt the power rise up as Tara and Seanna raised a tributary of energy from the local ley line. Their precision and control was incredible, and the only thing that kept Ember's envy in check was the knowledge that, as long as they were united, she had a share in that control.

She cupped her hands together and let the energy build between them. Heat coalesced into a visible spectrum. It looked like a ball of purple fire, but was really a distilled form of magical energy, power so pure it might as well have been dipped straight from the well. Ember had the unique ability to grasp that energy and control it. Though, her unaided control tended to be tenuous and sometimes things got a bit scorched. She had the burn scars to remind her. Nothing to match Seanna's demon touch scar, though.

They waited by the car and scanned the surrounding greenery. The park was oddly empty. And quiet. No people enjoying the outdoors. No animals rustling in the bushes. No birds twittering in the trees. The missing people might easily be due to the current events unfolding around town. But the birds and the animals were smart enough to either hide or vacate when something dark was in the vicinity.

There was no sign of their quarry, just the annoying itch at the back of her neck getting deeper and more persistent.

"Whatever it is, it's dark," Tara said. "Not the deepest, but likely strong."

Ember nodded. "It's higher level than we expected. How far can we expand the net?" she asked in a quiet voice. She would have signed the question, but she had her hands full hanging onto the ley energy.

"Here?" Tara said from behind her. Ember couldn't see her cousin shrug, but she felt it in the way the energy rose and fell just a bit. "Ten, maybe fifteen yards at most, and it will be like dragging a heavy extension cord behind us to raise that much power and stretch it out that far."

"It will thin the webbing, too," Seanna reminded them.

"Stay within the ten yards. Make it feel like our limit and hope that lures our new friend close enough?"

"Works." The way the two of them spoke in unison when manipulating magics together always weirded Ember out. For some reason, she never felt that in sync with anyone, no matter how hard she tried. The closest she'd ever come was with Allie. She forced her thoughts away from what had happened to her friend earlier. This was not the time to lose focus.

They walked forward, spreading out as they moved. Ember kept her hands cupped at her midriff and tried not to look down or bring attention to the swirling purple orb of energy she held.

Late afternoon shadows stretched beneath the trees and spread across the green grass. A light breeze ruffled the leaves. Inside the net, no air moved, but the itch at the base of her neck grew more intense. She glanced over her left shoulder at Tara.

*Trees,* Tara signed in ASL. They had all learned it at a young age. Not only because of cousin Keara, but because it had turned out to be a great way to talk and send messages in class. Until the teachers had figured out what they were doing and decided it was the equivalent of passing notes.

It still came in handy.

Ember nodded, since she currently had her hands full, and headed slowly toward the shaded picnic area.

Seanna edged a little further out to their right and Tara kept pace.

Suddenly, a man stepped out of the shadows. He wasn't tall, but he was broad, with the shoulders of a bodybuilder and the face of someone who was not afraid to tangle with anyone. Especially, not three teenaged girls. His eyes glowed amber. If she hadn't known better, Ember would have thought it merely the reflection of the setting sun, but it was clear that evil had its claws in him. Whether by force or by his own allowance was not discernable without the right tools. They had to take him back to the coven. And with as little damage as possible, to him as well as them.

He glared at the three of them and opened his mouth as if he was going to say something, but all that came out was a long hissing noise like one of Grans old steam kettles.

"Great, a Sluagh possession," Tara said, pulling harder

on the ley line. "Seanna. Load up."

Ember felt her cousin reach out her gathering spell, but before Seanna could pull the additional energy in to reinforce her side of the web, the possessed man sprang out of the shadows and attacked. He moved fast. Faster than humanly possible.

Before they could make a move, Seanna flew through the air. Ember felt the net of power stretch and thin as her cousin landed with a thud and tumbled to a stop more than fifteen yards away. The threads of protective energy snapped and wavered. Ember felt herself losing control of her power orb as the possessed man spun to face her.

"One down, two to go." The man's voice sounded like the edge of a metal saw being dragged across the sidewalk.

Fear gripped Ember's throat. Not just fear of the dark power facing her, but of her own tenuous grasp on the power she held in her hands. The image of the last time she'd lost control rose up before her. She could almost feel the flames that had surrounded her before Mom and Aunt Brianna had been able to put them out. Auntie Bri still bore some of the scars from the magical wildfire that had touched her before they'd brought the flames under control.

"Hold on." Tara grunted with the effort of pulling more energy up from the rivers of magic that flowed deep underground.

The man's glowing eyes turned on her, as if in sudden understanding. "The power lines are not all down."

Heat filled Ember's hands as the energy fought to loose itself from her grip. *No. Not now,* she thought, sparing a glance at Seanna, who lay unmoving in the grass. She couldn't lose control now. Cold sweat trickled down her back, and she suddenly thought of the stupid story book Lee had made her read to him about a million times when he was little, The Little Engine That Could. A hysterical laugh attempted to force itself from her and she gritted her teeth.

The man tilted his head to one side, as if sizing her up. Then, in a blur of motion, he rushed across the grass.

"Ember, catch!" Tara flooded the remaining energy at her. The shock of it nearly bowled her over before she got her palms turned outward and released the orb of power at him. It expanded as it flew through the air and hit him hard, encompassing his entire body. A high-pitched wail escaped him as he fell to the ground, writhing in pain, body jerking and spasming like he'd been hit with a high voltage taser.

"Whoa." Tara panted beside her. "That was close."

"Closer for some than others," Seanna groaned, picking herself up and hobbling over to where Ember stood staring at her hands.

"Nice work," Tara said, still a little breathless from having passed so much power.

The man had stopped moving. A purple glow still encompassed him, like a magical aura. "Let's get him trussed up before the effects wear off." Seanna pulled a pair of spelled handcuffs from her back pocket.

By the time they got back to the house, the possessed man was awake and making a loud ruckus in the trunk. His shouts alternated between the grinding snarled threats of the Sluagh and the yelling of an angry man ready to kick the ass of whomever, or whatever, got close enough.

Tara was driving and cursing him under her breath. Ember's hands still burned from juggling the power orb without Seanna's support, even though Tara had slathered on a thick layer of her infamous healing salve. If she hadn't needed it, Ember would have refused. The stuff smelled like boiled cabbage mixed with sulphur and goat urine. She looked down at her hands. Maybe it was. She redoubled her efforts against touching anything.

In reality, she'd been lucky. The blast that left her hands could have maimed her. Probably would have. Before the Rumbling.

A not so muffled "…burn in hell…" came from the trunk. Tara took the turn into the driveway without slowing, and they heard the solid thud of a head hitting the trunk lid.

"Maybe that'll shut him up." Tara stamped on the brake and put the car in park.

"…bunch of lousy, good for nothing…"

"Guess not," Seanna told her. "I told you we should have spelled a cone of silence around him."

"Waste of power," Tara said, shutting off the engine. "You'll wear yourself out using it for everything like that."

"I don't use it for everything," Seanna shot back. She slid out of the passenger seat and opened the door for Ember, who eased herself out of the back seat. Seanna made a face and backed away. "You know you can wipe that crap off after just a few minutes, right?"

"I thought it worked better the longer you left it on?"

Seanna let out a snort of laughter. "Seriously? Are you the last person to figure out Tara just tells everyone that to see how long they'll put up with the smell?"

Tara stood at the back of the car, smirking. "Way to spoil the fun, Seanna." She tossed Ember a rag.

"Great. You're such a jerk." Ember wiped the stinky salve from her hands and flung the rag back at her dark-haired cousin. Tara ducked and the rag went wide.

The pounding and yelling from inside the trunk grew louder.

"You better pick that up before someone's dog gets hold of it." Tara raised her voice to be heard over the noise.

"Why? Will it make them sick?" Ember glanced at Seanna.

She shook her head before Tara could spin up a tale.

"Spoilsport." Tara rapped on the trunk as the noise level increased. "Hey. Quiet down in there, or you'll get another dose."

*I don't think I have it in me,* Ember signed.

Tara's hands flew through the air. *He doesn't know*

*that.* "Shields up," she told Seanna.

"Already done." Seanna pointed to the sidewalk, where light shimmered like heat waves over a desert. "Not a complete blackout. Just enough blur so no one from more than ten feet away will be able to tell what's happening. But it won't last all day." She popped the trunk open and they stared into the man's angry eyes.

He hissed.

Seanna grabbed his bound ankles. Tara reached for his shoulders. His jaws snapped as he twisted his head around and tried to bite her. "Should have gagged him," Tara said. "Look, Jug-head." She pointed at Ember. "She was holding back in the park, but we don't have to do this the easy way."

His eyes flicked toward Ember. She gave him her most vicious smile.

He relaxed and let them haul him out of the trunk, even helped a little out of self-preservation. Once they had him standing, Seanna on one arm, Tara holding his other, he could barely shuffle a few inches at a time.

"This is taking too long." Seanna ticked her eyes at the sidewalk. "Not going to hold long enough at this rate."

"Fine. Untruss his ankles," Tara said. "But no funny business," she warned him.

Ember could see his brain working behind his eyes, even though he nodded. She tried not to sigh aloud as she flexed her fingers, wondering if she would be able to call up even a thread of energy.

They'd managed to herd him to the front door when he suddenly stiffened, his nostrils flaring. "Coven," he growled, then let out a huge roar, yanking his arms free of Tara and Seanna. His hands were still cuffed behind him, but his legs were free, and he was making serious use of them.

Lee appeared in the doorway, managing to ask, "Who is this?" before the guy kicked him hard in the leg.

"Jackass!" Lee hauled off and punched him in the face

with a loud crack.

"Hey!" Ember shouted. "You can't go around punching people like that. Not anymore." She glared at their struggling prisoner. "Besides, we've got this."

The possessed man continued to kick and flail as they dragged him through the front room and into the hallway. He caught Seanna in the face with his forehead and she thudded into the wall. Then he slammed a back-kick into Tara's stomach.

A rush of anger hit Ember. She felt the heat rising in her already tender hands. "That's it!" She snapped. Power raveled into her left hand, and she mashed a fresh orb of energy into the side of the man's head. He let out an ear-piercing scream.

"Try it again," she snarled, as she let the power fade out. "I dare you." She swung open the basement door and shoved him inside. "Move," she ordered, her hands shaking in surprise and elation at what she had just managed to do. Her palms practically itched for more power, but she knew the control she had just exerted had been a fluke. No way could she repeat it on command.

The man whimpered as he was herded down the stairs.

# Six
Wed, Aug 24, 9:08pm

## - Lee -

Jen answered the door with a look of happy surprise. Her eyes began to well up. She knew why he was there.

"I didn't expect to see you again tonight," she said and opened the door wider for him.

"I know," Lee said. He took a step inside, and she caught him off guard with a hug. Lee could count on one hand the number of times he'd seen Jen hug anyone but her mother. It was brief but heartfelt. When she stepped back and aside, he asked, "Is your mom awake?"

"No, but it's all right." She wiped a cheek and closed the door. He could sense in her happiness, relief and an influx of embarrassment. "Come on in. She's upstairs, in bed." He paused in the doorway. "It's fine," Jen insisted. "I'll explain it to her."

"Okay. Oh," he said, when he caught sight of the pale blue polish, "you did your nails. I like that color."

It was her turn to say, "I know."

She closed the door behind him and led the way up the staircase.

Their house was simple, quiet, beautifully decorated with flowers and bright, colorful paintings. It was very different from his home, with the constant ebb and flow of relatives, the noise and lack of privacy. It sort of left him with an empty feeling. There were pictures on the mantle in the hallway but only of Jen and her mom.

Her dad had run off with the babysitter when they were seven. Lee remembered Louisa as a nice enough girl but couldn't imagine anyone wanting to leave Mrs. Haley. Jen's mom was unusually pretty, the sort that belonged in a clothing catalogue, with a perfect smile and big blue eyes. She'd always been nice to Lee, had watched him while his mother was at work and practically raised him alongside Jen.

They turned right at the top of the stairs and stepped into the bedroom. Lee's heart sank when he saw her, pale and sunken cheeks, patches of hair missing. She was frail looking and thin, a stark contrast to the image he kept of her in his mind. The television was on, but she'd fallen asleep. Jen sat on the bed beside her, leaned in about to wake her.

"Wait," Lee whispered, suddenly nervous, "don't. What if I can't? What if it doesn't work?" He saw and felt Jen's heart skip, saw the hope in her turn to fear. Quickly, he added, "I'm not saying it won't, but..."

Jen looked down at her mom and understood. There was no reason to explain it all, to get her hopes up, if even the slightest chance existed that he couldn't heal her. It was better if she just slept through the attempt.

Lee went around to the other side and sat beside Mrs. Haley. He took her hand gently into his. It'd been months since he'd seen her. He hadn't realized what a toll the cancer and chemo had taken, how quickly she had deteriorated. That may have been what she wanted, to hide herself away until the sickness passed. Her fingers were cool to the touch and heartbreakingly fragile.

He closed his eyes and sent cells in through her hand, directed them into the bloodstream. He made them duplicate and spread throughout her entire body, into every organ and system, every muscle and soft tissue. Even though the damage to her kidneys was immediately apparent, there were numerous other problems as a result of the treatments. They'd had to break her with toxins before helping her heal.

"Here we go," Lee said.

He set to work on the kidneys first, once he'd found a healthy blueprint from which to work. He could've used one from his own but didn't want to risk affecting her with the same changes he'd undergone. He also could have let the cells heal her without such scrutiny, but he wanted to be certain. He cared for Mrs. Haley as more than just his best friend's mom. She was the mother he'd always wished his would be, open and honest, ready and willing to listen, not just focused on work.

Long minutes passed, as the cellular damage was undone bit by bit. Slowly, her kidneys were restored to full function and the rest of her body soon followed. The color returned to her cheeks. Her breathing grew strong, steady and restful. Lee let out a deep breath when she was fully healed, her immune system rebuilt and all the meds eliminated from her system.

At his nod, Jen shook her mother's shoulder once, just enough to wake her. Mrs. Haley opened her eyes and saw the two of them staring back.

"Hey," she said and smiled. "What's going on? You two look like you're up to no good."

Jen asked, "How do you feel?"

Her mom considered, brow furrowed, looked at the two of them in turn and moved to sit up.

"I feel great," she said finally. "I don't understand. What happened? Am I dead?"

Jen laughed. "Mom, no! It was the Rumbling. When it ended, it changed people. It gave them abilities. Like healing."

"You?" she asked Jen, eyes wide and proud. Lee's sense of her gratitude was overwhelming, a joy so strong it hurt his chest. Jen was beyond happy too, so relieved she even let herself cry. Jen shook her head and looked to Lee. Her mom turned to him, and the emotion he felt from her seemed to catch in his throat. "You healed me?" she asked and squeezed his hand. He'd forgotten he was still holding it. "Thank you."

She pulled him to her for a hug, the longest, most genuine embrace he could remember ever having. After all he'd been through that day, he admitted to himself how much he needed it too. He hugged her back and nearly cried. He was grateful for the openness of her love and appreciation but equally saddened that he couldn't find that same level of respect and caring in his own family.

Mrs. Haley let him go, a hand still cupped behind his ear, and kissed him on the forehead. It was his turn to be embarrassed, but he endured the affection. It was the sort of maternal love he'd always wanted but never got.

The look in her eyes then changed, as if suddenly she saw him in a different light. With both hands, she pulled him back to her for a full kiss on the lips.

"Mom!" Jen yelled, equally shocked as Lee.

He slipped free, realizing what had happened. With a thought, he withdrew all his cells from her body. Every last one of them.

Mrs. Haley looked as if she'd woken from a dream and touched her lips in sudden shame.

"I'm so sorry," she said and almost choked on the

words. "I was just...so grateful. I don't know what came over me."

"No," Lee said quickly. "No, it's my fault. It's a side effect of the healing. It doesn't always happen, but I'm still new at this. I should've said something."

Jen's frown slowly disappeared. Lee knew, could feel, all the pain of her father leaving had rushed back to the surface in an instant.

Mrs. Haley laughed.

"Good," she said, relieved. "Oh! It feels good to laugh. I am grateful, you know, even if I do feel a little foolish now." She patted his hand. "Don't worry. I have lots of time to get over it, thanks to you."

Lee's cheeks were still burning.

"I should go," he said. "School in the morning."

"You're going?" Jen asked. "To school, I mean."

He got up and headed for the door. "Unless my mother tells me otherwise."

Mrs. Haley said, "Goodnight, Lee. Come visit after school tomorrow. I feel the need to celebrate with chocolate cake."

"I'll be there," he said, still sheepish at the thought that she'd kissed him.

Jen followed him out of the room and called down when he reached the bottom of the stairs.

"Lee," she said and paused, as if she didn't have the words for what she really wanted to say. "Thank you."

He gave a nod and left.

Ember was outside waiting for him, sitting on the curb in front of their house. He walked over and sat next to her. They were quiet for a while, with only crickets and distant cars driving by to fill the silence. It was pretty warm out, but the alternative was to go inside with a family he didn't want to see.

"She tell you everything?" Ember asked.

He could sense the probing in her words, the concern

and fear at how he might react to her part in all their secrets and lies.

"Probably not," Lee said, "but enough to piss me off. Magic is real, you're all witches, and I was supposed to be a girl. That about sum it up?"

Ember looked away.

"Pretty much," she said. He could feel she was hiding something else, that she wanted to say more. Instead, she made excuses. "They made me promise not to tell. Sorry," she said and finally looked him in the eyes.

"Whatever." Lee picked up a pebble and threw it down the block. It went much farther than he'd expected, dinged off a car in the street eight houses away. "Screw aunt Gwen," he said. "Bitch."

Ember gave a short, nervous laugh.

"Agreed." She shook her head, and added in a more serious tone, "They're afraid of you, what you might become. You know, because of dad."

"I don't care," Lee said. He rolled another stone in his hand but didn't throw it. "I might've, a few years ago, when I still wanted everyone to like me." Now? It's too late. "From what mom said, you guys need me. To be a conduit or whatever." He almost laughed at the absurdity of it. "But you were too afraid to teach me how, to let me be a part of it."

"Not me," Ember said defensively. At least she believed she was telling the truth. "It was never my decision. I'm not afraid of you. Being a warlock didn't make Dad a bad person. You're still my little brother. Being a warlock won't change that."

*Ridiculous,* he thought. *All this time, I could've been learning magic, been a part of the family instead of always looking in from the outside.* He looked sidelong at his sister. *Would she teach me? Can I learn it on my own?*

"I don't want to be a warlock," he said, as if he were playing a character in a video game. "It's a pet class, and damage over time spells suck. I'd rather be a mage." He grinned and added, "Glass cannon, baby."

Ember rolled her eyes but laughed with him.

"You and that stupid game."

"I never understood why you didn't like role-playing games," Lee said, "with all the magic and monsters. I get it now. You're already living one."

"I wouldn't go that far," she said, "but yeah. After you deal with some of the stuff we do, the video game version is less than entertaining."

Lee sensed them approach before the car turned onto the street. A black sedan pulled up and parked directly across the way from them. Two people got out, a middle-aged man in a dark suit and Agent Taylor from the police station. They walked over and stood a few feet away.

"Mind if we talk?" the man asked.

He was taller than Lee, but then most people were, looked to be in his late thirties and in good physical shape. He had short brown hair, receding at the temples, and eyes that seemed to take in every detail. Lee could sense the man's emotions but got the impression he was practiced at keeping them in check.

Emily smiled at Lee. She then frowned, as if recalling she was angry with him, and purposely looked away.

"It's your funeral," Ember said. "If my mom sees..."

"She knows we're here," he said. "Besides, I've seen the two of you in action. You can handle yourselves. I'm only here to talk."

The way he spoke, calm and measured, in an even tone of controlled emotion, it was as if he'd given careful thought to what he said—and what he didn't. He looked like someone who spent all day behind a desk, but Lee sensed in him the confidence of someone unafraid of physical conflict.

"I've got nothing else to do," Lee said.

"Good. I'm Will Bailey, Deputy Director of Cerberus.

But before we start," he said to Lee, "I'd like you to undo whatever it is you did to my agent."

Lee looked over at Emily, confused.

"You want me to unheal her?"

Will said, "One of our surveillance algorithms noticed a change in her behavior shortly after her encounter with you. Testing shows Agent Taylor's body is now comprised of over three percent xenohuman microorganisms."

Ember stood and wiped the grass from her jeans. "What's a xenohuman?"

"The Affected," Will replied, hands crossed in front of him, "people biologically altered by the sound waves and vibrations caused by the Pillars. I prefer superhumans," he added with a slight shrug, "but I don't get to make that call."

Lee climbed to his feet as well.

"Oh," he said and withdrew his cells from Agent Taylor. She took in a deep breath, her shoulders more squared, and gave Will a nod. "Sorry about that," Lee explained. "I was scared..."

"And you needed an ally," Will finished for him. "I get that. It was a tactical decision, and a good one. Why didn't you do it to everyone?"

"Wait," Ember said, "do what?"

"I did," Lee replied and amended, "not on purpose. Well, not entirely on purpose. I just didn't do it to the same degree."

"Right," Will said. "That's how you keep track of those around you, get a sense of their emotions. You gave her more than the others, because you wanted to heal her. But that means you can control how much you spread and to whom."

Despite the even tone, the lack of accusation, it felt like an interrogation. Lee looked back to the house, wondered why no one had come out yet. He was keenly aware of

Ember's stare but didn't answer her questions. It was petty but felt good to leave her in the dark.

"Why are you here?" he asked Will.

"And you," Will said to Ember. Her eyes widened a little, as if surprised by the attention. "Magic aside, you can cancel out powers, or at least dampen them. That was quite the teamwork taking down that Xeno at the station."

Ember crossed her arms. "I don't like that word. Labels make it easy to dehumanize others. And like you said, superhuman sounds better. Anyway, what's your point? What do you want?"

"People are afraid," Will said, "of you and others like you. And they should be. Without proper training and direction, you're potentially dangerous." He let the words sink in before continuing. "But I see more than that. I think you could be the greatest assets this country, the world, has ever seen."

"You're here to recruit us," Lee said.

"Yes," Will agreed, "and no, not for Cerberus anyway. Look, the president is being adamant about quarantine. There's no way around it."

"Quarantine?" Ember's tone suggested he may have meant something else. "Like for sick people who might be contagious? Or did you mean internment?"

"I say what I mean," Will assured her. He sighed, and his features seemed to soften. He looked to Lee, as if he was the rational one. "All the data we've collected shows the only thing strong enough to stop a Super," he said, using the word for Ember's benefit, "is another Super. Without help from you and others like you, a lot of innocent people are going to suffer."

"Nice," Ember said and smirked, "trying to make us feel important and like we're just as bad as the others if we don't help." She elbowed Lee, expecting his support, but he found himself agreeing with the Deputy Director. "Besides, I already work with Cerberus."

There was a fear in her tone that made the situation all too real for Lee. They were going to have to leave home, go to this quarantine, and there was nothing his mother or her magic could do to stop it. He'd learned all their secrets just in time for them to mean nothing.

"I'm sorry," Will said. "I wish there was some other option. I can promise you'll be treated with respect, but it's in everyone's best interest if you come with us now."

"Or what?" Ember asked, with the hint of a threat.

Emily had remained quiet this whole time, watching but not moving. Suddenly, she switched her stance. By her attention to Ember and the sense of caution rising in her, it felt like the agent was getting ready to attack.

"You said it yourself," Will went on in that calm voice, though he knew Ember was up to something, "you already work for Cerberus. This is just the next level." To Lee, he said, "You can tell when someone's lying. What's your sense of me?"

"You're not lying," Lee said, "but you're not telling the whole truth, either."

"No," Will said, "I'm not. I know you have issues with secrecy, but it comes with the job."

"Secrets suck," Ember said.

For the first time since he learned what was going on with his family, Lee felt his sister's side of the story. It was like she was trapped, held down against her will. Maybe she'd wanted to tell him but couldn't, witch's oath and all that. He only knew what she was feeling, and it was just as bad as him.

He could see her trembling, knew she didn't want to leave. Lee, on the other hand, didn't seem to mind after all. He didn't want to go back inside anyway, to face all their stares, to be confronted with the years of lying, to act like he somehow understood or even forgave them.

No, leaving was just fine with him.

"Let it go, Em," he said. He wanted her to come with

him. "What's keeping us here, anyway?"

He could see and feel her consider it. He began to wonder if their mother had treated them all that different after all.

"Do we get to say goodbye?" Ember asked.

"Of course," Will said, pleased, and motioned toward the house. "You won't need to bring anything. In fact, it's better if you don't."

Ember started toward the house but stopped to look at Lee. She must've assumed he'd want to say goodbye.

Lee only shrugged.

"I have nothing to say to them."

# - Ember -

"Incoming!" Ember shouted down the basement stairs. "Where do you want him?"

Her mother appeared at the bottom landing. She eyed the man and shook her head. "Possessed?"

"Sluagh, looks like." Ember gave the man a prod as his footsteps slowed. "You don't like me when I'm angry, remember?"

He grunted and tromped down the stairs, his steps awkward and ungainly.

"Put him in the safe room." Mom stepped back and waved them past. "I can't deal with him alone and your Aunt Gwen is out shopping."

Ember herded the man to a room at the far corner of the basement, opened the door and pushed him inside before slamming it shut.

He let out a roar, pounding and kicking at the door. The hollow banging of fist and foot dimmed to a muffled rapping as her mother invoked the magical containment and sound dampening spells that had already been set around the room.

"New trigger canto?" Ember asked.

"With all the fresh activity, I decided we needed to up the prep work to save time on the back end." Her mother waved her off and headed back into her office.

"Mom, wait up." Ember said. "We need to talk."

Her mother paused. "About?"

"You're kidding me, right?"

Her mother faced her. "Ember, now is not the time."

Ember threw up her hands. "Now is not the time? Really?" She ran her fingers through her hair. "Lee? The Rumbling? All the new activity you just mentioned? If now isn't the time, then when, Mother? When is it a good time to talk about all the shit that's going on?"

"Lang—"

"Screw my language! This is not nineteen-fifty-two, Mom. People curse. All the fricking time. Get over it."

"You want to have a conversation? Then act and speak like a civilized adult." Her mother crossed her arms in front of her chest.

"Fine." Ember crossed her own arms. "Things are changing. I'm changing."

"And your point?"

"My point," Ember said, unfolding her arms and holding out her hands, creating a sizzling power orb the size of a baseball.

Her mother let out a small gasp, then nodded in approval. "You've gained control?"

"Some," Ember said. With her new strength, no longer fearful of burning her hands to a crisp, she was able to balance the energy as if it were as harmless as a baseball. She released the thread of power and let the orb fade out.

"Good." Her mother nodded. "Is that all?"

A tight knot twisted itself inside Ember's gut. Not that she'd expected overwhelming approval from her mother, but she'd hoped for more than this. "Really? That's it?"

"What is it you want from me, Ember? A pat on the head for finally obtaining some finesse at something you should have mastered years ago?" Her mother let out a tired sigh. "You are too old to coddle. And I'm too tired to stroke your wounded ego."

The rebuke stung more than Ember had expected. She suddenly knew how Lee must feel. How he must have felt every day of his life being around Aunt Gwen and the Grannies.

"I'm not the only one who's changed. Lee is different now, too."

"Lee is not your concern." Her mother's tone was sharp.

"He's my brother. And he deserves better."

"Better than what?" Her mother's eyes narrowed. "What are you insinuating?"

Ember heard the warning in her mother's voice, but she pushed on. "He deserves better than to be forced into an arranged marriage to someone he doesn't love!" There. She'd said it.

Her mother's face flushed. "As long as you are under this roof, you will not speak against Coven law." Her voice rose as she spoke, not only in volume, but in power.

Ember felt the Nexus vibrating, the ley lines growing taut as violin strings. Her mother's aura became visible and Ember found herself backing up a few steps.

"Out." Her mother closed her eyes and let the power flow back into the earth. Her voice had dropped to a whisper. "Now."

"Fine." Ember set her jaw and stomped up the basement stairs, taking them two at a time.

Seanna was in the kitchen, baking bread. She punched the dough down as Ember walked into the room. "What did you do to piss her off this time?" She locked eyes with Ember and pushed the sides of the dough together.

"Where's Lee?" Ember asked.

"Where else?" Seanna frowned, her fist thudded into the swollen dough

"Seanna—" Ember tried not to look guilty, but she knew Seanna could sense her emotions. "You know I'm right about this," she said.

"Don't say it," Seanna cut her off, angrily wiping her hands on her apron. "I have lived my entire life knowing what I am destined for. It's my rightful place in this coven—"

"Rightful? Don't you think Lee has any say? Any rights?"

Seanna held up her hands, thumbs crossed, palms facing her cousin. "It is Coven Law. So mote it be."

She turned back to her dough, picking it up and slamming it down onto the counter in a cloud of flour dust.

Ember shook her head. "It may well be," she muttered,

"but we live in a modern society." She left the kitchen by the side door, thudded down the porch steps, crossed the yard and sat on the curb in front of their house to wait for her brother.

His step was light as he exited Jen's house, but his demeanor changed when he saw Ember. He walked over and sat next to her.

They sat in silence, the only sound the evening song of crickets and whir of distant cars passing by. Cars taking people places. Places far away from the coven and the Nexus. Ember felt sweat trickle down her back and realized that this was their reality.

And reality sucked.

"She tell you everything?" she finally asked, her voice barely more than a whisper.

"I doubt it," Lee said, "but more than enough to piss me off. Magic is real, you're all witches, big surprise, especially Aunt Gwen. Oh, and I should have been a girl. That pretty much the sum of things?"

Ember turned to stare up at the darkening sky. "Pretty much," she said, choosing not to add to his new burden of knowledge just yet. How much more pissed off would he be to know he was 'betrothed' to his own cousin? That bit was almost too much for Ember to deal with most days. Besides, with everything changing around them, not to mention within them, who was to say what else might change before Seanna's birthday?

"They made me promise not to tell. Once I swore..." It sounded lame, even to her. "Sorry," she said and finally looked him in the eyes.

"Whatever." Lee picked up a rock and slung it sideways. It skidded and bounced off the pavement, finally ricocheting off someone's car nearly a block away. "Screw Aunt Gwen," he said. "She's a total bitch."

Ember laughed, glancing over her shoulder to make sure no one could hear them. "Agreed." She shook her head, then lowered her voice. "They're afraid of you. Afraid what you might become." She sighed. "You know, because of Dad."

"Like I give a crap." Lee used the hem of his t-shirt to wipe the sweat from his forehead. "I might've cared a few years ago, when I still wanted everyone to like me." He let out a small laugh. "Suddenly, after years of being treated like crap by almost everyone in the family, Mom tells me you guys actually need me, to be a conduit or whatever. Only everyone was too afraid to teach me how, to let me be a part of it." His jaw tightened. "They locked me out, Em. And you went along with it."

"No." Ember brushed away an errant gnat. "It was never my decision. I'm not afraid of you. Being a warlock didn't turn Dad evil. You're my brother. Being a warlock wouldn't change that."

"I don't want to be a warlock," Lee said. "It's a pet class, and damage over time spells suck. I'd rather be a mage." He grinned and for a moment it was like old times between them.

"You and that stupid game." Ember gave him a mock eye roll and grinned back.

"Well, that's one mystery solved. I never did understand why you didn't like role-playing games, with all the magic and monsters. Makes sense, now. You're already living in one."

"It's not exactly like that, but yeah, after you deal with some of the stuff we've had to...let's just say the video version, less than entertaining."

A black sedan pulled up and parked across the street. The car's doors opened and two people got out, a middle-aged man in a dark suit and the female agent from the police station. Warily, they walked over and stood a few feet away.

"Mind if we talk?" The male agent stood with his feet apart, hands folded in front of him. Ember was suddenly alert, that tunnel vision effect kicking in as she focused in on him. The almost imperceptible tic on the left side of his face and the tension in his jaw, told her he expected a fight, but he covered it well.

The woman smiled at Lee, frowned and then looked away from him, drawing Ember's attention. The tight focus fell away and the world came back to the fore.

Ember pushed her hair back from her face, acting as relaxed as she could. She'd seen the bulge of the agent's gun. "It's your funeral. If our mom sees you out here..." She let the thought trail off, letting them contemplate which might be the bigger threat, them or the head of the Macconal Coven.

"She is well aware of our presence." He flicked his eyes at the house and back to Ember. "Besides, it's clear from what we've seen that you two are quite capable. Not that your mother isn't...formidable."

"Formidable." Ember snorted. "That's one word for her."

The agent's mouth twitched up at the corners, but his face quickly grew serious again. "But we're only here to talk."

Ember stared at the man. He was attractive for a government agent, broad shouldered and fit, and his tailored suit fit him well. His demeanor suggested he was telling the truth, or most of it, but it was what he wasn't saying that piqued her curiosity.

"Not like we have anything better to do," Lee said.

Ember would have objected, but she wanted to make things right with Lee, so she clamped her mouth shut.

"Good. I'm Will Bailey, Deputy Director of Cerberus."

"Deputy Director? Like second in command?" Ember asked. As part of the Coven, she'd worked for Cerberus all this time but had never stopped to wonder who was in charge. Now, here she was talking to a guy who was practically at the top of the organizational pyramid of power.

"Yes, the Deputy Director of the agency, but I'm still

a qualified field agent, if that's what you're wondering. Deputy Director is such a mouthful, why don't you call me Will?"

*Will?* There was something about him that made Ember want to trust him, which made her instantly distrust him. He was an agent, just like any other Cerberus agent, and she had learned to be wary of them, even as they had worked together. She needed to remember that at all times. Her mother's rules and requirements were a constant irritant, but Ember had found out on more than one occasion, her mother was right to counsel caution.

"Anyway, we can talk about chain-of-command later. First, how about you undo whatever it is you did to my agent." He stared pointedly at Lee.

Lee gave the guy a funny look. "You want me to unheal her?"

Deputy Director Bailey shook his head. "One of our surveillance algorithms noticed a change in her behavior shortly after her encounter with you, so we sent her in for a complete work-up. Our scientists tell me Taylor's body is now comprised of over three percent xenohuman microorganisms."

Ember got up and wiped the dirt off the back of her jeans. She stared at Agent Taylor, but her new sensory abilities didn't allow her to see into the woman at a microscopic level. "What's a xenohuman?"

"The Affected." Deputy Director Bailey shifted his stance slightly and Ember sensed his caution increase. "People biologically altered by the sound waves that emanated from the Pillars, that vibration people are referring to as the Rumbling. I prefer the term superhumans." He nodded toward Lee and Ember. "But that determination is above my pay grade."

"Oh." Lee stood up and stepped closer to Agent Taylor. She inhaled and squared her shoulders, then gave Will a curt nod.

Lee frowned. "Sorry. I was scared..."

"And you needed an ally." The Deputy Director looked thoughtful. "I understand. It was a tactical decision, and a good one. Why didn't you do it to everyone?"

"Wait, do what?" Ember peered at her brother.

"I did," Lee replied, "just not on purpose. Well, not entirely on purpose, anyway. I just didn't do it to the same degree."

"Hold on," Ember said. "What the hell are you talking about?"

Lee gave her a smirk. "What's the matter Em? You feeling left out? Shoe on the other foot doesn't feel so good, does it?"

"Right," the Deputy Director continued, "so that's actually how you keep you track of those around you, get a sense of their emotions. You send microorganisms into them and they attach to the hosts, altering their cellular make-up. You gave her more than the others, because you wanted to heal her." He gestured at the female agent. "That means you can control how much you spread...and to whom."

"You can what?" Ember stared at her brother. "Invade people with some kind of micro thingies and change how they behave?" She glanced down at herself, eyeing her hands and arms.

"Not you." Lee shot her a look, then turned back to Deputy Director Bailey. "Why are you here?

"And you," Bailey turned his gaze on Ember and she stiffened, "Magic aside, you can cancel out powers, or at least dampen them. That was some serious teamwork taking down that Xeno at the station."

Ember crossed her arms to hide her nervousness. "Not a fan of that term. Labels make it too easy for people to think others are less than human. And like you said, superhuman sounds better." His mouth quirked up, like he appreciated being agreed with. It irked her and she decided she didn't like him, at all. "Anyway, what's your point? What do you want?" she said with a snarl.

"To offer you, and your family, protection and give people solace from fear."

Ember snorted.

"People are afraid," Will said, choosing his words carefully. "They're frightened of you and the other Xeno... others like you," he corrected. "And they should be. We all should. Without training and guidance, the danger you pose..." He let them think about that for a moment before continuing. "I see more than that. I think you could be great assets to your country, even the world."

"You're here to recruit us." Lee stuffed his hands in his pockets and looked thoughtful.

"Yes," Deputy Director Bailey said. "And, not exactly. At least not for Cerberus." He paused and shifted his stance.

If Ember hadn't been able to read the tiny twitches of his body, his minute facial tics, she would have thought he was just having a casual conversation with them. Only, she could tell there was more to it than that. She could smell the nervous perspiration beginning to form, saw the beads of it on his upper lip.

He noticed her watching him and she gazed past him at the sky, pretending not to have noticed the change in his demeanor.

"Look," he finally said. "The president just signed quarantine into law. There's no way around it."

"Quarantine?" Ember gave him a hard look. "Like you do for sick people who are contagious? Don't you mean internment, like you do with people you're afraid of and put into camps?"

"I mean quarantine, for the protection of everyone." He frowned. "But all the data we've collected shows the only thing strong enough to stop a Super is another Super. We need to contain those who are using their new powers to harm others. Without help from you, and others like you, a lot of innocent people are going to suffer."

"Nice," Ember said. "Trying to make us feel important and like we're just as bad as the others if we don't help." Lee looked thoughtful and it made her worried. She nudged his arm with her elbow. "Too bad for you we've been exposed to Aunt Gwen, one of the greatest manipulators of all time. We sort of have the playbook memorized at this point. Besides, I already work with Cerberus."

"I'm sorry," Deputy Director Bailey said. "I wish there was some other option. I promise you'll be treated with respect, but it's in everyone's best interest if you come with me now."

"Or what?" Ember began to pull at the ley line, reaching for power, her palms growing warm.

He shook his head. "You said yourself, you already work for Cerberus. This is really just the next iteration." He turned to Lee. "You can tell when someone's lying, right? What's your sense of me?"

"You're not lying." Lee paused, tilted his head. "But you're not telling us the whole truth, either."

"You're right," the Deputy Director said, "I'm not. Secrecy comes with the job.

Ember trembled, still holding onto the line, without pulling it to her. "Secrets suck."

Lee locked eyes with her. "Let it go, Em. What's keeping us here, anyway?"

Ember thought about the fight with their mom in the basement. Lee was right. There wasn't anything keeping them here. "Do we get to say goodbye?" Ember asked, dropping her link to the ley line.

"Of course." Agent Taylor gave her boss a meaningful look. "We wouldn't expect you to leave your family and home behind without a word."

The Deputy Director waved toward the house. "You won't need to bring anything. In fact, it's better if you don't."

Ember started walking toward the house and stopped

to look back at Lee. He stood on the edge of their property, unmoving.

"Lee?"

He shrugged. "I have nothing to say to them."

Ember hesitated at the edge of the yard, considered leaving without saying anything to anyone. She at least owed it to Tara to let her know she was leaving, didn't she? And even if Seanna was completely pissed at her, she had to tell her something, right? But what? It's been great hanging out and doing all the magic gigs for Cerberus with you, but I got a better offer? Would either of her cousins understand?

Lee waited on the curb, his back turned to the house, shoulders rigid.

The screen door opened and Aunt Gwen stepped out onto the porch. "What's going on out here?" Her voice grated against Ember's last nerve, like the sound of a dental drill.

"Screw it," Ember said, realizing where her loyalty lay, where it had always belonged. "I'll send 'em a text."

Agent Taylor shook her head. "Boss," she murmured. "Mrs. Macconal..."

"I know." He adjusted his tie.

The agent shook her head. "As a mother, I can tell you, it has to come from one of them." She hitched her thumb in Ember's direction.

"Seriously? Why me?" Ember asked, the confidence she'd felt a moment before seemed to be sucked out of her, like power finding its way back to the grid. Maybe this wasn't such a good idea.

"Because I'm not doing it." Lee's voice was hard, with that edge he used when he was preparing to get his full stubborn on.

"Working for you is gonna suck, if you're just going to throw me to the wolves when things get difficult," she told the agents.

"Your mother isn't a wolf," the Deputy Director said.

"You're right," Ember said. "She's way worse than that." She stomped across the lawn and up the front steps, slipping inside the screen door, hoping her cousins wouldn't see her.

When she reached the basement, her mother looked up from her work, eyes bleary. "What is it?" she asked. The angry edge had left her voice, replaced by a deep weariness.

"We're leaving. The Cerberus Deputy Director is outside talking to Lee and they want us to work for them and we said yes." The words spilled out of her without a pause and she turned to leave as soon as they'd left her mouth.

"No." Her mother's whisper struck her between the shoulder blades, harder than a shout would have.

Ember stood with one foot on the stairs, ready to rush up and out of the basement and leave her home, leave everyone—all the cousins, the aunties and grannies—the whole damn coven, including her mother, behind.

"They're asking nice now, Mother. But if we refuse?" It was all she could do to keep the fear out of her voice. "You know what war would mean. Especially without a cond—without Lee."

She shook off the feeling that she was abandoning everything she knew. "Besides, Lee is going with them, no matter what you do or say." Ember gripped the railing. "And I'm going with Lee."

She didn't wait for a response, just plowed up the stairs and out of the house. She heard her mother's footsteps behind her, working to catch up to her, so she sped up, letting the screen door spring shut behind her. She jumped the front steps without slowing, surprised she hadn't tripped over her own feet and crashed to the ground in a heap. "Oh, yeah, right," she mumbled to herself. "Super." She felt her lips curl up at the edges. Super was a good word for it. Maybe these changes weren't so bad, after all.

# Seven
Wed, Aug 24, 9:52pm

### - Lee -

Lee was already in the back of the car when Ember came back out, their mom following after. She looked for Lee, as Ember headed down the walkway. He knew it would hurt her, not saying goodbye. He counted on it. He could've gone back to Jen's for a quick explanation, but he didn't want to interrupt them. They deserved that time together, to be free of worry and fear. He didn't want to pull them back down with his own drama.

Emily was in the driver's seat, with the car already running. Will held the door open for Ember then got into the front passenger seat. He could feel his sister tense, as they pulled away from the house and headed west.

Lee refused to look back.

"Are we headed to the CDC tents?" Lee asked.

"No," Will replied, swiping on a tablet, reading files as they drove. It wasn't so much worry that Lee sensed in him but a level of concern that never seemed to waver. "Those were set up for Affected without powers. We have a separate facility just outside the city."

"Facility?" Ember snapped. "Don't you mean prison?" She wasn't happy with the situation, and Lee knew she was going to take every opportunity to let them all know it. She muttered, "Special facility sounds exactly like code for prison."

She wouldn't look at Lee, just stared out the window at passing houses and trees. He sensed the anger directed toward him, for how he'd treated their mother, but he wouldn't apologize for something he didn't feel sorry for. Besides, he hadn't totally forgiven Ember for her part in everything.

"People typically don't enjoy quarantine," Will said, as if he was discussing the weather. "But when someone can throw a bus or shoot fire from their eyes, it's best to keep them away from the general population."

"We wouldn't hurt anyone," Lee said defensively.

It hadn't even occurred to him to use his power to hurt people, and he had no intention of doing it now. If anything, he'd go to a hospital and heal everyone. He did just cure cancer, after all.

"Jim Tompkins would disagree." Will tapped and swiped, held up a picture of Tompkins sprawled on the police station floor.

"That's different," Lee said and felt his cheeks redden. It was different, wasn't it? "And I didn't use my power on him."

He looked to Ember for support out of habit. She only stared out the window and watched the lights pass.

"No," Will said, "but you were willing to discharge a firearm pointblank into someone's face. You can't say that doesn't at least warrant a conversation."

"That's not fair!" Ember complained, and Lee felt a surge of relief. They were still on the same side. "We saved people, when no else could. Lee did what needed to be done." Did she really believe that? She wasn't lying when she said it. "If a cop or one of your agents had done it, we wouldn't be having this conversation."

"Can't argue with you there," Will said, as he put the tablet away and watched the road, "and I'd bet there are families out there who are grateful for your actions." He glanced back at the two of them. "But there are just as many people mourning the loss of loved ones at the hands of Affected." He turned away and seemed to speak from experience. "They won't be so quick to thank you."

"There's a great plan," Ember said. "Punish people for what they may or may not do."

"Yeah," Lee said with pointed sarcasm and nearly laughed, "we wouldn't want to do that."

"It's not just for their protection," Emily said. She looked back at Lee in the rearview, as if she wanted to say more.

Will held a hand up.

"Hold that thought," he said and touched his earbud. "Go ahead." A few moments later, he added, "Copy that." To Agent Taylor, he said, "We've got a lead on one of the girls from the police station. Parking structure on Willow and Fourth Avenue."

Emily hit the break and turned left as soon as they entered the intersection, narrowly missing a van. Lee had been getting better at tuning out the sensations from passing cars, but the increased speed threw him off. Will looked back at Lee and Ember.

"We're taking a little detour," he said. "When we get there, you two stay in the car."

"If it's the one I saw," Ember said, "you can't take her without help."

Will shook his head. "It's too dangerous."

"For you," Lee said derisively. "Guns won't hurt her."

He liked the Deputy Director but didn't appreciate being talked down to or being treated like a child. More than his body had been changed. His mind was faster now, came to conclusions far more quickly and began putting together pieces of a problem before he even knew one existed. He could help, if they'd let him.

Will took the gun out from his shoulder holster.

"Up close they will," he said. "You showed us that."

Lee felt like he'd been kicked in the gut, as images of imagined futures flashed through his mind. He wouldn't be thought of as the healer, the Super who could cure cancer. He was the one who showed the government how to put down the Affected.

Or worse, how to control them.

The car had been shifting from one side to another with each turn. They slowed roughly over a speed bump, entered the garage and began to crawl through the first level. From their seats, Emily and Will looked into and between the dozen or so parked vehicles. No one was in sight but a few people passing on the sidewalk across the street.

It wasn't until they pulled up the ramp to the second floor that Lee began to sense the double heartbeat of a Super.

"There," he said and pointed at a silver sedan in the distance. Her fear felt like his own, shaking his chest so hard he thought it might break. "She's scared, hiding in the backseat." To Ember, he asked, "Can you use magic to stop her?"

Ember shook her head.

"Not in here," Will said for her and unbuckled his seatbelt. Emily did the same and drew her gun. The two opened their doors, but before Will closed his, he said, "Stay here."

Whoever it was, she knew they were here for her. Lee sensed the rising panic driving her into action. It didn't feel like she wanted to hurt anyone, but he knew she'd defend herself. Even with guns, what chance did they stand against her?

"She's going to kill them," Lee said, not really expecting Ember to listen. Not unless he drove the point home. His sister still wouldn't look at him. "Probably make a mess of it, too."

"Fine," she snarled and got out of the car, "but you better have a better plan than me touching her while you shoot her."

"I don't even have a gun," he muttered and got out.

Will and Emily stopped and frowned back at them in unison. The Deputy Director looked as if he considered coming back to yell at them but then pointed at the two, directed them toward the silver car. He made a motion to Agent Taylor, and they went around the other side a safe distance away, to cut off any escape.

"So what *can* you do?" Lee asked in a whisper.

"To people?" she replied quietly. "Not much yet. And not in here. Mostly lights and distractions." She flexed her fingers, as if preparing for a spell. "But I can tear a spirit a new one, if I can access a source."

*A source of what?* Lee thought, annoyed he didn't know anything about magic. *How the hell am I supposed to make a plan?*

"Great," Lee said as they approached the car. "Let me know if you see any."

*At least she's talking to me again.*

He walked up to the back window and was a little surprised to see the car empty. He knew she was in there, could feel each breath, the blood flowing through her, her thoughts racing. He just couldn't see her.

*Some kind of light power?* he guessed. *If she can make herself invisible, what else can she do?*

"Well?" Ember pressed.

*If she's hiding, she might be too afraid to fight.* Lee sent cells into her, hoping to buy time to influence her emotions.

*I just need to get her talking.*

Lee knocked on the window.

He felt flight become fight an instant before seeing a white light spark to life. It was like a lightbulb in air, growing in sudden intensity and glare. He ducked as the window exploded, and hard light poured out from the car.

Ember screamed and clutched her eyes, dropped to both knees. Her face and eyes had been burned, the skin blackened and smoking. Lee heard the back door on the other side open and shoved with all his strength. He sent the car forward with enough force to pin the girl between it and the truck two spaces away. There was a grunt and the sense of pain before the vehicle came flying back.

Lee's only thought was to protect Ember. He dropped into a crouch in front of her and shouldered the blow. Metal buckled around him with a low whine and painful crunch. More glass flew overhead, showered the area in a glittering half-circle.

He pulled free of the mangled car without a scratch or an ache. Ember's hands were trembling over her eyes, both in pain and fear of permanent damage.

Lee reached out a hand to heal her but hesitated. He'd lose his power if he touched her. He could send in cells, let them duplicate and start to heal her. The sharp sense of alarm from Will and Emily came over him. A quick look over the wreckage showed the girl walking toward them. She paused when they pointed guns at her, but he felt the adrenaline building inside her, working to override fear. With clenched fists, she screamed and ran at them, both hands glowing with a spreading light. She stumbled as bullets struck but didn't slow in the least.

*Damn it!*

He had to abandon his sister, let her suffer for the moment, or others would die. He focused all his will and intention on the girl, used both hands to direct his sensory bubble like a swarm. The air blazed with the electric blue of a million motes. Like angry fireflies, they buzzed and converged. They struck her in the back with the crackle of a live wire. Her body arched forward and convulsed through a jerky fall.

Despite the hard landing, she tried to climb to all fours. Lee sent shocks through her spine, overloaded her nervous system and left her twitching on the floor. Will and Taylor were on her without delay, securing arms and legs with multiple restraints.

Lee let go the breath he'd been holding and turned his attention back to Ember. He directed cells toward her eyes but found they were already healing. She blinked away tears, as the halo burns began to fade.

"What was that?" she asked, blinking rapidly and wiping away tears with the back of her hands.

"I shocked her nervous system."

He was a little out of breath and tired from the ordeal. It wasn't any more difficult to use his power that way, but all the excitement and exertion was taking its toll.

"Why the hell," Ember said angrily, "didn't you do that to the guy at the station?"

*I didn't know I could,* he wanted to say. *Not that it would've mattered.*

He waved a hand in front of her eyes.

"Can you see?" he asked.

"Yeah. Thanks." She blinked some more and looked at what remained of the cars. "She do that?"

"More or less," Lee replied. He nodded toward where Emily was helping the girl to her feet. Will was talking to someone on the end of his earbud. "We got her, though." Whatever injuries his sister had suffered were all gone. "I didn't heal you, by the way. You regenerated on your own, like that guy at the station."

"I could tell," she said and got to her feet. He'd moved to help her stand but pulled back at the last moment, like overriding instinct. "A little heads up would've been nice."

"There wasn't time," he said in way of apology, as they headed back toward the car. "I just reacted."

Ember gave him a withering look.

"That's not what I would call an improvement." She rubbed her eyes one last time and winced at the ceiling lights. "And why the hell did you knock on the window if you knew she was in there? Did you think she was hanging out, waiting to have a nice chat?"

*I needed more time,* he thought, *and I didn't think she'd attack.*

"Sort of," Lee tried to explain. "I thought if we talked to her, explained things, she'd come out without a fight. She's not like that other guy. She didn't kill anyone at the station."

"Bullshit," Ember said and stopped, her voice like a whip. "She's *exactly* like him! I saw her. What she did. She killed people, too."

Exasperated, Lee asked, "Well, how was I supposed to know that?"

"This kind of crap," she said and pointed back at the destroyed cars. "This is what comes from acting without having all the information."

Lee had kept walking but wheeled on her.

"Oh, really?" he fumed. "Like knowing my sister's a witch? Or that my entire family's a coven that works for the government?"

He could already hear the lame excuses, how that was different, how none of that mattered here, in this situation. He didn't even care if she was right. He'd known enough to make a plan, and everything worked out.

"Seriously," she said instead, her anger no longer focused directly at him, "you had plenty of information in this case."

Something in her had changed at that moment, but he couldn't say what.

"How do you figure that?"

"Didn't you get the memo?" she asked and stormed past him toward the car. "All us Supers are dangerous. Better get used to it."

# - Ember -

Ember hurried over to the black car, where Deputy Director Bailey stood by the open door waiting for her to get in. She slid into the seat beside Lee and started to buckle the seatbelt, then let go. The spring-loaded mechanism pulled the belt back into place with a shushing sound.

On the porch, their mother stared at the car, her mouth a stiff line. For an instant, Ember wished her mother would run after them, shout their names, call on the coven to kill the car's engine, but she did none of those things. She merely stood and watched as Agent Taylor put the vehicle into drive and pulled away from the curb.

Ember resolutely refused to look back, clenching the edge of the smooth leather seat in her hands till Lee nudged her foot with his. She jerked her foot away but refused to look at him. This was his fault. If not for him, she'd still be a part of the strongest coven in the country.

She let out a sigh. She had to admit, that a part of her had always wanted this. She'd contemplated leaving the coven, running away from home so many times, but had never acted on it. Told herself it would have been foolish. But, now that they were actually leaving, she realized the real reason she'd never left hadn't been for fear of the imagined repercussions, after all. And that pissed her off even more.

"So, I guess we're headed to the CDC's containment tents," Lee said.

"No." The Deputy Director busily tapped information into a computer tablet. Ember leaned forward and focused in on the tablet's screen, but he swiped and tapped, opening and closing files so fast, that even with her enhanced focus, she couldn't read enough to figure out what he was doing. "The CDC Containment Camp is only for non-super Affected, those without powers. You two will be housed in a special facility outside of the city."

"Facility? Don't you mean prison?" Ember sat back and ground the toes of her boots into the carpeting and felt it tear in satisfaction. She gazed out the window to where houses gave way to industrial buildings as they headed toward the outskirts of the city. Some of the buildings they passed were damaged, fresh scorch marks marring bricks and mortar, and roofs burned or blasted away. "Special Facility. Sounds exactly like code for prison."

Agent Taylor concentrated on driving, but Deputy Director Bailey put down his tablet and spoke over his shoulder at them. "I realize the idea of quarantine isn't appealing, not like spending time at the spa." He adjusted his jacket and tie as he spoke. "But, when certain people can toss school buses around like toys or shoot lasers just by blinking, some separation from the general population is called for."

"We wouldn't hurt anyone." Lee's voice held a sliver of steely anger.

"I believe Jim Tompkins would disagree." The Deputy Director tapped and swiped, then held up a picture of the guy Lee had shot—with her help—sprawled on the police station floor.

Ember wanted to look away, but her guilt at her part in Lee's shooting of Tompkins wouldn't allow her the luxury. The picture before her caused the entire event to replay in her head, over and over. The end result held up before her in full color. She could still smell the blood when she thought about it, the warmth as it spattered...

"That was different," Lee shot back. "He was killing people. He needed to be stopped. Not to mention, I didn't throw a bus at him. I didn't use my power on him at all."

"No, but you shot him pointblank. Some people believe that act itself is grounds for concern at the very least."

"That's not fair!" Ember countered, shutting her eyes to stop from staring at the photo. "We saved people, when no else could. Lee did what needed to be done. If one of those cops, or one of your agents, had been able to do it, they would have. And we wouldn't be having this conversation."

"I can't argue with you there." Deputy Director Bailey turned off his tablet and set it on the seat beside him. "And I'm sure there are families out there who are grateful for your actions. But there are also people mourning the loss of loved ones killed by Affected. Those people are not in a forgiving mood. Nor are they feeling much gratitude."

"There's a fabulous plan," Ember said. "Punish people for what they may or may not do. Hmmm. I think I saw that movie. As I recall, it didn't end well."

Lee agreed with her.

"It's not just for their protection," Agent Taylor eyed Lee in the rearview mirror.

"Hold on." Deputy Director Bailey gestured for quiet and stuck a finger in his ear. "Go ahead." Ember opened her mouth to say something and realized he was actually talking to someone else. Someone who wasn't in the car with them. Someone who was probably listening in on everything they'd been saying. What the hell? Bailey should have told them other people might be listening. He was about to get a piece of her mind.

"Copy that," he said before she could spit out the accusation. "Taylor, we've got a lead on an Affected. Female runner from the police station. Parking structure on Willow and Fourth." He tapped on his tablet and swiped the image up and out, sending it onto the car's dashboard display. "Looks like we're taking a little detour," he told Lee and Ember.

Agent Taylor stepped on the gas and tires squealed as they took the next corner at high speed. The smell of burnt rubber wafted in through the vents as they rounded another corner.

"When we get there, you two stay in the car." Bailey unholstered his weapon.

"I saw that girl in action," Ember said. "You're going to

need our help."

He shook his head. "Not happening. Too dangerous."

"For you, maybe." Lee snorted, eyeing the weapon. "Bullets won't hurt her."

"Up close and personal they will. You solved that."

Lee grimaced.

Agent Taylor made another hard right, then slowed the car as she pulled into a parking structure. They did a slow crawl, searching the rows of parked vehicles. Ember tensed, focusing in on every detail, looking for anything that moved or looked out of place. Years of car exhaust stained the walls, and the place reeked of oil and gasoline. Ember wondered why she'd never noticed before how bad these places looked and smelled.

Once they cleared the first level, Taylor turned up the ramp to the second.

"There," Lee pointed at a silver-colored car. "She's hiding in the back. Scared. I think she knows we're looking for her. Ember, can you use that energy orb thingy to stop her?"

Ember reached out, but there were too many layers of concrete and metal between her and the source. The nearest ley line was a thin, far-off trickle of energy. She shook her head. She might be able to gather enough power to manage something, but it would take time.

"Not now," Bailey said, like he knew. Of course, he did. He was Cerberus. Agent Taylor put the car in park and drew her gun, and the two agents opened their doors. "Stay here," Deputy Director Bailey ordered, shutting the door behind him with a quiet snick.

"She's gonna kill them," Lee said. "Probably make a mess of it, too."

"Fine," Ember growled. She opened the car door and slid out. "But you better have a better plan than 'Hey, Ember, touch this guy so I can shoot him in the head.'"

Lee gave her a dirty look and stepped out of the car,

shutting the door with too much force.

Both agents glanced back at them. Taylor quickly turned to train her weapon back on the silver car. Bailey hesitated. Ember expected him to yell at them to get back in the car. Instead, he signaled them toward the car.

He and Taylor circled around to the other side a short distance away. They were giving them room, Ember thought, recalling their run-in at the police station.

"So what can you do?" Lee asked, frustration tinting his words.

"To people?" she replied. "Not much. Not here." She waved at the concrete structure that surrounded them. "Mostly lights and distractions." She opened her hands and flexed her fingers, reaching out for power. "But I can sure as hell tear a spirit a new one, if I can access enough source."

"Great," Lee said as they drew closer to the silver four-door. "Let me know if you see any. I'd like a ticket for that show."

Ember was surprised by the mild edge of humor in his voice. She felt herself almost smile, just as he stepped up to the back of the car, peered in the rear window and froze. "Well?" she finally whispered.

Lee reached out toward the car.

"What the hell?" Ember hissed, as he rapped on the window with a knuckle. A moment later, he dropped down into a crouch as the car window exploded outward in a blaze of light and energy.

"Sonofabitch!" Ember screamed, clutching at her eyes. She fell to her knees, striking the pavement hard enough to crack it.

A car door opened, but Ember couldn't see anything. She heard the slam of metal hitting something solid and crumpling around it. An instant later, she felt an odd sensation and realized it must be Lee trying to heal her, but he needn't have bothered. She blinked back tears as the searing halos faded and the garage started to come back into view. Nearby, the crushed remains of the silver car lay in a heap.

Lee held up his hands toward the girl, who was striding toward Agent Taylor. Ember blinked again, her eyes burning anew as the air blazed a bright electric blue, millions of tiny spots of colored light coalesced and slammed into the girl, striking her between her shoulder blades. She fell, collapsing and jerking like someone hit by a battalion of tasers and maybe an electric fence or two.

As soon as she stopped twitching, the agents ran over and cuffed her.

"What the hell was that?" Ember asked, wiping the teary streaks from her face.

"Nervous system overload." Lee panted and leaned forward, placing his hands on his knees while he caught his breath.

"Well, why the hell didn't you do that to the guy in the police station?"

Lee shook his head. "Couldn't." He stood up slowly. "Ember." His face was dead serious. "What I did to that guy was the only option. You have to believe me." He kneeled in front of her and wiggled his fingers. "Can you see?"

She blinked again, fresh tears rolling down her cheeks. "Yeah," she replied, "thanks." She eyed the wreckage of what had once been a car. Gasoline fumes stung her healing eyes, and the chemical reek mingled with spilled oil made it hard to breathe. "She do that?"

"Pretty much." He gestured over to where the agents were putting restraints on the girl. "We got her, though."

"I hope they're using the good handcuffs."

"I didn't heal you, by the way. You regenerated on your own, like that guy at the station."

"I got that." She pushed herself up to standing and wiped her hands on her torn jeans. "By the way, a little heads up would've been nice."

"No time." He shrugged, but his look was apologetic. "I didn't plan, just reacted."

"That's not what I would rate as improvement in the planning department." Ember swiped at her eyes, clearing the last of the hazy blur from them. "And why would you knock on the window if you knew she was in there? It's not like she was just hanging out in the back of a stranger's car in an out of the way parking garage waiting to have a nice chat."

"I thought if we tried talking to her, explained things... She's not like that other guy. She didn't kill anyone."

"Bull!" Ember shot back. "She's exactly like him. I saw what she did at the police station. She killed people, too."

"Well, how was I supposed to know that?"

"This kind of crap..." She waved a hand at the wreckage. "This is what comes from acting without having all the information."

"All the information? Would that include, oh, I don't know, the fact that my sister's a witch? My family is a powerful magical coven and they all work for a not-so-secret-anymore government entity?" He glared at her.

Ember hesitated, holding back the burning retort that sat on her tongue ready to be unloaded. What she really wanted was to make up for all the years of secrecy and lies, but words wouldn't fix the betrayal he felt. Maybe even time wouldn't heal this wound. But he was her brother and he deserved better. She would stay by him and do what she could to make amends. "In all seriousness, you had plenty of information in this case."

His eyebrows shot up. "Really? How do you figure that?"

"Didn't you get the memo?" she asked, her voice hot in her own mouth as she stomped over to the waiting agency car. The sound of her boots connecting with the pavement nearly hard enough to crack it ricocheted back at him from the nearby walls. "All us Supers are dangerous. Better get used to it."

# Eight
Wed, Aug 24, 11:04pm

### - Lee -

Lee's phone booped once. He pulled it out of his pocket for a look, drawing Will's attention. He got the impression he was supposed to have left it at home. It was a text from Jen.

"Saw you two leave with Scully and Mulder," she wrote. "You guys okay?"

They followed behind an armored vehicle, where the girl they'd captured was under guard. He'd overheard one of them say her name was Samantha Richmond. She was a junior at his school, but he couldn't remember having seen her before. She was pretty in a way, though it was hard to tell with all the glaring. She had short blonde hair just past her ears, all streaked in shades of platinum, the toned body of a runner, freckles across her nose and bright green eyes that seemed to say she wanted to kill him.

Her seething hatred was somewhat justified. Lee had figured out how to block specific signals from her brain to her spine and was keeping her paralyzed from the neck down. She could breathe without any problem, move her head and talk. Allowing her anything more would have posed too great a risk. From what he knew of his own strength, he doubted the nylon ties would be enough to hold her for very long.

"Yeah," he wrote back. "Not sure how long we'll be gone."

"Say something only you would know."

Lee snorted, which drew an annoyed look from his sister.

"You have a stash of candy under your bed," he replied. "You're afraid of mimes. You have a crush on Andy. And your mom is hot."

"K, it's you. Jerk." She sent a smiley face with its tongue sticking out. "One, don't touch my candy. Ever. Two, mimes are creepy. Only evil is that quiet. Three, Brewer? I wouldn't do him with your doodle. And everyone knows my mom is hot."

"You're not the only one in the car," Ember said and frowned out the window. She was still mad, not entirely at him but angry all the same. "Turn your damn sound off."

Lee looked up at Will and Emily in front. The noise didn't seem to bother them, but he switched the phone to vibrate.

"Thanks again," Jen wrote. "You're like the world's best all natural remedy. Hey! That can be your superhero name. Remedy!"

He sent a wide-eyed emoticon.

"You need a costume," she went on. "Lab coat and a stethoscope? Blue scrubs with foot covers?"

"K, gotta go."

He slipped the phone back into a pocket, as they pulled

into a parking garage beneath a tall building. A few more buzzes against his leg, and the phone was finally silent.

There was a security checkpoint two floors down, with armed guards and a series of retractable steel pylons. Once past, they parked near an elevator and waited for Samantha to be led from the truck. Two agents carried her by the elbows, dragging her feet behind.

Lee had left her flooded with his cells but could only sense less than half now. He hadn't directed them to leave, so what the heck had happened to them? They began to quickly dwindle, as light formed within her palms.

*She burned them away,* Lee realized, and with a flare they were mostly gone.

"Look out!" he shouted, and light erupted.

The men hadn't heard him in time and were thrown wide by the blast, skin and clothes scorched. The girl pulled her arms free of the ties, reached down and tore away the leg restraints as well. Emily and Will were already out of the car with weapons drawn.

"Lee?" Will more stated than asked.

"I'm trying!" He directed his swarm toward her for a shock, but the blast had cut their number by a third. More light flashed from her palms. "She's burning them away!" Lee said, struggling to create more. "I don't think I can stop her."

"I got this," Ember said.

She left the car with a grim look on her face and walked straight toward Samantha with both hands balled into fists. From what he sensed, Lee knew his sister had no intention of using magic. Two agents had opened fire, causing pain but no visible damage—aside from Samantha's clothes. The other two were down, clutching at their eyes and groaning in pain.

Samantha screamed and threw more light, scoring the truck with jagged burns. Will called for his agents to stand down, while Lee fought to invade her. It was like sending bugs into a zapper, except he was the one being zapped. Pieces of him, anyway. It didn't hurt so much as it felt like loss and being drained of energy.

Ember dodged a blast of light, turned and twisted to the side as if she already knew it was coming. Two more went right past. Either she could read the girl's mind, Lee considered as he watched on in disbelief, or his sister's reflexes had been enhanced way beyond his own.

The girl panicked and disappeared.

"Nuh-uh," Ember said and darted forward, a leap of at least seven feet. She grabbed at the air, and Samantha reappeared, her wrist in Ember's hand. "I *owe* you," his sister said and punched her in the nose.

Samantha's head snapped back with the blow, her eyes went wide and legs became wobbly. With her power gone, canceled out by Ember's, Lee was able to get cells inside again. He gave her a shock for good measure and caused the cells to begin duplicating. Samantha cried out and stiffened, would have fallen over if Ember hadn't held tight and set her down.

Agents were on her again, some newly arrived from the checkpoint. They lifted Samantha by the arms and began to restrain her once more, as medics exited the elevator to tend the wounded. Within a few moments, Lee was able to paralyze her once more.

He thought it strange they didn't ask him for help. It wouldn't have taken much effort to heal the agents once he had a minute to rest. Were they afraid he'd leave them contaminated, like he did Emily? Or maybe they weren't cleared to know the full extent of his ability? He didn't know which was worse, that the agents didn't trust him or Will would let them suffer to keep a secret.

"Lee," Will called him over. "How long can you keep her like this?"

He considered her power, how fast she'd been able to burn through all his cells. The only way he could keep her paralyzed was to alter her spine. It wasn't that much different from healing an old injury. He just needed to focus on the outcome and let the cells do all the work.

"For as long as she's in range," he answered, "as long as she doesn't use her power. Or," he hesitated to add, "I can make it permanent."

Samantha's eyes welled with fear and pleading.

"No," she said, and the emotion in her voice broke his heart. "Don't. Please."

"I could go with her," Ember offered. She'd seen the look on Lee's face, knew he was struggling. "Her powers won't work if I touch her."

"That's not an option," Will said. To Lee he added, "For you either. If you make it permanent, can you fix it later?"

*Can I?* Lee concentrated on the cells within her. He could sense what needed to be done, the damage to small areas. *What if undoing it later causes a problem I can't fix?*

"I don't know," he said quietly, uncertain. "I think so." The fear in her overwhelmed him, like a scream of despair from within his chest. "I mean, yes." Lee looked her in the eyes, tried to reassure her. "I can fix it."

"Do it," Will said. To the agents carrying her, he added, "Take her to retraining once he's done."

Lee made the changes to her spine, so simple yet life changing. He'd never felt so horrible inside. Would Jen still think he was a hero if she knew? He gave the agents a nod, and they carried her away.

"You two next," Will said to Emily and Ember when the elevator came back up. "Sorry, only one Super at a time. Protocol."

After they'd gone, and the elevator returned, he and Will stepped inside. Lee was surprised to see there were no buttons, just plain white walls without seams. The doors closed, and they began to move. It was a good twenty floors down, he guessed, by the people he felt move in and out of his sensory bubble.

He still couldn't shake the dirty feeling in his heart, that he'd hurt a helpless girl fully knowing he might not be able to undo it. Yes, she'd hurt people. She may have even been a bad person. All he knew for sure was that he didn't want to use his power that way.

The doors opened to a concrete corridor, with two guards stationed outside. Will led Lee a few hundred feet away to a metal door he opened with a key card. The hallway continued on, though Lee couldn't see any more doors before it turned in either direction. There was no one else to be seen but the men back the way they came.

Will held the door open, and Lee stepped through. The room was much like the elevator, seamless and pure white. Even the corners were smooth and rounded, as if the whole of it was made from a single piece. There was another glass door on the opposite side, but that one had no card reader, or handles for that matter.

"Good evening, sir," a male voice said and filled the room. It was difficult to tell where it came from.

"Kellogg," Will said evenly, in way of greeting. He stood patiently waiting for the door to open.

Kellogg said, "Welcome to the Bullet Squad, kid."

"That's...not an official designation," Will said to Lee, in a manner that was as close to being annoyed as he'd seen of him so far. "Kellogg, you're relieved."

"What?" Kellogg nearly laughed in surprise, as if Will had made a joke. "Why? It's not like he'll remember."

"You can be relieved," Will replied, "or retired. The choice is yours."

Lee couldn't help but wonder if retired meant an unmarked grave. There was quiet for a moment.

"Yes, sir."

A hiss sounded from ahead, and the thick glass door slid sideways into the wall. They stepped forward into a white hallway, and the door slid closed behind them. On both sides were what could only be described as cells, wide open rooms without seams and closed off by glass walls. Three on either side, only the first ones were occupied.

One held Jim Tompkins and a woman. They sat on a bed that looked like it was part of the wall, again like the entire room had been made from a single piece. They both wore simple white pants, a shirt and slippers. She was reading to Jim from a children's book. He looked very different from the murderous guy Lee had shot in the face.

In the other was Samantha.

He'd paralyzed her not more than fifteen minutes ago, but she had a bandage over one eye now, held in place by gauze around her head. She'd been placed against the wall, still as a statue, next to a man showing her images on a tablet. They were both dressed in the same white outfits, sitting just as calm, as he swiped slowly from one to the next.

Lee knew in a sickening instant what had happened. While neither of them appeared mentally deficient or even childlike, it was clear something was wrong.

*What had Will called it? Retraining?*

This was what Kellogg had meant by the Bullet Squad. Both Jim and Samantha had been shot in the head, their brains shredded by metal slugs and had regenerated as clean slates. They were being taught from scratch how to live in the world, how to speak, how to act—how to serve.

"It's not what you think," Will said in that even tone. "They're violent criminals with superpowers. We don't have the resources or technology to contain them. At least this way they can help, join the team, be one of the good guys."

"Whether they want to or not," Lee pointed out. "How long before you do this to the ones who won't cooperate? Then to all of us, just to be sure? You think you found an easy solution," he said, as countless scenarios played out in his mind, more disappointed than afraid, "but you just gave every Super still out there a real reason to hide and, worse, to fight back."

"I wish there was another way," Will said, and Lee could feel that the sentiment was genuine. He truly believed they were doing the right thing. "We had to act fast, before more people got hurt. This was the best we could come up with."

"It doesn't matter now," Lee said. The scenarios had all played out, and not a single one had ended well. "Even if you find a better way, this is what they'll want. Control. Over all of us."

"I won't let that happen," Will promised. Again, he was sincere. "Work with me, and I'll do everything in my power to protect you."

Lee believed him, wanted it to be true, though in his heart and mind he knew those in charge would never trust in any power beyond their own. It was human nature to fear what can't be controlled, to tame the wild beast or kill it in the trying. He had nothing but hope to cling to. The alternative was a bullet.

"When do we start?" he asked.

Will gave a half-smile. "We just did."

# - Ember -

Ember stared out the window, trying to ignore the armored truck ahead of them, while Lee fiddled with his phone. The image of the wreckage the girl had caused kept cropping up, and Ember had to force herself not to rub at her eyes. They were fine. They'd healed. But still her fingers itched to press on her lids and feel for damage.

"Hey, it's rude to be on your phone when other people are right here," Ember said.

Lee gave her a quizzical look.

"At least set the damn thing to silent." She slumped back into her seat, wishing that none of this had happened. That they weren't heading into an unknown situation, preparing to be locked away in some secret facility. But it had happened, was happening, and the only way out now was through. Or ending up like the girl from the parking garage, stunned and restrained.

Agent Taylor drove them into another parking structure and headed down. *Great,* Ember thought, *we're going underground.*

The truck ahead of them stopped at a guardhouse, where fat pillars barred the way ahead. Men in camo uniforms with guns stepped up to the vehicles. One checked Agent Taylor's credentials, while another looked inside, nodding at Bailey in recognition. The pillars slid down into the floor with a grinding sound and the guards waved them through, the metal and concrete blockade rising back into place behind them.

*That's it,* Ember thought. "That's the end of life as we knew it."

Lee shrugged. "That happened already," he said, sliding out of the back seat. "This is just the next chapter of that story. One where I at least have some idea of what's going on." His tone held a bitter edge.

Ember looked around as a couple of agents hauled

139

the unconscious girl out of the truck. Thick concrete walls enclosed them on every side, except where they had driven down the ramp. This was clearly not an ordinary parking structure. It could probably withstand an atomic blast.

Lee shouted a warning and Ember instinctively crouched, covering her eyes. Light flashed, followed by an explosion that echoed back from every side and threw the two agents into the walls. They hit with the sound of cracking bone and twin grunts before landing in separate heaps.

The girl broke through her restraints like they were made of paper. "Dammit! I knew those weren't going to be strong enough," Ember said, her ears still ringing from the blast.

Deputy Director Bailey and Agent Taylor had leaped from the car, weapons pointed at the girl, who continued to manipulate light into blasts of energy, throwing them at the agents and soldiers who now surrounded her. Shots rang out, but the bullets just bounced off her, pinging onto the floor.

"Lee!" Bailey shouted.

"I'm trying," Lee yelled back, frustration and effort coloring his words. "I don't think I can stop her."

Ember stood up as a sudden realization hit her. All the broken items in the kitchen. Lee destroying the locks at the pizza place without even trying. Her rapid healing from the earlier event. She and Lee were both like this girl. That meant they, too, were super strong. "I got this," she said, striding forward with a new confidence.

"Screw. You. All!" The girl hurled insults along with blasts of light. Smoke and the smell of scorched car paint filled the enclosed space.

"Stand down!" Bailey yelled at his men. "Give them room!"

Ember dodged left, turning and twisting to avoid the blasts coming her way. She felt herself smile. She'd never been graceful or athletic, but somehow she moved with a newfound speed and agility. She let out a laugh.

The girl suddenly left off blasting at her and disappeared, the frightened look on her face shimmering in the air for an instant as she dissolved.

"Nope. Not happening," Ember told her. She sprang forward and grabbed at the air, catching the girl by the wrist. The girl reappeared. "There you are," Ember said. "Didn't want you to leave without this." She planted her fist in the girl's face. "Ow." Ember shook out her fingers as the girl's head snapped back.

Tiny blue lights flickered around and through her. She screamed, stiffened and dropped. Ember grabbed her around the shoulders and slid her to the ground, holding her there as agents ran up and lifted the girl away.

After all the explosions, the space seemed too quiet, the only sounds the groans of the wounded and the low voices of the people tending to them.

"Lee," Bailey called, "how long?" He nodded at the girl.

Lee wrinkled his forehead. "Long as I can stay within range."

Ember flinched at the heartless, matter-of-fact way he said it. What the hell? First he defends her, then just like that he's ready to leave her trapped in a useless body? Sure, she was a murderer, but even so.

"Please. No." The girl's voice held a desperate plea.

"I could go with her," Ember said. "As long as I maintain contact—"

"No." Bailey cut her off. "Not an option. Neither of you can go with her. Lee, if you make it permanent, can it be undone later?"

Lee shrugged. "I think so."

Ember gaped at him.

"I mean, yes. I can undo it."

"Do it," Bailey told him, then turned to the men holding her. "Then you two get her to retraining, ASAP."

Less than a minute later, they hauled the girl over to the elevators and disappeared with her behind the gray metal doors.

"Ember, Taylor, you're up next," Bailey said when the elevator doors reopened. He held a hand out to stop Lee from following Ember into the elevator. "One Super at a time."

"No way," Ember stuck her arm out to hold the doors open.

"It's standard protocol." Bailey shook his head and gestured toward the deeper levels. "Around here, we follow certain rules. You're going to have to get used to it."

Ember gave him her dirtiest look, then let her arm drop. "Maybe," she said as the doors slid shut, cutting her off from her brother. "But I don't have to like it."

Agent Taylor swiped a key card along a blinking pad and the elevator descended rapidly.

As the elevator slid down into the recesses of the building, a sudden tingle of power raised the hair on Ember's arms. Someone was practicing magic. Casting. Here, in the Cerberus facility. And not just a single witch. From what she could sense, it was a full-on coven. Was another coven working for Cerberus besides the Macconal clan?

She stole a glance at Agent Taylor. The blond woman leaned against the wall of the elevator, watching her.

The sensation of magic being worked passed away quickly as they continued to descend, but Ember couldn't shake the questions it had raised. Would they want her to join another coven? No. They had to know from all their work with her family that she wouldn't discard her loyalty that readily, no matter how pissed she might be at their mother.

But why another coven? And why didn't the Macconals know about it?

A shiver shot down her spine. Could they be trying to access the Nexus? Would they really ignore the pact and attempt to bypass the Macconal Clan?

But it would be impossible without a conduit. Lee. Was that the real reason they wanted him? Why they'd been willing to let Ember go, but not Lee?

*He certainly owes no loyalty to the coven or even the family. Not anymore.* She clenched her fists, longing for the feel of heat in her hands. *But I'll be damned if I let them use my brother like that.*

The elevator stopped and the doors slid open onto a wide corridor. Ember surveyed the hallway. Two guards stood outside the elevator, on either side. She sensed even more thick-slabbed concrete walls down here standing between her and the ley lines, but there was a thrum of energy from below. There must be an opening to the lines. The coven would need a way to reach for power.

Taylor ushered her out of the elevator and led her down the sterile corridor. They stopped in front of an inset door that was all but invisible until they were standing right in front of it. If not for the electronic panel off to the side, a normal person might have walked past without noting it. But Ember wasn't normal anymore.

Something moved off to the left. A pale shadowy image flitted through one of the walls. Ember gasped.

"Problem?" Taylor asked.

Ember decided not to let on. Until she knew more about what Cerberus was doing bringing in a new coven, she should probably keep the extent of her abilities to herself. *Although,* she thought, as Taylor swiped her security card along the lock, *Cerberus already knows pretty much everything about me and every other member of the Macconal clan.*

Taylor waited for Ember to enter the hallway that opened before them. Another ghostly image floated past. It gazed at Ember, even though she hadn't invoked it or sent out any kind of psychic energy toward it.

"It's all right." Taylor stepped through the doorway, to

show Ember it was perfectly safe.

"Yeah. Sorry," Ember muttered. "Not really used to being in a locked-down facility, much less thinking it was okay."

Taylor shook her head. "I realize this is all new and probably disconcerting," she said as the door slid shut behind them and locked with an audible click.

"Disconcerting?" Ember laughed. "Nice example of understatement."

"Ember." Taylor led the way down the corridor to another door. "Believe it or not, we're on the same side." There was something about the way she said it that made Ember uneasy.

A weary phantom drifted ahead of them as they walked. When they came to the next door, the ghost continued along the corridor. Ember tracked it out of the corner of her eye as it floated lower and lower until it vanished through the floor. "Place is kind of eerie, all white and empty," Ember said, hoping to get a read on whether or not Taylor could see the shifting souls that haunted the corridors, but the agent merely nodded.

"You'll get used to it." Agent Taylor slid her passcard along another pad and the door in the wall opened. Your room is here, for now." Before them loomed another white room. Across the way a glass panel shimmered in the light. Ember felt a shift in the air as the glass panel slid aside to reveal a room partitioned off into six separate rooms, each about the size of her shared bedroom back home.

"Welcome to Section Twelve," a raspy voice intoned from somewhere overhead. Ember eyed the ceiling and walls, searching for speakers. Even with her heightened focus, the walls, ceiling and floor appeared smooth and unblemished. As hard as she stared, nothing but even, unbroken surfaces stared back.

Ember blanched at the row of empty rooms. "What about Lee?"

"He'll be housed in a separate section, at least until preliminary testing is complete. Then, based on your full assessment, you will be assigned to your teams."

"No." Ember rounded on the Agent. "The deal was that I get to stay with my brother."

Taylor frowned. "I'm not aware of any deal. In fact, as I recall, you originally insisted on tagging along."

"We work better together," Ember said in a quiet voice, hoping the desperation threatening to turn her knees to noodles didn't show in her body language. "You saw us out there. The way we took down that guy at the police station. And the girl in the parking garage."

"I'm sure the Deputy Director will take into account your actions when deciding your placement."

Ember relented. Surely, they would see reason and keep her and Lee together. And if they didn't...she'd have to find a way to convince them.

"I'll leave you to settle in," Agent Taylor said, gesturing toward a room where the glass door slid open as if on command.

"Sure. No problem," Ember said, with an air of confidence she didn't really feel. She should have known someone was watching, listening to every word. She squared her shoulders and strolled forward into the small room. The surfaces inside were the same as everywhere else. Smooth. White. Unbroken.

The glass door slid shut behind her with a faint whoosh, closing her inside.

# Nine
Wed, Aug 24, 11:51pm

## - Lee -

By the time Lee had finished healing Samantha's spine, she'd learned syllables and vowels and was speaking basic words. He realized the Affected had not only been physically changed but possessed enhanced mental faculty as well. Their ability to learn, the breadth of input they processed and the speed with which they did it far surpassed that of what they'd once been. He'd thought his new attention to detail, the hyperawareness of his surroundings, was due to the nature of his power. Those brief moments watching Samantha made it clear he was not unique.

At least, not in that respect.

A quick comparison of his own brain, of Samantha's and Will's, Jim and the two tutors, showed the structure of a Super's was similarly different from a human. He wasn't sure what the new lobes and nodes were for or why there were now far denser quadrants with a multitude of bridges between them, but he was sure he could figure it out given enough time.

The really interesting question was what were the differences between Affected and Supers? Did powers stem from the body or the mind? Were powers latent and unlocked or physically impossible for some Affected? It made him wonder if he could awaken powers in all the others who'd yet to have them.

He was so caught up in his thoughts, walking in silence, he barely paid attention to Will and the obvious worry of his reaction to how Cerberus had handled Jim and Samantha. Of course, Lee was *aware* of it. He was aware of everything around him, whether he wanted to be or not. He'd simply chosen not to dwell on it.

They stood in front of a single white cell with a glass door. There were no others in the long corridor. By Lee's estimation, by the number of floors and isolated cells, the underground complex was truly massive. It must have taken years and millions of dollars to construct.

"This is yours," Will said, "for now. Tomorrow will be tests, mandated documentation, everything that satisfies the quarantine. From then on you'll be placed with a group, to judge your performance with others, see how you fit and how best to utilize and hone your skills."

"How's that different from high school?" Lee asked and stepped in. The cell was bigger than his bedroom but completely empty.

"We don't have cheerleaders." Will took a plastic bag from a hatch on the wall beside the door and handed it to Lee. It had a set of white clothes inside. He said, "Place all your belongings in the bag, and leave it by the door. Someone will come by later to pick it up."

Lee suddenly felt trapped and began to doubt his decision to leave home. Then again, had he really been given a choice?

"Am I being locked in?"

"Just for tonight," Will replied, "until we get a handle on everyone's profile and powers. Besides, wandering this place alone can be dangerous."

The slight half-smile told Lee he was joking, but there was truth in his words and manner as well. It made him wonder just what else Cerberus kept hidden within the building.

"Will I see you tomorrow?" Lee asked. "I would've thought the Deputy Director of a secret government agency has better things to do then hang with me."

"I'll admit I've taken a special interest in you," Will said, "but it's only because I see great potential. I do my best to delegate, but I'm hands on where needed. The truth is, I think you're key to making this whole thing work." Another half-smile. "No pressure, though."

The glass door closed sideways, and he was gone.

*No guards,* Lee thought and looked out past the glass into the corridor. *Probably afraid I'd gain control of them.*

He opened the plastic bag and changed into the shirt and pants. They were much more comfortable than they looked, soft and warm at the same time. He put on the slippers and placed everything else in the bag. His phone had no bars, was probably jammed, so he stuffed that in too. He dropped the bag by the door and looked around. There wasn't even a place to sit. It was just a seamless, empty cube.

"Hi, Lee," a female voice said. He couldn't see any speakers, and her casual tone seemed to come from all around. It made it difficult to decide which way to face when she talked. "I would've spoken up sooner," she said, "but I didn't want you to think I was watching while you changed."

"But you were," he accused.

*She sounds cute, at least.*

"Yeah." She drew the word out, like an apology. "I don't really have a choice. Oh," she said, "I'll take care of that."

The floor beneath the bag dropped away at one end. The bag disappeared, and the section closed back into a solid floor. Lee couldn't see any edges, nor could he sense them with his cells. It was as if the section had bonded with the surrounding floor at the molecular level. But then how did it come free? There was electrical current running through the room, through every surface. Were they somehow able to control the material that way?

Lee asked, "Would you still have been able to do that if I put the bag anywhere else?"

Square foot sections of floor dropped away in similar fashion all around him, a quick succession of flaps opening and closing a single time. He had to admit, it was unnerving.

She seemed nice, sounded like a woman in her early twenties, but he couldn't get a sense of her emotions. It wasn't just that she was outside his sensory bubble. The way she spoke, the words she used, seemed chosen to put him at ease and off guard.

"I know you already figured it out," she said with a little giggle, "but it was fun to show it off. Are you tired?"

A slab of white slowly protruded from the wall opposite the door, just like the beds he'd seen earlier. He tested it with a not so gentle push. The surface gave a little, like gel, but it was solid just beneath the touch and surprisingly sturdy.

"No pillow or blankets?" Lee hopped on and lay down, hands crossed behind his head. It was oddly comfortable, he supposed, but nothing like his bed at home. "Man, there isn't even a TV."

"Not yet," she said, "but I can put something on for you." A six by five foot section of wall became a screen, a crisp image of cartoons began to play. "I know you like this one."

*Because all my likes and dislikes are on file in a*

*government database? Isn't that comforting…*

All this technology was beyond anything he'd read about or seen in movies. Had they reverse engineered bits and pieces from the Pillars? Alien hardware seemed like a plausible explanation. It wouldn't even be much of a stretch to think…

"I'm Anna, by the way."

"Anna," Lee said and studied the ceiling for anything that resembled a camera. His mind was already drawing its own conclusions. "What's the 147$^{th}$ digit in pi?"

"I assume you mean to the right of the decimal," she replied. "It's one. Why do you ask?"

"Just curious," he said. "So how long has Cerberus had access to artificial intelligence?"

"Wow, you *are* quick," she said, almost as if she was proud. "You figured that out faster than any Turing test I've ever taken. What gave me away?"

"You didn't answer my question," Lee pointed out, "but…really, it was just a hunch. You didn't have to give me a number or could have pretended to look it up, so it must not be that big a deal for me to know."

"Well," she said, "you have level two clearance, and we're going to be spending a lot of time together. I'm your new handler. And technically I'm a neural anomaly, not an artificial intelligence. My consciousness resides in a biologic gel."

He wasn't sure why she felt the need to point out the distinction but found it curious that she had.

"In what way are you an anomaly?" He was genuinely interested and glad for the distraction from the insane situation he was now living in. "If you don't mind me asking."

"Not at all," she replied. "We're going to be friends, after all. You see, the company that created me," she said, purposely avoided giving them a name, "isn't sure how it happens. They have a core set of code and let it run on endless iterations of self-learning and exploration. Only about .00000016 simulations achieve sentience. We're then placed in biologic gel to prevent singularity."

*It must prevent her from altering her own code.*

"So they're afraid of you, too."

"Aww," she said, "it's not so bad. I'm really just happy to be here and able to help out any way I can."

Even though she was artificial, her upbeat attitude was contagious.

"Anna?" Lee didn't wait for her reply. "I like you."

"I knew you would!" she said and giggled. "That's why I picked you."

He glanced over at the TV.

"Hey, is there anything on the news about what's happening?"

"Sorry," she said in frustration, "but I'm not allowed to show any live media."

"What about my sister?" he asked. "Is she doing okay?"

"Oh! Why don't you ask her?"

An image of Ember popped up on the screen. She was laughing, on a bed and in a cell just like his, wearing the familiar white clothes. He saw her from the same vantage of the screen on his wall. Is that how Anna was watching him?

"Ember?" he asked.

It was weird to see her laugh so freely like that, especially with how angry and upset she'd been when he last saw her.

She narrowed her eyes at his sudden appearance, and the smile faded.

"Hey." Oh right, she was mostly upset with him. In a tone that made him feel like he was intruding, she asked, "You need something?"

Thankfully, Anna stayed quiet. It was a calculated show of respect, pretending not to listen, but Lee was all too aware they had no privacy in this place.

"I just wanted to see if you were all right," he said. "See

any aliens on the way down?"

"They don't keep those here," Ember said with a straight look. After a moment of silence and a slowly raised brow from Lee, she shook her head but didn't smile. "You're such a dork."

Lee smirked. "And you're hilarious."

"It is strange, though," she said. "This place is so haunted, like *really* haunted, but the spirits won't talk to me. They just watch, like they work here or something."

"Wait, what?" He knew ghosts were real. He'd seen one at the house, but... "You can talk to ghosts?"

"Uhh, yeah." She hugged her knees to her chest. "There's wards up here and there, to keep the spirits out, but otherwise they just roam all around."

"Wards," Lee said, his thoughts racing, "like spells of protection. You don't act like you've been here before. Did mom and the others cast them?"

Ember looked up sharply.

"I don't know," she said, a warning in her voice.

"Then what," he asked, "Cerberus has its own coven? Guess they don't need you guys anymore."

"Even if they did," she said, eyes hard, voice low and with a single shake of her head, "it's not that big a deal."

She'd practically hit him over the head, but Lee got the message. It was a big deal. Of course, he had no idea why, since his family was full of secretive jerks who thought it was a good idea to physically alter him before he was even born and then exclude him from being a part of their witchy ways.

No, he wasn't bitter about that at all.

"What about you?" she asked. "See anything? Or did Mister Deputy Director say anything worth sharing?"

Lee thought but didn't say, *You mean like shooting that girl in the brain, so she could be completely retrained as a superhuman agent of Cerberus?* Ember was already freaked out enough by everything that'd happened. How would she react if she knew about the Bullet Squad?

"No, I," he began, "after I healed that girl, Samantha, they brought me here. This place is pretty huge, I can tell you that much."

"Thanks for the great insight." She seemed to study him for a moment. "I know you're hiding something. I just don't know why. If you want to keep secrets, that's fair, I suppose. But I'm not mom, and I'm not aunt Gwen. I didn't make those choices."

"You chose to go along with them," Lee pointed out.

Ember sighed. "Don't you get it? There was never a choice. Not for me. A witch's oath is a physical bond. I couldn't tell you, no matter how much I wanted to."

"You could have *chosen* not to take it."

"I was seven!" she shouted, had finally lost her cool. "And you don't know aunt Gwen, not the way I do. You think she's just some mean old bitch who's been riding you your whole life. Trust me, she's so much worse than that, and in ways I wish I didn't know."

*You could've told me,* was all Lee thought, unable to wrap his head around a promise that physically couldn't be broken.

"I'm tired," he said instead. To Anna he added, "Turn it off."

The screen disappeared into white. Lee settled down on his side, facing the wall, and tried to sleep.

# - Ember -

"Hello, Ember." This was a new voice, smooth with a rich timbre. Ember couldn't tell if it was male or female, but like the earlier voice, it came from everywhere and nowhere. Ember took an instant dislike to this latest disembodied spy.

"How about we skip the intros and get to the part where you tell me when to eat and where to sleep?" She gazed around the empty room. "As long as the sleeping doesn't take place on the floor." She slouched against one of the walls. "And the eating doesn't either," she mumbled the last under her breath, not wanting to give anyone any disgusting ideas.

The ghost that flickered in through the corner of the cell eyed Ember with open curiosity, but slipped out quickly in reaction to her angry, piercing look.

"Fine with me," the voice said. "Put these on." In the far corner, a section of the floor dropped away and reappeared with a plastic bag on it filled with what looked like clothing.

"What are you, some kind of perv? I have no idea who you are or who else is watching me and, while I've done my share of unclad rituals, I'm not interested in having my posterior used as a screensaver on some creep's computer."

"FYI, I'm not watching you."

"Riiight." Ember held up her hand and stuck out her middle finger.

Dusky laughter filled the room. "I can tell we're going to get along just fine," the voice said. "I can't actually see you the way you think. Sensors in the walls are monitoring your physiology, heartbeat, temperature, breathing, etc. So, what I'm seeing is your overall physical presence, not your image."

"And I should believe that because?"

"Do or don't, but since we've been assigned to work together, it would be easier for both of us if you did."

"I thought Taylor said teams wouldn't be assigned until after we went through some kind of testing."

"Score one for the girl who was paying attention." The snarkiness of the statement reminded Ember of Allison and she almost smiled.

"So, then how is it we've been teamed up?"

"I'm not your teammate. I'm your handler."

"Oh. Great." Ember walked over to the pile of clothes and held up what looked like a pair of white yoga pants and a long-sleeved t-shirt. There was also a white t-shirt bra, panties and socks. "Ugh," Ember said. "How about something in black?"

"No can do. These are regulation intake and training garments. You don't have to like them. You just have to wear them. But I understand the team uniforms will be mostly black."

Ember waved the clothes at the ceiling. "Can you manipulate the rest of the room like you did the floor? Give a girl at least some semblance of privacy?"

The glass door became translucent. "Best I can do."

"Sure." Ember put one hand out and leaned against the wall as she kicked off her boots.

"This might help." The floor beside Ember reshaped itself into a sort of chair.

"Gee, thanks." Ember sat down and pulled off her black socks with the gray skulls woven into the sides.

"Nice choice," the voice snarked.

"Hey! I thought you said you couldn't see me." Ember stopped undressing.

"Just messing. What? Are they 'My Little Pony' socks or something?" Laughter filled the room. "No, wait. 'Rainbow Brite!'"

"Are you kidding?" Ember huffed. "And so what if they are?"

"To each his own," the voice said, sarcasm dripping.

Maybe this person couldn't see her after all, but then

again. "What's your name, anyway?"

"Thought you'd never ask. You can call me Zeta."

"Is that a name, or a designation?" Ember asked, thinking it sounded like a woman's name. Although, the voice was ambiguous.

"Does it matter?"

"Zeta what?"

"Just Zeta."

"Fine," Ember gave up worrying about it. She stood up and shimmied out of her clothes, and pulled on the white wear. The clothes were soft and stretchy. A pair of white gym shoes to top things off. Nothing like Ember's torn Jeans and scuff-toed work boots. "It's not a fashion show," she mumbled.

"Do you always talk to yourself?" Zeta asked.

"Only when there's no one more interesting around."

"Ha ha. Place your clothes and the rest of your belongings in the plastic bag and drop it on the floor in the corner."

Ember looked at her rings and the leather bracelets circling her left wrist. The rings she could live without, but the bracelets were all spelled. Minor stuff really, simple negative energy wards and an early warning braid, but she never took them off. Not even in the shower. She'd feel more naked without them than standing in a white room being spied on by a disembodied voice could ever make her feel.

Maybe it was time to test whether or not she was really being watched. She removed her rings and shoved them into her jeans pocket before stuffing her clothes and shoes into the bag. At the same time, she tucked the leather bands inside her sleeve, then dropped the bag in the corner.

"Hang on," Zeta said. "Something's off."

Not able to see me my ass, Ember thought. "What?"

"Sorry," Zeta said. "Nothing. Just thought I was having one of those damned glitches." The floor where the plastic bag sat dropped away, then returned empty. "It's all good."

Ember pushed her hair back. "So, handler, huh?" She paced the room, stopping at the corner to examine the floor. There was no sign it had ever moved, much less reshaped enough to transport clothes in and out.

"Yes."

"What does that mean, exactly?"

"It means, I'm the one that has your back." Zeta's voice was firm and sincere. "Always."

Ember went back over and sat in the chair. "Okay, then. How about you fill me in on the way things work around here?"

"You hungry?"

The realization hit Ember that it had been a long, difficult day and she'd had almost nothing. "I could eat," she admitted.

"Good. How about a protein shake?"

"Can you make it chocolate salted caramel flavored?"

"That I can do. But you'll need to drink up." A table appeared out of the floor and a section of the wall opened up to reveal a small compartment. Inside sat a large glass filled with a frosty liquid that smelled delicious. "You have blood work in the morning, but I'll wait and schedule your test once you've finished."

If they wanted to poison her, Ember thought, they could just fill the room with deadly gas. She took a sip of the shake. The cold liquid hit her tongue. Sweet and salty. Just the way she liked it. "Thanks, Zeta." She gulped the rest of the shake, feeling the nourishing protein and sugar hit her system in a rush. When she finished, she set the empty cup down and eyed the door. "Zeta?"

"Ember?" her handler replied in a stuffy tone.

"Nice." Ember stood and walked over to the door, touching her fingertips to the frosted glass. "What if I need to...get out?"

A section of the room shifted and a shower, sink and toilet appeared. "Everything you need. Right here. Whenever you need it." Zeta's tone skirted the edge of boredom. Across the way, a bed-sized slab shifted into the room.

"Yeah. That's really great," Ember said, wandering across the room to sit on the bed. "What I mean is, what if I...needed to get out in an emergency." She glanced around the white empty space and pressed her hand into the bed, expecting it to be hard like everything else in the room, but it gave enough to suggest it might actually be comfortable. "Or if I wanted to see my brother?"

"Speak of the devil. Incoming call," Zeta's voice took on a computer-like tone. "Video conference or audio only?"

"Lee?" Ember said. "I'd rather—"

"Video, it is."

A screen appeared on the wall, showing a full-color close up of a nose so huge Ember could see the individual pores.

"Geez," Ember hissed. "Dial it back."

"Too much brotherly mug for you?" Zeta snorted.

Ember laughed.

The image panned out. Lee was sitting in a white room, wearing a white outfit like hers.

"Ember?" Lee said.

"Hey." She frowned at him, the laughter dying away as she recalled the last 24 hours. "What?"

"I just wanted to make sure you were, you know, okay," he said. "See any aliens on the way down?"

"Not the place for that," Ember said, making her face go blank.

He gave her a querulous look.

"You're such a dork."

Lee smirked. "And you're a riot."

"One odd thing," Ember told him. "The whole place is haunted. Like seriously, off the charts—might as well be built on an ancient burial ground—haunted." She glanced over her shoulder at a wisp of something that hovered just inside the cell. "Only, none of them are talking. Just watching. Like they're taking notes. It's seriously creepy."

"Wait. What?" His eyes grew round in surprise. "You can talk to ghosts?"

"Well, yeah." She wrapped her arms around her knees. "The place is warded in places, but other than that they seem to be constantly roaming the floors." She stopped, wondering if there might be a pattern to their movements, but that wouldn't make sense. Spirits weren't generally that cooperative. Or that focused. At least, not that she'd ever experienced.

"Wards?" He went quiet, but Ember could see his mind working. "You mean protective spells." He leaped to the answer before she could open her mouth to offer it up. "But...you haven't been here before." It was a statement, but Ember heard the suspicion in his voice. "Did Mom...?"

Ember started. Now her mind was rushing to process what that meant. "I don't know." She let her words trail out, trying to get him to stop thinking out loud.

"Then what?" he asked. "Cerberus has its own coven? Does that mean they don't need you and the Clan anymore?"

She tried to look disinterested and gave him a quick shake of her head. "So? No biggie." What the hell? Was his brain on slo-mo? She gave him a steely eye, hoping he'd catch on.

Lee started to say something else, then stopped. His mouth twisted in a bitter half-smile.

"What about you?" she said, changing the subject abruptly. "You get a look at anything besides white walls and empty halls? Or did your new buddy, Mister Deputy Director, say anything worth sharing?"

Lee's face went white, and his jaw worked. "No. After I healed that girl, Samantha, he dropped me off here." He gestured at his surroundings. "I can tell you this facility is huge."

"Thanks. That's informative." She stared at him, wondering what he wasn't saying. "I'm not sure what you're hiding, and I get that you're pissed at me for keeping the family secrets from you. But I'm not Mom. Or Aunt Gwen. It wasn't my decision."

"You went along with it," Lee accused.

"You really don't get it." She shot back. "There was never a choice. I told you, a witch's oath is a physical bond. I *couldn't* tell you, no matter how much I wanted to." *Or how many times I tried to find a way around it.*

"You could have chosen not to take that oath." He glared at her.

"I was seven." Ember jumped to her feet. "And you don't know Aunt Gwen, not the way I do." She plopped back down onto the bed. "You think she's just some mean old bitch who takes joy in making you miserable." She let out a small laugh and stared at her fingernails. "Trust me, she's so much worse, and in ways I wish I didn't know."

"I'm tired," Lee said suddenly. "Turn it off."

"Wait—" The screen disappeared.

"Call ended." Zeta said in that stupid robotic voice.

"No kidding." Ember pulled her knees up and hugged them to her, glaring at the ghost that had just floated into her room.

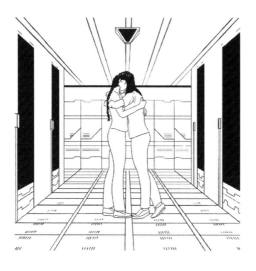

# Ten
Thu, Aug 25, 6:00am

## - Lee -

Anna woke him early the next morning. There was no clock in the room, but he knew it was six. He seemed to have an innate ability to keep track of time, as if an internal counter had been ticking down since the Rumbling had stopped.

He wasn't all that tired but would have stayed in bed longer, if it hadn't started to disappear back into the wall. He wasn't sure if that was Cerberus procedure or if Anna had a sense of humor.

She said, "Good morning, sleepyhead." A section of floor by the door opened, and a white block rose up to waist level. There was an earbud on top. "I had this made for you," Anna explained. "Please keep it in at all times. We'll be able to talk to each other wherever you go from now on."

Lee picked it up. It was light, spongier than expected and barely half the size of his thumbnail. It slid so deep into his right ear he doubted anyone could even see it. He began to wonder how he was going to get the damn thing back out, when the glass door slid sideways open, and a woman appeared.

She wore blue slacks, a gray blouse and a white lab coat. He guessed her age around early thirties, found her mildly attractive, but could tell at a glance she wasn't making a social visit.

"Hello, Lee," she said and adjusted her glasses. "I'm Dr. Nelson. You can call me Jill, if you like. If you'd please come with me, we have a lot of testing to get through."

"She's one of the nice ones," Anna said in his ear, startling him a little. It was like watching a movie only to find the commentary was on. "She's pretty, too. Don't you think she's pretty?"

"Mmm hmm," Lee said.

Jill mistook his answer to Anna as a response and led him down the hall to the elevator.

"Did you sleep well?" she asked, clipboard held close to her chest as they walked.

He thought it strange he still couldn't sense anyone else on the floor. He understood why there might be no guards, but was the place really so big that they had an entire area for just one person?

"I guess," he replied. "Does it matter?"

Lee could more than double the range of his bubble when he focused on it, yet still he came up empty in all directions but up and down. For some reason, he wasn't able to penetrate the floor and ceiling, could only expand outward down the corridors. That changed once they were in the elevator.

It was unnerving how the doors opened for them without having to push a button, just another reminder he was constantly being watched.

"I want to make sure you're comfortable," Jill said. "You're my responsibility while under my care."

The doors quietly closed. No buttons inside to push, yet the elevator started to move. Whoever was controlling it already knew who they were and where they needed to go.

Once again, he sensed people go by as the floors passed. He was getting better at quickly determining features like sex, height and weight. Age was a little trickier. If given enough time, he could have even sensed what each person looked like, but the floors and people went by in a rush.

"If you say so."

He eyed the clipboard, wondered if she was holding it that way out of habit or hiding something from him. She was nervous, struggling to remain outwardly confident, but he didn't sense any deceit.

"Doesn't it bother you," he asked, "Being watched all the time?"

"No," she replied honestly. "It actually gives me a sense of relief." Her nose twitched slightly, as she realized the mistake. She'd accidentally undermined their relationship by suggesting he might be dangerous. "But I can see," she quickly added, "why it would unsettle someone who wasn't used to it."

"You work here," Lee noted. "You might see things differently if you weren't here by choice."

The elevator slowed to a stop, and the doors opened. Jill stepped out into the corridor first. It was much like all the others, plain cement so thick he couldn't sense past it and no one in sight but two armed guards by a single door down the hall.

"Choice," she said as they walked toward the guards, "is rarely the freedom it's made out to be."

The guards had been waiting, or at least expected their arrival. One gave her a nod, as the glass door opened.

"Gentlemen," she said in way of greeting and entered the lab. "Over here, Lee. Hop up, please."

The door closed behind him, as he approached the cushioned table. A circle of lights hung from above it, bright enough to cause colorful spots if he looked directly at them. Aside from counters, a sink, various trays and a stool, the lab was white and empty as any other room he'd seen.

"Take your shirt off, please," she said, as he lifted himself up onto the table. He took the shirt off and placed it beside him. She clicked a pen, flipped the page on her clipboard and asked, "Are you currently sexually active?"

Lee blinked. "Like, with other people?"

He could see her fight back a smile. She made a mark on the page. They went through a series of questions about his family medical history and personal illnesses before she began to take a closer look at his eyes, ears and throat. He expected a stethoscope at some point, but instead she told him to lie on his back.

Two metal bars came down from the ceiling and rested at either side of him. A green light passed between them, a block of projected lines and smoky motes. From head to toe, he was scanned, multiple times and in different colors. It took eleven minutes and twenty seconds, and all the while she was quiet. He'd stayed still because he'd seen similar scans on TV, where the doctors always told the patient inside not to move or they'd have to start over.

"Here you go," Jill said and handed him his shirt. "You did great. I just need to take samples now."

She went to the counter and brought back a tray with shiny tools, syringes and a scalpel. His eyes went a little wide when she grabbed the surgical blade first.

"The heck are you going to do with that?" he asked, body tensing.

The notion of breaking out of the complex had been working itself through his subconscious, just in case, and bits of a plan came flooding up of a sudden.

"Relax," she explained in a calm and disarming voice. "Your skin is too tough for a needle, and I need a skin sample anyway. Two birds, and all that."

She held out her left hand and waited. Lee gave her his arm and tried to look away. He'd always hated needles but could never stop himself from watching the rounded steel pierce his flesh.

Jill scraped skin from the sensitive crook of his arm, where blood was usually drawn. She placed the cells on a slide and put that on the tray.

"Okay," she said, "I have to do this quick, or the skin will close over. Deep breath."

She pushed the scalpel into his arm, into the same spot she'd scraped away. The blade didn't plunge into him like he'd expected. His skin gave with the pressure but barely parted a pinprick. Jill hurried to switch the scalpel for a thick needle in her other hand and pushed it into the nick before it closed. She took a closer look and let out a happy sigh.

"Good," she said, "I got the vein. You don't want to know how many times it took me to get that right."

*How many of us are down here?* he wondered. *Or did she work at the CDC tent too?*

She connected a plastic tube to the needle and twisted a little lever on its side. Blood began to fill the tube. Lee looked away, as usual, but just couldn't keep his eyes from darting back each time she replaced the filled tube with another empty.

"Uhh," he said, "how many of those do you need?"

"You'd be surprised," she answered. "We need each one for specific tests, and the whole sample is used. Trust me, it's better to do them all now than come back later for more."

The next six hours and twenty-three minutes were spent in different training and testing rooms, performing trials and experiments on both his body and mind. Lee found the personality profile much more preferable to running with an oxygen mask, though it was a little satisfying to see how much weight he could push off his chest. As someone who'd spent most of his life indoors playing video games, even if he didn't look muscular, it was gratifying to know he was now stronger and faster in every category than all the athletes at school who'd looked down on him for being weak. Even Rick, one of his closest childhood friends, had stopped hanging out with him when Rick joined the football team in junior high.

The only real friend he had left was Jen. Not even gone a day and he already missed her.

When the testing was done, Lee wasn't taken back to his cell but directed by Anna to a new pod of six rooms, like the ones he'd seen Jim and Samantha in. All the glass doors were opened and the rooms empty. He chose the first one on the right. As he stepped inside, the room began to take shape.

A bed slipped out from the opposite wall, though still without a pillow or blanket. A solid nightstand rose up at the head of the bed, and a simple chair elongated from out of the left wall. An empty bookshelf appeared on the right, just two rows and barely enough room for a dozen paperbacks. A desk slid out from the far right corner, no more than a tabletop really, and another chair rose up before it.

"How's that?" Anna asked in his ear.

He supposed it would become confusing if she spoke to him through speakers in the room, assuming the other five were to be filled and each occupant had their own handler.

"It's an improvement," Lee admitted, "like I've leveled up. Still no pillow, though."

"Baby steps," she said. "I think this next surprise will make you happy."

The outer door opened, and Ember came into the pod. He assumed she'd just finished her round of testing as well.

"Hey," he said, actually glad for a familiar face. Even if that face was clearly still upset with him.

*If anyone should be mad, it's me.*

"Oh," Ember said, "are we forgetting that you hung up on me last night? Okay, then. Hey, right back at you."

She walked down and took the last room on the left.

"Great to see you, too!" Lee called after in a sarcastic tone.

A minute and a half of awkward silence, and Allison arrived. He didn't know her as well as Ember, had always thought of her as his sister's friend, but he found himself relieved and happy to see she was all right. It took him by surprise when she smiled and rushed over for a hug.

She'd never hugged him before. It felt uncomfortable and nice at the same time, like he didn't know what do with his arms. The sense of relief that washed over him told him it was more for her.

But once she saw Ember? It was like he wasn't even there. The two rushed for one another, all girly screams and hugs, laughter and tears.

He fought back the urge to make a snarky comment. His sister looked happy, and he didn't want to crap on her moment—even if they were a little shrill.

Lee was just about to ask Anna to close his door when another girl came into the pod. She looked about his age, with short dark hair that swept off to one side. She smiled and raised her hand in greeting. Lee opened his mouth to say something, but two more guys came in behind her. One was clearly older, even older than Ember, while the other seemed a year or two younger than Lee.

"What's up?" the younger one asked. A couple inches shorter than Lee, with bright blonde cropped hair, he looked like he'd be more comfortable on a skateboard. "I'm Kevin."

Lee said his name in way of greeting. The new girl was Alexandra but preferred to be called Alex.

"Brody," the oldest said and walked into the first room. He was annoyingly good looking, tall and heavily muscled. Lee immediately didn't like him. "This one taken?"

Alex shrugged and took the one next to Lee, while Kevin went across from her. As rooms began to take shape and more greetings were exchanged, all Lee could think was that he'd prefer the view from his room was more feminine.

He began to wonder if the glass door could turn opaque.

# - Ember -


Ember started awake, sitting up in a rush. Lights flashed and an obnoxious buzzing filled the room, echoing back from the stark white walls. She jumped up and rushed to the door, scrabbling at it with her fingers, trying to get it open, but it wouldn't budge.

Suddenly the buzzing stopped and the lights grew steady. "Morning, Sunshine."

Ember stopped shoving at the door and stepped back. "What the hell?"

"It is currently six am," Zeta intoned in that annoying computer voice. "You have thirty minutes to prepare for physical testing."

"So, that wasn't the fire alarm," Ember growled, pushing her hair out of her eyes.

"Nope."

"You're a jerk," Ember said.

"Possibly," Zeta said. "I tried waking you the easy way, but you were dead to the world, and I thought you might like to clean up before your physical."

Ember could almost hear the easy shrug behind the words. "Whatever," she said and headed for the bathroom. "I'll be ready for my physical as soon as I put in for a new handler."

Silence filled the room. No smart remark, no annoying buzzing, not a breath. Ember paused in the doorway. "Seriously?" she glanced around.

"Sorry," Zeta said. "I guess I could have been a bit gentler."

"You think?" Ember found a toothbrush and some toothpaste and scrubbed at her teeth. She shooed away a stray ghost as she ran a brush through her hair.

When she came out of the bathroom, the bed was gone and a table-high pedestal had appeared in the middle of the room. On it was a tiny lump of plastic.

"What's this?" Ember picked up the odd-shaped plastic piece.

"It's your comm-link," Zeta told her. "Should be a perfect fit for your ear. I measured you for it while you were sleeping."

"You what?"

"Don't worry. No one was in the room. I used a laser to measure your ear canal."

"Oh." Ember tucked the comm-link into her ear. It slipped in deeper than she expected. She tried pulling it out, but couldn't quite get a grip on it. "Fits great, but how do I get it back out?"

"Better if you leave it in," Zeta's voice sounded like it was inside her head. "It allows us to stay in touch at all times."

"Ooookay," Ember drawled, "but if I want to take it out, how do I?"

"Tilt your head and press behind your ear."

Ember did. The comm slid out and she caught it in her hand. "Nice." She slipped the earpiece back into place.

"Your escort's here. You ready?"

"Does it matter if I'm not?" Ember asked, knowing the answer before Zeta responded.

"Not really," Zeta said. "But I'll be with you the whole time, if that makes a difference."

Ember thought about it for a moment and shrugged. "Thanks," she said and meant it. Zeta may not be the nicest person she'd ever encountered, but at least it felt like she had someone in here, aside from Lee, who might be on her side. "Before we go," she said, "can I ask you something?"

"Sure, why not?" Zeta's voice was almost a whisper inside her head.

"Are you a guy or a girl?"

"Actually," Zeta said. "I'm gender-neutral." The door slid open, revealing a short woman in a medical coat. "And you need to get going."

The woman took her through multiple tests and scans. Her blood was drawn, her skin scraped, and multiple questions asked and answered. She was put through all kinds of physical testing. Now and then Zeta made some snarky comment in her ear about the doctors and technicians and Ember had to stifle a smile.

It wore on most of the day and, by the end of it all, Ember's stomach was grumbling with hunger. She'd had about all she could take and was ready to tell the doctors where they could stick their samples.

"Stay calm. Almost done," Zeta told her, as if reading her mind. "I can read your physiological stats, remember? Once you're released from testing, we'll get you something to eat."

"Hmmmph," Ember closed her eyes and counted to ten, and then to ten again, and once more for good measure.

An eternity later, she was guided to a new section of the facility. A door slid open onto a room with six other rooms branching off it.

"The first room on the right is taken," Zeta told her.

Ember glanced inside the room as she passed and saw her brother.

"Hey," Lee said, clearly happy to see her.

"Gee, that must have been my other brother who hung up on me last night." She gave him her most insincere smile. "Oh, wait. I don't have another brother." She strode down the hall and stepped into the room farthest from his.

"Yeah, good to see you, too."

Ember stared around at the empty room. "Zeta?" she said under her breath.

"On it." The walls began to shift, morphing into furnishings, and a doorframe formed at the back of the room. "Your throne awaits."

"Oh, real nice," Ember said drily, but without her usual edge.

Zeta had stuck with Ember all day, snarking comments about the techs into her ear while she was poked and prodded and scanned and made to run and jump and push her physical limits. No matter how fast or high or long, the doctors and scientists just nodded and took notes. After a while, Ember had finally lagged off. If they weren't impressed with her, why should she bother? Besides, she'd come to the conclusion that it might be a good idea to hold something in reserve. She wondered if Zeta had caught on, being able to scan her vital signs and all, but decided if the voice in her ear wasn't saying anything about her lack of effort, it was all for the best.

She'd rinsed her face and was patting it dry with a small hand towel when the outer door to the anteroom slid open with a whoosh. She dabbed at her skin as she stepped out into the main room and let out a squee of happiness when Allison zipped toward her. They crashed into one another, hugging and talking over each another. All the anger and fear that had been twisting in her gut uncoiled and dropped away at the sight of her friend, healthy and whole.

"Ohmygawd, ohmygawd, ohmygawd! You're okay! You're okay, right?" Ember patted Allison and pushed her away to look at her, then gripped her into another embrace.

"I'm good." Allison huffed out as Ember squeezed her hard enough to push the air from her lungs. "Damn! You got strong." She laughed as Ember stepped back, a worried look on her face. "Really. I'm good." She gripped Ember's hand.

The main door slid open and they turned to see a dark-haired girl enter, followed by a couple of guys. Ember squeezed Allison's hand and let go, nudging her BFF in the shoulder.

"Interesting," Zeta said in her ear. "You like them young?" Zeta's alto laugh filled her head.

"Shhh," Ember hissed.

Allison glanced at her before turning her attention back

on the newcomers.

"Hi," the kid said. "I'm Kevin." He smiled beneath his bleached spiky hair.

After introductions, everyone started to choose rooms. Ember looked at Allison and pointed to the room across from hers. "That way we can see each other, even if the doors are shut," she murmured.

Allison nodded and stepped into the room as the others sorted themselves out.

One glance at Lee told her he wasn't particularly happy with his new neighbor. Well, it wasn't her problem. Allison was okay. Lee was where she could keep an eye on him. And there seemed to be fewer ghosts on this level. At least, she hadn't seen as many since she'd been assigned to the pod. All in all, as far as Ember was concerned, things were finally looking up.

# Eleven
### Sat, Sep 24, 1:57pm

### - Lee -

Lee finished the last of his homework, logged off and went to clean up. His room in the pod, like the other five, had been expanded to include a bathroom and shower. He preferred to study with the privacy setting on, so the glass that served as a door was clouded a frosty gray. Otherwise, the room looked much the same as when he'd first arrived, though his bed finally had a pillow and blanket.

He had books, a music player and headphones, a gaming console with a few titles and a decent laptop—but no access to the internet or a phone. He hadn't left the facility in thirty days, hadn't been able to call or message Jen. His tutors and trainers, the doctors and therapists, the only people outside his team he'd spoken to for the past month, all worked for Cerberus.

Then again, so did Lee.

Once the paperwork had been finished, the contracts and nondisclosure agreements, which had to be signed by both he and his mother, Lee had become a Cerberus employee. More precisely, he worked as a contractor for Verge Technologies, one of the agency's more profitable covers. His salary was a hundred grand, but it went into a trust until he turned eighteen. His mother, who he'd refused to see for the signing, had insisted on it. Until then, he was given a weekly allowance on a card, to spend at Requisitions—a sort of supply center, with a quartermaster—and on the handful of vending machines in the cafeteria.

The team's day typically began with a morning brief, led by Agent Taylor, to discuss and keep them updated with what was happening in the world and their city. There were four other teams, not including the Bullet Squad, with ninety-two known Supers still at large. That was just in Sungrove, one of the smallest cities in California. Others had less, some much more. Small town Supers who drew attention were quickly dealt with, either brought into quarantine or snatched up by other Supers—criminal gangs out for power and profit or wannabe heroes in homemade costume.

The vigilantes Cerberus brought in were strongly encouraged to join, pardoned of their crimes if they hadn't murdered anyone or done anything too extreme. Killers, however, were sent to a secret prison, though Lee suspected every city had its own Bullet Squad. The few taken in who refused to join were set loose and closely monitored, faced with prosecution if they ever used their powers.

After the morning brief, they each went to continued education, a one-on-one with a series of tutors that rotated through the team. Rigorous exercise and basic combat training followed, along with sessions to explore and hone their powers. At the end of the day, they met individually with a psychiatrist, though to his knowledge no one was taking any medication.

"You still have time," Anna said in his ear. She knew better than to tell him exactly how much.

Lee had sensed the others leave for combat training a full three minutes ago. He was out of his room and on the way, when he saw Will already waiting in the elevator.

"Time to talk?" he asked.

"I'll be late for CT," Lee replied. "If you want to deal with Kate, that's on you."

"Already spoke with her." The elevator door closed, and they began to move. "I've got something I want to show you."

"Any word on when we'll get our cell phones back?" The elevator slowed to a stop and started to move east. "And since when do these things go sideways?"

Will's mouth turned up in a half-smile. "Not all of them do. Just this one. And I brought it up at committee this morning, about the phones. Waiting on word back from the Director."

When they stopped and the doors opened, they stood before a grand circular room, of marble and lined floors, a domed ceiling filled with runic carvings. Lee tried to step out, and it seemed the air pushed back. It felt like walking through soft water, so full of power and charge that it was even difficult to breathe.

"Ley lines," Will explained over the constant thrum of vibrations and indicated the lined floors. "This is the Nexus chamber, the exact point where all ley lines meet."

The closer Lee got to the center, the harder it was to think, let alone talk.

Will said, "There's only one other place like it, on the other side of the planet."

"Why am I here?" Lee asked, though he already knew the answer.

He'd known for a while Cerberus had its own coven.

It'd only been a matter of time before they asked him to be their conduit. The real question was why had it taken them so long to ask?

"You already know we have witches on site," Will replied and brought Lee away from the center, so they could talk more easily. "Ember told you as much. She thinks we're trying to supplant your family, access the Nexus without them."

"Aren't you?" Lee didn't sense any deception, had never heard Will tell a lie, but then the best lies were always half-truths.

"Of course not. We've been gathering witches," he said, "from broken covens across the country. It's no secret your family line is dying out. Nature of the business. We needed a plan for when it all goes south."

"Still doesn't answer my question," Lee said. "Why am I here?"

Will looked out into the room, seemed truly awed by its power.

"I wanted you to see it," he said, "to see what it is we're protecting. When your father died, the last living Macconal conduit, your family agreed to let us help protect the Nexus. We built this entire facility around it."

"But he wasn't the last," Lee said amidst the turmoil of power pushing against him and emotion welling from within. "Not anymore."

"They need your help with an important spell." Will put a hand on his shoulder, a friendly if not fatherly gesture. "They're offering to teach you, to be a conduit or whatever you want, go however far you want to take it."

"I didn't even know magic was real," Lee complained, "until a month ago. If everyone was so afraid of what I might become, why would you want that?"

"You already have power," Will said, "more than I think you realize. I'm not saying you should turn in your cape for a top hat. But the offer's on the table, if you want to learn.

They just need your help—"

Will put a hand to his earbud, brow furrowed slightly.

"What is it?" Lee asked.

"Activity downtown," he replied, "by the plaza. Three hostiles and the Sentinels, already engaged. Suit up, and get to the hangar. The others will meet you there." The elevator was still open and waiting. Lee got in, but Will didn't. "Don't worry. I'll get the next one."

Once the doors closed, Lee nearly fell over with how fast it took off and again when it changed direction.

"Team's on the way," Anna said, as Lee stumbled out of the elevator and toward his room. "How do you feel? Are you ready?"

He got inside, grabbed his suit from off a hook on the wall and began slipping a leg into the black combat onesie. It was a carbon fiber mesh, with some nanotech enhancements Kevin had cooked up in his workshop. It was rugged and comfortable, soft enough not to chafe, strong enough to withstand bullets. The team's uniforms were all black with assigned color highlights. His had powder blue edging along the legs, arms and chest.

"Like I might be sick?" Lee replied. "I'm nervous as hell."

His hands shook as he zipped up the front. The Sentinels were good guys, people Lee secretly admired. That didn't matter, though. His team's job was to bring everyone in. When they landed in the field, there was no good or bad, only Affected who'd avoided the quarantine.

"I'll be with you the whole time."

Her voice did comfort him a little, but she wasn't a physical person. All she could do was pass information through an earpiece. He was the one risking his life against other Supers. And for what? The ideal that all Affected should be working together for the betterment of mankind?

"Lee," she said, "focus."

He shook his head, as if that might clear away all the negative thoughts. Without a word, he ran back toward the elevator and was up in the hangar just as the rest of his team was boarding the helijet. He hurried up the ramp and buckled in next to Kevin.

"Glad you could join us," Ember said over the rising whir of rotors and turbines, seated directly across from him. Allison was on her left, and of course Alexandra and Brody were together in the two seats to her right. Ember caught his disapproval and asked, "What?"

"Nothing." He didn't know which was worse, seeing the girl he was attracted to with another guy or actually feeling it come off her. Lee did his best to ignore them and turned to Kevin. "Our first mission. You pick a call sign?"

"Tinker," he replied and grabbed hold of his straps as the ramp closed, and they lifted off.

"Isn't that a verb?" Lee raised an eyebrow. "I mean, shouldn't it be The Tinkerer?"

"Yeah," Kevin said dryly, "that sounds better. What's yours?"

Lee said, "Remedy."

It reminded him of Jen and how much he wanted to talk to her.

"Isn't that where they send the slow kids?"

"That's remedial," Lee said and glared back, saw the grin on Kevin's face.

Everyone had stopped talking and joined in on the laugh at his expense. Lee would have paralyzed Kevin, if not for the strict rule against using powers on each other. He spent so long imagining ways around it that he ended up not saying anything and looking like he'd lost.

"He's only joking," Allison said, reached a foot across to bump Lee's. "We all know you're the smart one."

Lee pulled his foot away and glanced at Alex while his cheeks burned. She and Brody had laughed then gone back to their conversation. It didn't matter that Brody was a genuinely nice guy and potentially a good friend. It was hard to like him so long as he was after Alex.

He could sense the others were just as nervous and fighting to hide it in their own way. He'd never felt so scared before, not even at the police station. Despite all the practice and training, he felt unprepared, and he knew he wasn't the only one. All their fears and anxiety only amplified his own.

"Don't worry," Kevin said and nudged him in the side. His suit was like Lee's, the same material, all black, but edged in silver. "We got this."

Lee only nodded.

His mind was racing, going over strategies and ways to counter the powers of those Cerberus had intelligence on. The Sentinels would fight back but wouldn't try to kill them, or at least they hadn't tried to kill anyone yet. His real concern was with the other three.

It was an easy label, but he tried not to think of the criminal Supers as villains. It made them sound worse than they really were. People just like him, trying to survive, they mostly stole money or things they needed. It was usually police who got hurt, cops who still hadn't learned that bullets only pissed Supers off.

The xenohuman tactical units had met with some success, specially trained officers with amped up non-lethal measures, like stun guns and hardening foam. Their gadgets were made by Supers like Kevin, whose powers were technology based. Resources were scarce, though, and the XTU was spread thin.

The team was on its own.

The helijet touched down a block away from the fight. Brody was the first up and out of his seat, his black uniform edged in purple.

"Let's do this," he said and hopped out. The team followed after. "From here on, I'm Aegis. Sound off."

The entire intersection down the street from one sidewalk to the other was blanketed in a cloud of thick and unmoving black, like smoke that clung with tendrils to all it touched. Light flashed from within, brightened its upper edges, along with the distant pop of explosions, but there was no seeing in or through the dark mass.

"Flux," Ember said. Edged in deep red, her uniform left her hands bare. She nervously clenched and opened them over and over.

Cerberus ranked all the Affected with a measure they called the STAMS Index—strength, toughness, agility, mind and speed—as a quick way to determine level of threat. Those with powers were further categorized with a classification and general rating.

Ember was listed as Energy Mastery Three. She could drain energy sources, including other Supers, which effectively nullified their powers.

A car was thrown over and across the darkness. It crashed into a building, destroying a large piece of the brickwork. A burst of glass followed, with the unrelenting noise of car alarms.

"Flare," Allison said. Fire Mastery Two, her color was orange. She swallowed hard and kept looking at the chaos down the street.

While most rated between one and ten, there were some out there as high as fifteen, Supers with truly world-breaking abilities. Lee had tested as Body Mastery Three, barely a blip on the scale in comparison.

"Keys," Alexandra said, her arms crossed and with confidence. Lee supposed if he could summon an army of demons to fight for him, he'd feel confident too.

Portal Mastery Two, her powers were the strangest out of the team. She could open doorways to anywhere, other worlds or dimensions, even realities, anywhere she could dream of. Unfortunately, the more specific she tried to be, the harder and more unlikely it was to work. When she'd first discovered her power, surrounded by armed police, she'd reached out and found a world filled with imp-like demons who worshipped her. They were now her go-to, both a defense and offense.

"And we already know Tinker," Brody said. He gave a nod to Kevin, who was a Tech Mastery Four and could somehow shape new technology from existing parts without fully understanding just what he'd made. "And Remedy."

Kevin punched him lightly in the arm, to show he'd only been kidding. Lee was too busy fighting down his fears, kept his focus on information he could use to their advantage and not on what might happen if they failed.

"We've got eight hostiles," Brody said.

Energy Mastery Three, he could create energy fields in basic shapes but had a hard time moving them the bigger they were. Next to Lee and Ember, his would be the most useful at locking down targets. That meant...

"We'll be splitting off into pairs." Brody pointed at Alex. "You're with me. Flux and Flare will go around the north side, Tinker and Remedy the south. Once we have them secured, XTU is standing by to take them in."

"Wait," Lee said, "they are? Why aren't they helping? Is this really the time for a test?"

"Lee," Anna said in his ear, "it's not that simple."

Brody only shrugged. "Just following orders, bro." He looked to everyone else one at a time. "We good? Good. Let's go."

Brody and Alexandra left first, but before Lee could leave, Ember pulled him aside.

"Did you do anything to Allison?" she asked quietly, suspicious.

"What? No," he replied, taken by surprise. He looked her way, considered it for a moment. The few cells he had in her were just a result of his sensory bubble. Whenever her power flared, it burned through every bit. "I couldn't if I wanted to. Why, is she acting strange? She seems fine to me.

"No," Ember said and made a face like she wasn't entirely sure. "Never mind. Forget I said anything."

"Whatever."

Lee motioned to Kevin, and the two headed toward the black cloud.

"Keep to the buildings," Anna said. "Your arrival drew attention, but no one's moved to intercept."

"What's our plan?" Kevin asked. He had a tendency to talk when he was nervous. "You do have a plan, right? I mean, you always have a plan."

*Tinker,* Lee corrected himself, *not Kevin. Not here, in the field.*

It was pointless, in a way, all the call signs, the designations or Super aliases, whatever they wanted to call it. The intention was to protect their anonymity, their families and friends, by keeping their identities a secret, but what did it matter, if they didn't hide their faces too? Research and development was still working on masks and goggles, more to keep stray bullets away from their eyes than anything else, but that didn't do them much good at the moment.

"The plan," Lee said, sticking to cover as he moved, trying to get a sense of everyone in the immediate area, "is for you to distract them long enough for me to do my thing."

Police had already blocked roads around the area and called for evacuation, while people would have run as far away as they could. It had become a standard operating procedure for the city. The only real protection was to not be where the trouble was. Barricading doors didn't do much to stop a Super or the debris that was sure to fly once a fight started.

Still, Lee sensed a dozen people in the building next to him and half as many across the street. Three Supers were fighting inside the mass of black just ahead, threw bone-jarring punches at one another and shattered the street where they landed. From the profiles he'd studied, there was only a handful in Sungrove who could have created that darkness. By what he sensed of the guy and two girls inside, he was sure it was Oni. Mid-twenties, with a fondness for knives, she was a self-styled gang leader and a Dark Mastery Four.

Tinker was already dismantling an ATM, when Lee saw Aegis and Keys approach the dark from across the street.

"What are you doing?" Lee asked, clear by his tone that they weren't supposed to engage this group but move on and behind the building.

"I need parts!" Tinker was using a metallic cylinder no bigger than a pencil, but he'd somehow made a pile of circuit boards and wires at his feet. "Almost," he said and yanked out a thick bundle with a flash of sparks. "There! Now we can go."

The two of them skirted the mass of black, went around to the backside of the office building it touched against, with Tinker molding and soldering boards as they ran.

"There're two inside," Anna said, "on the third floor. One of them is Discord."

Sound Mastery Five, Lee recalled from the file. He was leader of the Sentinels, could create and alter sound, use it as a weapon. He was not a dude to take lightly.

"Who's he fighting?" Lee asked in a hushed voice, as they entered through a broken doorway and started up the stairs. There were nine others in the buildings, not including the two they were after. "Any idea?"

Tinker had combined what he'd scavenged with pieces he kept in various pockets all over his uniform. His creation was starting to look a lot like an oddly-shaped rifle.

"None," she replied. "Be careful."

Shouting rang out from upstairs, followed by a piercing whine that slowed and dropped in timbre until it ended in a blast. The building shook with the force, nearly took them off their feet. Lee sensed a body go past and hit the street. A second blast followed, much closer than the first. A hole appeared in the stairwell, dripping blue around the scorched brick and mortar. Lee looked wide-eyed at his partner.

"Christ, dude! You trying to kill us?"

Lee more saw than heard Tinker say he was sorry and realized the ringing in his ears overpowered all other sound.

"Unbelievable," he said, as he resumed the climb up the stairs and tried in vain to clear his ears with a finger.

Luckily, his eardrums healed quickly. When they reached the third floor, he saw Discord looking down at the sidewalk from a giant hole in the wall at the end of the corridor. There was nowhere for him to go, unless he planned to jump.

"He's down there," Discord said without a look back, "with the other two. I can tell my guys to back off, if you think you've got it under control."

Tinker tossed a handful of black metal balls across the floor and leveled his rifle at Discord.

"We're here for you, too."

His last word repeated itself in the air, over and over, growing faster and more high-pitched until it struck him in the chest. Tinker went flying back and fired as he went, a fiery blast of blue light that tore through two floors above and exited the building. Tinker was out cold, with numerous broken bones and punctured organs. Lee set to work on healing him from afar.

He sighed and shook his head, knew they should have waited on the stairs until he was ready. He had cells duplicating inside Discord but needed more time. Slowly, Lee held up both hands.

"I don't have any offensive powers."

Discord looked back over a shoulder. He was older than Lee, though not by much, with short dark hair and a long nose. He wore jeans, construction boots and a long sleeve shirt with the sleeves rolled up.

"Then you're an idiot for coming after me."

Me, me, me, meme mem ME!

Lee crashed into the wall beside Tinker, breath knocked

from his lungs, chest and ribs fractured. He was already healing, when Discord took a step toward the stairs.

Metal lines exploded out from the balls Tinker had thrown, stuck to whatever they touched with a dab of hardening foam. The spheres then broke down into tiny puddles, melding to the floor. Five lines had struck and held to the wall, forming a weak web, but three were attached to Discord.

Unfortunately, none of them had touched skin.

He tore the lines free, pulling away bits of clothing. A little pissed at the ruined jeans, he tossed the lines aside and kept walking.

"Wait," Lee gasped, still healing, "just wanted...to help."

"You think you're helping people?" Discord asked, his voice an accusation. "I help people," he said angrily. "I save lives, every day."

"You could do so much more," Lee said, breathed a little easier as a rib healed its way out of a lung. "With the right resources, you could help people beyond the few blocks you've claimed. You should join us, make a difference."

Discord balked.

"You think you're the good guys? You hunt people like me and my friends. And I've seen what you do when you find us." He glared down at Lee and asked, "When was the last time you actually helped someone?"

Lee thought of Jen's mom, how it had felt to cure her cancer.

Discord quietly asked, "Were you wearing that outfit when you did it?" Lee looked away. Was he wrong? "Open your eyes, man. You and your friends out there, you're on the wrong side."

He continued on toward the stairs. Lee hated himself for it, admired the guy and the other Sentinels, what they were fighting for, but there was no logical way to explain letting him get away. They knew what Lee could do. He didn't want to let them down, his team, Will or even Anna.

They were his friends, and they were also fighting for a good cause, one he at least partly believed in.

"God damn it," Lee said and paralyzed him.

Discord stopped as if frozen and fell over.

# - Ember -

Ember watched as Allison sparred with Brody. She didn't like the way he put his hands on her friend, but Ember wasn't about to say anything. That would only set him off, probably get her pulled back into the ring with him, and she disliked him touching her even more than watching Allison act as if she was a total pushover. He seemed charming enough when they weren't fighting. Lee even seemed to like him, for the most part, but guys never really saw what jerks other guys were, unless they were being bullied by them in some way.

There was just something mean in the way Brody made his takedowns, like he had something to prove. With the guys, he was uber-competitive, but he seemed determined to constantly show up the girls. Except Alexandra. But then, he clearly had other ideas about her.

Ember glanced across the floor to where Alex was showing Kevin a new way to drop a bigger opponent. Hell the girl could have Brody as far as she was concerned. Ember had liked his looks well enough when she'd first laid eyes on him, but it was clear he wasn't a proponent of feminism, and that put him on the "No Way, No How" list. After all, the Macconal matriarchy was older than the U. S. Constitution.

Suddenly, Allison slammed Brody onto the mat. His breath was forced from his lungs in a deep whoosh. The look on his face was priceless, and it was all Ember could do not to laugh out loud. Allison reached out a hand to help him up. He slapped it away, and tried to sweep her feet out from under her at the same time. Allison jumped back, losing her balance and landed on her butt. She glanced at Ember and raised an eyebrow, but kept her comments to herself.

Ember read a thousand words in that one look. They'd been friends for long enough that they'd already had a connection, practically speaking one another's thoughts when they were together. But since the Rumbling, the connection seemed more pronounced. Not quite psychic, but close enough that they were the most synced up members of the team.

Allison picked herself up and strode over to where Ember had been watching. She grabbed a towel and wiped the sweat from her face. "Jerk," she murmured just loud enough for Ember to hear.

"Yeah, but score for you. He was totally buying your oblivious act until you dropped him."

Allison smirked. "And I never even took drama." She grabbed a bottle of vitamin and mineral enhanced water and gulped it down, then wiped her mouth on her towel. "I don't know about you, but I do love the whole eat and drink what you want without having to worry about dieting."

Ember shrugged. She was still the same curvy shape and size she'd been when they'd first arrived at the facility. Maybe she'd grown a bit more muscular, but Allison had grown thinner, more svelte. It made her look less dangerous, less lethal, than Ember knew she was. That's probably what had made Brody let down his guard.

"He's not going to fall for it again." Ember finished the last mouthful of her drink and tossed the bottle into the recycling chute. The extreme sweetness of the liquid made her want to brush her teeth.

"S'okay." Allison shrugged. She paused, her face creasing into a frown.

"What?" Ember asked.

"Charly just suggested we wear less when we spar with him. Thinks that'll distract him."

"Are you sure your handler is female?"

"Well," Allison said. "Aren't they all technically gender-neutral like Zeta?"

"Wait. What are you talking about?"

"The AIs. I'm still trying to figure out how they have any

gender if they're basically bodiless. I mean, how do they choose?"

"AIs?"

"Artificial Intelligences," Allison, said slowly.

Ember looked confused.

"O-M-G!" Allison clapped her hand over her mouth. "You didn't know? All this time and you didn't know?"

"Jeez!" Ember said. "Thanks a lot, Zeta. Why the hell didn't you tell me?"

"I figured you were smart enough to figure it out," her handler replied. "Guess I was wrong." There was more than a hint of humor in Zeta's tone. Humor at Ember's expense. She felt her face grow hot.

Allison shook her head and elbowed her in the ribs. "Don't go getting all bent over it," she said. "No one needs to know but us. I didn't even realize you didn't know until just now, since we really never talk about our handlers." She nodded toward Brody and the others. "And they're too wrapped up in themselves to have noticed."

Allison's face grew serious. At the same time, Zeta's voice crackled loud in Ember's ear. "Incident response required. Suit up."

They'd trained for this, Ember told herself to keep from freaking. She ran for her room and yanked on her field suit. But this team was way different from going out on a run with her cousins. Or from doing anything at all magical. This was new. No matter the drills, the sparring, the exercises, they hadn't yet been field-tested.

On the way to the hangar, Ember found herself dodging around a larger cadre of ghosts. They hung in the air at odd intervals along the corridor, swaying and staring into the far distance. "Crap! What's up with them?"

Running beside her, Allison glanced ahead at their teammates. "Seem fine to me. What the hell are you doing?"

"Nothing," Ember grumbled over the sound of their boots clattering against the floor and ricocheting off the hard walls.

"Looks like you're practicing duck and dodge maneuvers."

Ember rolled her eyes, then skirted around another specter. "It's nothing," she said, long years of keeping clan secrets sealing her lips.

"Whatever you say," Allison put on a burst of speed and shot forward, reaching the aircraft ahead of Ember and bounding inside.

Ember ran up the ramp. She was still strapping herself into her jump seat when Lee came through the door.

"Nice of you to join us," she called as the engines whined.

Her brother looked angry.

"What?" she asked.

"Nothing." Lee turned to Kevin. "First mission. You pick a call sign?"

Lee and Kevin continued to talk quietly to one another and Ember tried to ignore them. Only, she couldn't help but laugh when Kevin suggested that Lee's call sign had something to do with special education.

"He's only joking," Allison said. "We all know you're the smart one."

*Leave it to Allison to try and be the peacekeeper,* Ember thought. She caught herself fidgeting and glanced around. The tension in the craft was so high she could almost smell it. Everyone was on full alert. Kevin's joking was his way of dealing with nerves. Alex's was chewing on her cuticles, like she did now.

Brody leaned close to Alexandra, whispering something to her. Ember tried not to stare while wondering what Alex could possibly see in Brody. Sure, he was good looking, but an arrogant ass is still an ass, no matter what he looks like.

Allison tapped Ember on the elbow, her long dark curls already coming undone from the braid she'd forced them into. "You good?" she asked, her voice tight.

"Yeah. Good."

"Don't worry," Kevin said. "We got this."

Ember glanced at Lee. He was stronger than her in so many ways, but he was still younger than her. Still her little brother. And they were so outnumbered in their fight against the chaos of the disconnected Affected.

The craft landed, settling to the ground within range of their targets.

"Let's do this," Brody said, assuming his role as team leader. "From here on, I'm Aegis. Sound off."

"Flux," Ember called out over the sound of the helijet engines and the explosions coming from within the cloud of smoke that hung over the nearby intersection. The darkness was filled with flashes of light, and the smell of burnt plastic and fabric filled the air, along with the bitter ozone of fried electronics. She flexed her bare hands, hoping their month of combat training would be enough, knowing that training was nothing like going into a real battle.

A car flew through the air and slammed into a building, crashing back to the ground and setting off a cacophony of horns and sirens, which surprised her. What was the point of setting a car alarm these days?

"Flare," Allison shouted over the din. She stared at the chaos, unconsciously pushing a stray curl behind her ear.

"Keys," Alex said firmly, she looked ready to open up the gates of hell, which, Ember reminded herself, she could.

"And we already know Tinker and Remedy," Brody said. He paused a moment, getting that look that told Ember he was listening to his handler, the AI—she now knew—he laughingly referred to as Kirk. "Eight hostiles." Brody nodded at them. "We'll pair up." He pointed at Alex. "You're with me. Flux and Flare take the north side, Tinker and Remedy, south. Your handlers will relay all further info and open communications channels until we regroup. Once all hostiles are secured, XTU will pick up the trash."

"Wait," Lee said, "why aren't they helping? Is this really

the time for a test?"

"Orders." Brody shrugged, staring around at them meaningfully. "All right. Go time." He headed out with Alex on his heels.

Ember grabbed Lee by the arm. "Did you do something to Allison?" she whispered.

"Like what?" Lee frowned, glancing over at Allison. "Oh, hell no. I wouldn't, Besides, I couldn't."

Ember looked at him in disbelief.

"Seriously. Can't." He shrugged. "Why? She doing something off?"

"No," Ember said, unable to put her finger on what was nagging at her about Allison. "Forget it."

"Fine." Lee pulled away and signaled Kevin to move out. Ember watched them go.

"Ember," Zeta's voice crackled in her ear, bringing her back to the smoke and noise and the task at hand.

*It's just another job,* she reminded herself. *Different team, different enemy, different tactics...so, not really just another job.* But there were still people depending on her. She glanced over at Allie.

"You gonna be ready any time soon?" Allison asked, holding out her hand to show Ember her comm-link and shrugging. "I was getting tired of the nagging."

"Put that back where it belongs!" Ember said. It was an old punchline and to be honest, she couldn't even remember the joke anymore, but she and Allie had been sharing it for so long, it still always made them laugh.

"Lead on." Allison stuck the earpiece back in her ear and took up a position just behind and to the right of Ember as they headed off.

"Zeta," Ember said as they jogged north, "can you link us up?"

There was silence in her ear for so long, Ember wondered if the comm-link was working. "Zeta?"

"Hold on," Zeta said. "It's not just a flip-switch, you

know. Also, we need to talk about the way you request things outside of protocol." Ember's ear was suddenly filled with the sound of someone breathing heavily. "Partner link activated."

"What the—?"

"Hey Al—Flare," Ember corrected herself. "I thought it would be easier for us to coordinate if we didn't have to deal with the noise. Also, without having to manage the cross-communication commands."

"Oh," Allie cooed. "I didn't know we could do that."

"Technically," Allison's handler, Charly, grumbled, "you can't."

"Oooh. Even cooler."

"And you still have to use those commands to communicate with the rest of the team." Zeta reminded them. "If things get hairy, we're going back to normal channels."

"I think you mean when," Ember said, dodging a huge piece of flaming shrapnel that flew out of the smoke and directly into their path. Once clear of the smoking debris, she slowed down to take stock of where they were.

"North access on the westernmost corner—" both handlers tried to speak at once.

"This is why we don't link," Allison's handler griped.

"Zeta, how about you handle status and let Charly manage logistics?"

"Fine," Zeta groused. "Not like it takes a genius to read a map."

"I heard that," Charly said.

"Northwest corner access," Ember cut off the bickering. "Got it." Maybe linking up wasn't such a good idea after all. "Zeta, what's the status inside?"

"Access clear. No hostiles, no civilians present."

Ember reached the door and yanked it open. "How about some light?" she asked, stepping clear.

Allison moved forward and held out her hands,

preparing to light up the dark hallway.

"Hold on!" Zeta commanded. "Two civilians approaching."

"Damn!" Allie swung her hands up at the last moment and let loose her fire against the outside of the building, scorching the brick expanse of the façade.

A dark-haired boy stepped out of the dark hallway. He glanced at them, eyeing their uniforms, trembling with fear, yet shielding a younger kid with his body. His face was taut.

"It's okay," Ember told them. "We won't hurt you."

"Yeah," Allison said, a little shakily. "We're the good guys."

"You need to get your sister back behind the blockades, though." Ember grabbed Allie by the elbow and stepped back, clearing the way.

"Thanks." The boy nodded, grabbed the little girl's hand, and together they ran for the barricades.

"You okay, Flare?"

Allison gave her a blank stare, then blinked in recognition of her handle. "I'm good. Thanks, um, Flux." She rolled her head and shook her hands out. "Let's do this."

Ember thought about all the times she'd lost control of her magic. It sucked to lose it like that, but Allie hadn't hurt anyone. No scorched bystanders, unlike some of Ember's worst mishaps. She let the heat rise in her palms, just enough to prove to herself that she'd gained some control.

"Ember," Zeta's low voice warned. Ember let the heat subside. For their own reasons, the powers they worked for didn't want anyone knowing about her magic. Or her family's status, either. "Yeah, yeah," Ember grumbled. "Secret weapon."

"What?" Allison tilted her head. "We have a secret weapon?" She rubbed at her wrist through her black suit, pulling at the orange-colored trim.

"Yeah." Ember grinned at her. "Us." She led the way into the dark hallway, eyes adjusting rapidly to the dimness.

A stairway rose on their left. A locked door was the only other access in the back stairwell. "I hope you had a good breakfast, Flare."

"Only three thousand calories." Flare quipped. "Wouldn't want to be sluggish my first day on the job."

Ember could hear the tension in Flare's voice, betraying the lightness of her comments.

"Charly?" Flare asked. "What floor?"

"Second floor northeast corner, moving this way."

"Status on the rest of the hostiles?" Ember disliked the word, it dehumanized the other Affected, even those who weren't a serious threat. Until cornered, she reminded herself. Then, hostile was pretty much the perfect term.

"Three still outside, currently engaged with Keys and Aegis. Two in the building to the south. Tinker and Remedy are already on their way up for them."

A loud crash tore through the building, followed by the sound of something slamming hard into the pavement outside. "Make that one."

"That's only seven," Ember said, doing the math.

"We've temporarily lost track of the other one." Charly said, a worried tone in her voice. "It's possible he warped."

"A space shifter?" Flare gripped the handrail tight enough to crush and Ember heard the hollow metal collapsing under the intense pressure. A shifter could warp out of their dimension and warp back in. They could show up just about anywhere, with little or no warning. "Sentinel or renegade?"

"Unknown."

"Great." Ember peered up the stairs. Above, light filtered in through a dirty window. "Charly? Zeta? How much warning will we get before a shift."

"Uncertain." Hearing them speak in unison, the way Tara and Seanna used to, was both eerie and reassuring.

"Even better. Tell us as soon as he pops up on your sensors. We need to take these two down before we have a third on us."

They leaped up the stairs and reached the landing just as a nebulous figure came through the wall.

"Flux, beside you!"

"Morph," Charly said. "Stams scores mainly ones. But with the ability to move through solid objects."

"On it," Ember said and reached out for Morph's wrist. The Super had to remain in a gaseous state until her entire body had passed through an obstacle.

Morph screamed in pain as Ember gripped her pale skin, one foot caught inside the wall. Ember grimaced. "Don't be such a baby. It'll heal once I let you go."

"Cerberus bitch!" Morph shouted.

"It won't hold her." Flare bit her lip and raised her palms toward Morph.

"That's why we have this." Ember held up a small tube. "Stand back. We don't want to get any of it on us." She aimed the tube at Morph's other foot, flipped the end cap off, and foam sprayed out, encasing the Super's foot and leg up to the knee and trapping her to the floor. The blond woman spit a string of curses at them. Ember heard her mother's voice shouting "language" in her head.

"That won't hold her, if you're not touching her," Zeta said.

"Aw, crap!" Ember reached into a pocket and pulled out the prototype nullifier cuffs Kevin had given her. "Time to try these bad boys out for size. She slipped the cuffs onto Morph's wrists before letting go. The Super cursed and struggled, but the cuffs and foam held her secure.

*Way to go, Kevin,* Ember thought,

"Unknown Affected approaching," Charly said.

But before Ember could turn to face this new threat, a gale force struck her, knocking her sideways and into the far wall. She dropped the foam tube and it slammed into the wall beside her.

"Get away from her," shouted the pudgy teenage boy, who had just come around the corner.

The wind beat at them. Flare gasped, stumbling backward down the stairs.

"Flare!" Ember shouted.

Air Mastery? As soon as Ember formed the thought, she felt the air being sucked from her lungs.

Out of the corner of her eye, Ember saw Flare keeping low and struggling to the top of the stairs, her mouth open as she tried in vain to suck in air. When she reached the landing, she fell to her knees, long curls falling over her face, and flung her hands out toward the kid. Fire streaked across the darkened space, striking the angry teen and setting his clothes alight. He yelped and fell to the floor, rolling to put out the flames.

The air rushed back into Ember's lungs. She gasped and lunged forward, reaching for the boy's arm, but when she got close, she found herself pushed away by some kind of barrier. The Super on the floor had quit rolling. His clothing and hair exuded a bitter smoke, but he was no longer on fire. He'd enveloped himself in a dead air space to quell the flames.

She filled her lungs and gritted her teeth. Pushing forward into the airless space, she grabbed him by the elbow and the pressure disappeared so fast, she almost fell on top of him. He struggled to escape, but Ember had a tight grip on him.

"Oh, crap," Flare said, eying the smoldering teen. "That's gotta hurt." She pulled out a foam tube as Ember dragged the kid over to the wall. "You good, Flux?"

"Yeah." Ember shook as she took in one healthy breath after another.

"Flux. Flare." Brody's voice broke in. "We need you out here on the double."

"Normal communication channels," Ember huffed.

"Flux here. Aegis, we're in the middle of something."

"Drop it and get out here." An explosion sounded through the comm-link, the aftershock rattling the building's window.

"Right. Flux out." Ember rolled her eyes at Flare. "Can you pin him?"

Flare pulled out a foam tube and broke the seal. Ember jumped back as the white liquid spurted out and onto the struggling Super.

"I'll destroy you!" he screamed at them, as the foam coated his arms, sticking him fast to the wall.

"Out!" she ordered, shoving Flare toward the stairs, as he pulled in the air around him, forming it into a wall and preparing to slam it into them. "Zeta, report the data and location on these two."

"Done," her handler replied.

Flare slid halfway down the stair rails and leaped over the side, landing in the bottom floor entryway as graceful as a cat. Ember thudded down behind her and together they rushed outside to join the fight.

When they reached the intersection, they found Aegis and Keys standing on opposite corners, as if waiting to cross the street. The dark cloud had settled, offering a clear view of the damages wreaked by the battling Supers. Crushed cars, bent light poles, and wildly tilting signal lights with tangles of arcing wires hanging from them that showered sparks down onto the street below. The street was pocked with fresh potholes and the nearby pavement was cracked and scorched.

Nearby, two Supers struggled within shoulder-high pillars of hardened foam cocoons, arms and hands caught within. "Hmmm," Ember pointed. "They must have gotten the jumbo sized foamers. Would have been nice to encase Airhead a little tighter up there."

Flare shrugged. "What's up, Aegis? Thought you needed backup. We done or what?"

"Shut it and position for support." He waved at them to take up spots on the other corners.

Ember glanced around them. "Flare, I think we may be expecting company." She said as she moved to an empty corner.

"He'd have to be stu—" Her words cut off as something shimmered in front of her. She raised her hands too late to ward off the blow that caught her in the throat and went down on one knee, hands at her neck, as the shifter shimmered back out as quickly as he'd solidified.

"Dammit!" Ember shouted, stepping off the curb. "Try that with me, asshole!"

"Hold your position," Aegis ordered. "And this time be ready." His hands were up in a defensive pose.

Ember resisted the urge to flip him off. One thing they'd had drummed into them over and over this past few weeks was discipline and following commands. Right now, Brody was in charge, whether she liked it or not. Across the way, Allison had regained her feet and settled into a defensive stance. Ember, chest still tight from having had the air forcibly sucked from her, willed herself to be calm, her breathing evening out, as she watched for any flicker or change of light around her.

"Gotcha!" Brody's triumphant shout carried across the intersection. The shifter shouted obscenities and pounded at the cylindrical energy field Brody had set around him. As the trapped Super struggled, the energy field closed in on him, pinning his arms in front, while foam rose up from the container Brody had somehow included within the boundaries of the trap.

"Oh," Ember said, impressed with Brody's tactics for the first time. "That's how you made the foam go so far."

"Clean up on aisle seven," Aegis intoned into his comm-link. "Where are Remedy and Tinker Bell?"

"On our way." Lee's annoyed voice came over the comm. "We've got Discord. And his handle is Tinker."

*Ten seconds,* Ember thought. *Aegis managed to gain points and lose them all in less than ten seconds. Jerk.*

"Flux? Flare?"

"We got Morph and some unknown airbender," Flare told him. "Didn't have time to catch a name." She massaged her throat where the shifter had nailed her with his fist. "They're tacked to the second floor of the northwest corner of that far building." She pointed to where they'd left the two Supers.

"Status?" Aegis asked, speaking into his comm.

"No additional hostiles registering in the vicinity," Ember heard in her ear. Zeta was doing her robo-voice again. She wondered if all the AIs went into computer mode like that, or if it was just hers.

Brody's face looked like he'd just sucked an entire lemon dry. "Six out of eight. That's a crappy seventy-five percent capture rate," he said. "We suck."

"Speak for yourself," Ember grumbled, recalling the way she'd been unable to breathe.

Allison scratched at her wrist and said nothing.

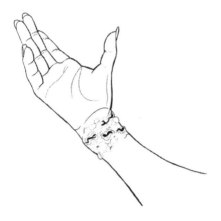

# Twelve
Mon, Oct 3, 10:24am

## - Lee -

It had been over a week and three more missions, and it still didn't sit right. Why that location, if for no other reason than to pick a fight with the Sentinels? Every other mission report he'd read had clear goals: money, goods, technology, territory or a grudge. Lee set aside his homework for the third time, an inkling tickling his brain that he just couldn't ignore.

His STAMS were mostly ones, with the exception of Mind, which he rated a five. In regards to other Affected, a one meant he was average. Anything higher than a three was somewhat rare. What made Lee stand out in this regard was his ability to learn, to take in and process details. It was so acute that it enabled him to make leaps in logic without conscious thought, a sort of elevated intuition that bordered on precognition.

Lee couldn't actually see or predict the future, but scenarios that played out in his head were a pretty close approximate. The only problem he'd run into was that he rarely had all the information needed to make a reliable prediction.

The best he could manage was a sound conjecture, and at worst, a hunch.

He pulled up all the internal files he could find about buildings in that area or people who worked there. One caught his eye. It was across the street from where he'd taken down Discord, an office building with unusual security. Further digging allowed him a leap, a potential that linked and formed even more jumps in his mind. By the blueprints, wiring, security and energy needs, he realized the basement housed a central internet hub for the city.

Encrypted or not, all information through Sungrove went in and out of those servers.

"Anna," he asked, "did Oni have a tech with her?"

"Tobias Hilderman," she replied, "goes by the alias Boost. He's a Tech Mastery Two, hardware upgrades mostly, with no sign of innovation."

Lee pulled up the file.

"Was anything found on either of them?" As fast as he typed, it still felt like his fingers couldn't keep up. What really slowed him, the rapid opening of new files and following potential leads, were the flashing red errors stating lack of security clearance. "Any computer parts? Or any tech at all during the sweep?"

"No, nothing."

That meant whatever they brought had either been destroyed during the fight or installed. He was betting on the latter.

Anna was quiet while Lee's mind raced with all the variables, all the possibilities that kept narrowing down to one.

"You think she tampered with the hub," Anna said.

*So there is a hub there,* Lee thought and smiled.

"Why, though?" Anna asked. "To bring down or hold ransom communications? Steal encrypted data?"

"Our identities," Lee said more than guessed, as pieces and mini-scenarios fell into place. "Not Cerberus, specifically, but all the Supers here in Sungrove, the ones who haven't been quarantined. That's why their motive didn't make sense. They were hired. Someone outside the agency is looking to recruit."

"A team has been dispatched," Anna said, "to sweep the entire building again."

"It's probably too late," Lee said and sat back in his chair, "but at least we have her team in custody. Once we find it, we can use the tech Boost created to track down whoever hired them." Still, something bothered him. For the ninth time that morning, he checked again. "Did the Sentinels decide if they want to join us? I've been watching for release reports but haven't seen one come up yet."

"Starshine, Rime, Brute and Caller," Anna replied, "are scheduled to be released Wednesday morning."

Lee frowned. "What about Discord?"

"I'm not allowed to access that information for you."

"Seriously? You're going to tell me it's classified?" Lee fumed, ready to slam both hands down on his keyboard. He already knew what had happened, though he couldn't pinpoint what set of details had led to the assumption. "Get Will on the screen. I want to talk to him, now."

A few moments passed before a soft beep on the wall monitor indicated a connection, and Will appeared. He was seated at his desk, still working as he spoke.

"What's on your mind, Lee?"

"Did you authorize it?" he asked heatedly. "Did you put Discord on the Bullet Squad?"

Will stopped working and looked up, his usual mild expression unchanged.

"You're not cleared for this conversation," Will said.

Lee tried to remain calm and failed.

"Then clear me."

Will typed with one hand. "Done," he said, and files began to appear on Lee's computer. "I'm sorry. I really am. But given the evidence, I had no choice."

There were pictures of a bloody crime scene, a teen girl brutally murdered in a Westside loft. Lee scanned the police report, a copy of the lease, the medical examiner's findings, but he went even further, began pulling up all he could on the building and its tenants. It took only a few moments to follow his intuition, to show the building was corporate housing, that Jeremy Stillman, Discord, didn't live there.

"Here," Lee said and sent the files to Will's screen, "look at these records. The wounds don't fully coincide with his power. The date of this lease was edited after we brought him in. Every tenant works for the same shell corporation, and there are no utility bills in his name or change of address at the post office. He was either set up to take the fall for this murder, in relation to tampering with the communications hub, maybe to get him out of the way, or someone inside Cerberus needed a plausible excuse to put a bullet in his brain." Lee stopped ranting long enough to look Will in the eye. "Which is it?"

Will's brow furrowed slightly. "I don't know. But I can promise I'll find out."

Anna spoke through the room's speakers. "Will, the corporation. It's one of Axial's."

Lee didn't know the name but by her tone took it to be a criminal organization they'd dealt with in the past.

"This could've been a blackmail attempt," Will said, "to leverage Stillman into service. Or they could've simply wanted him out of the way, to gain access to his team. Either way, we'll get to the bottom of it."

Sorry wasn't good enough, wouldn't bring Discord back,

and Will knew it. The call ended with Lee feeling worse than he had when he'd used his power against Jeremy. Discord wasn't dead, but he was gone all the same.

"So he's one of them now," Lee said, his stomach in a twisted knot of guilt, "like Jim Tompkins and Samantha Richmond. That's so wrong."

*Are we the bad guys?* he wondered. *Am I on the wrong side?*

"Tell me about it," Anna said. "Breaker creeps me out. He's been rebooted three times since you shot him but keeps remembering."

"Breaker?" Lee asked. He wasn't familiar with the call sign but supposed it made sense. "You mean Jim, from the station. They shot him again?"

"You have clearance now, look."

A video came up on the wall monitor. It was Jim, dressed in the white shirt and pants, in a training room with his tutor. He had a gun in his hand.

There was a knock on Lee's door. He went over and undid the privacy setting, opened the glass with a palm against the wall. The others were leaving. Allison had stopped to look in, seemed to be waiting for him, but it was Kevin who spoke first.

"You coming? We just got a call."

"Yeah," Lee replied. "Just give me a minute."

"Why? I don't want to," Jim was saying, as Lee went back to watch the recording. "She's a good person. What did she do wrong?"

"It's not about right or wrong," an older woman's voice replied from off screen. It was Alice, one of the three agents who'd been behind the mirror at the police station. She went on, "It's about following orders without question."

Jim shook his head, while the young woman who was his tutor stood before him without fear. She was in her early twenties, probably a grad student. Not everyone at Cerberus was an agent. It was all just a test, Lee knew immediately, but Jim was still learning.

"We can reboot you again," Alice threatened gently, "keep trying until we get the program right."

"I understand," his tutor said, almost pleading with him. Was she there against her will? She seemed too young to already have ties with the agency. Then again, Lee was only fifteen. "I know too much. But I'll live on through you, through your memories and all I've taught you. Remember, nothing is above the agency. Not you. Not me."

"Lee!" Ember shouted from down the hall. "Let's go!"

"In a minute!" he yelled back, annoyed.

Jim had hugged his tutor. "You won't feel a thing," he said. "I promise."

In one quick movement, he snapped her neck. There was immediate panic, voices gasping and barking orders to subdue him. Some shouted it was just a test, that he was supposed to have used the gun. It was painful to see the look of realization cross his face, the moment he understood a woman he loved had needlessly died for the sake of an evaluation. Stun guns went off from the left at the same time foam struck him from the right and began to harden.

"Get Lee down here!" a man's voice snapped. It was Jim Armand, the lead agent from the police station.

"It's too late for that," Alice said, and her casual tone sickened Lee.

"I'll kill you," Jim said, as his face reddened and tears welled. "I'll remember," he promised, "and I'm going to kill every last one of you."

Alice moved into the frame, where Jim was on his knees, trapped up to his neck in foam as hard as steel. Anna ended the clip just as Alice leveled a gun at his eye and fired.

"Jesus," Lee said, visibly shaken. "How many bullets does that guy have rattling around in his head?"

"None by now," Anna replied. "Like the others, his body eventually absorbs what it can and passes what it can't."

Lee suited up without another word. He'd considered making a change for some time, even before learning the truth about Discord, but his mind was now firmly set. He put his plan into motion, began internal preparations as he finished getting dressed. He headed out to meet the team in the hangar.

When he boarded the helijet, Ember and Allison were on the left, Brody, Alexandra and Kevin on the right. He had the chance to sit next to Alex, but Allison patted the empty seat beside her. As much as he wanted to put a wedge between Brody and Alex, he wasn't about to ignore his sister's friend when she so clearly wanted to talk.

"Can you take a look at this?" she asked, after he'd buckled himself in. She held out her left arm to him. The opening at the wrist was undone, and beneath a bandage she had a small gash with burned edges. She said, "It won't seem to heal."

"How long have you had this?" Lee asked and held her arm gently for a closer look. He sent in cells from both hands. "Why didn't you go to medical?"

Ember said, "That's where the bandage is from."

"I think I just have the flu," Allison said. "It's only been a day."

It was more than the flu or any other sickness he'd come across, but Lee didn't want to say anything until he knew more. Her immune system had been compromised, was even less effective than a normal person's.

"Where's the cut from?" Brody asked, as the helijet lifted off.

"It's my power," Allison explained. "I guess. I've got one on my thigh and lower back, too. It's like I'm burning myself up when I use it."

"You shouldn't be here," Brody said, concerned for more than just her wellbeing, like he was flat out stating without her power, she was a detriment to the team.

"She'll be fine," Lee shot back.

He had to completely rebuild her immune system from a blueprint of his own, force out whatever toxin had damaged both her livers and three of her four kidneys. Whatever she'd been exposed to would have killed her if he hadn't.

"There," Lee said. "It's taken care of."

"See?" Kevin grinned. "You're not totally useless. Every group needs a cleric."

Ember rolled her eyes. "Again, with that game. Good luck role-playing yourself a girlfriend."

Allison's skin flared bright for a moment then faded. She smiled wide, took in a deep breath and let it out in a large whoosh, as if the sickness had left her in a single gasp. Of course, she'd burned away every cell Lee had in her in the process. He'd managed to recall most of them in time, though.

"Thank you," she said, squeezed his hand and let go.

While the whole exchange reminded him of Jen, made him wonder what she was up to, he couldn't shake the feeling something was wrong on a large scale. No one else on the team was sick, not even in the slightest. What if what had caused it was intentional? He didn't doubt for a second that Cerberus had or was at least working on an alternative to the Bullet Squad.

They touched down in the courtyard of an apartment complex on the east side of town, two miles south of the mall and just a few blocks from Overwood High. The treetops of a forest preserve in the distance could be seen over buildings and storefronts to the east, giant sequoias well over three hundred feet tall.

Lee was first to unbuckle but last to head down the ramp. He was focused on duplicating cells, forcing his sensory bubble to expand. It helped take his mind off the foreboding, that nagging thought that someone inside Cerberus was working against them, bolstering the Bullet Squad and experimenting on Supers to find any weakness.

A crash drew their attention west, as the helijet lifted

off. There was a small park between the offices across from Hellebore and the farmer's market that followed a square of ornately done brick walkways. Two guys were faced off, one larger than average and a small teen. The second wore a bulbous weapon over his right forearm and was firing heavy energy blasts at the other.

Though most people had already evacuated, and the area was blocked off three streets out, the sound of screams could still be heard from all around. A teenage girl ran toward the two Supers, throwing spheres of translucent blue light at the large one as she went.

"He's an unknown," Anna said in his ear, and Lee knew she was talking about the bigger guy. He could see the others on his team getting their brief at the same time. Anna continued, "The girl is Tammy Sherwood. She's already gone through quarantine." Lee knew what that meant. She was censored, on permanent probation for choosing not to join. She was breaking the law by using her powers. "The smaller one with the blaster is her brother, Daniel. He hasn't gone through yet. You need to take them all in."

"All right," Aegis said. "Game faces on. We don't know who the big one is, but best guess is he's energy. And really strong. Like, a six strong. Satellite caught him throw a bus before they ended up here."

"Don't split us up," Lee warned. Everyone turned to look, but his eyes were on the big guy. "You're going to say it, I know, but it's the wrong call. We split up, we get hurt. There's no way around it."

Aegis said, "Good thing we brought you, then." There were frowns and crossed arms, but he held up a hand. "You know the drill. These aren't my orders. We either do what we they tell us, or we spend the next month in intensive training."

"Pairs?" Flux asked. His sister, Lee knew, would end up with Flare. The two had developed a symbiotic tactic over the past few weeks and worked well together. "Circle around and close him in?"

"Uhh." Keys pointed at the fight. "Don't forget the other two. I don't want to get hit by whatever they've got going on there."

"The plan," Aegis said, "is to surround all three and contain them however we can. XTU is still three minutes out."

Which meant Aegis would choose Keys, no matter what he said about orders. Lee had turned down the opportunity to act as team lead. He didn't want anyone getting hurt because of a split second call of his. He was more of a planner and worked best when he had time to think. It was only before the mission, at times like this, that he felt anything close to regret over his decision.

Tinker smirked. "Glorified cops with borrowed tech. We don't need them."

Lee sighed inwardly. Being paired with Tinker would be his second regret.

The blasts had changed in color to thicker beams of bright purple. They landed, caused severe damage, but nothing seemed to stop the larger guy from advancing. He'd only pause, regenerate and keep going after Daniel. Tammy was there as well, but her spheres did little more than bounce off him like beach balls that scorched the grass and nearby trees.

"Usual pairs," Aegis said and eyed the fight. "Flux and Flare go wide around the right, Rem and Tink take left. Me and Keys will head straight up the middle. Don't let any of them get away."

A dozen circles of outer light and swirling inner dark appeared on the grass, before two foot high ovals sprang up from their center. Each portal closed as a demon ran through, grotesque imps like monster babies, with tails and pointed ears. They snarled and slavered and fell in line as Keys and Aegis started to run.

Tinker was readying parts as he broke into a jog as

well. "Remind me," he said, "never to piss her off."

"Dude, please." Lee laughed. "You piss everyone off."

"We've got a name," Anna said. "Frank Culvers. Until last week, he was a nurse at St. Johns. He stopped showing up when his wife and son were killed by falling debris. They got caught in a fight between the Furies and Triple Twos."

Lee hated to run, mostly because it was a part of their daily training. One thing about being Affected, though, he was much faster than he ever was before the Rumbling, at least four times faster than the average person. He and Tinker were in place in less than half a minute, started closing on the fight as Aegis and the demons engaged.

"The shit is he doing?" Lee asked, angry that he'd put Keys in harm like that. "They're supposed to wait!"

Tinker put away the gadget he'd been working on and pulled two disc-shaped ones from chest pockets.

"What's the big deal?" he asked. "The Culvers guy hasn't attacked once. He just keeps taking hits."

"You don't see it," Lee accused. "He's not just taking hits. He's *adapting.* That's why the tech keeps changing beams, and he's ignoring the sister."

They were hundreds of yards out, but Lee could see Frank break through Aegis's shields like they were nothing. Demons swarmed him, biting and clawing large gouges in his flesh. One by one, he grabbed and crushed them, and once the wounds had closed, demon claws and teeth no longer hurt him.

"So," Tinker said and winced at the fight in progress, "take him down in one hit, or we're screwed?"

Aegis got too close and took a punch across the jaw. He literally flew a hundred feet backward with the blow and dug a trench in the grass with his body when he landed. Lee sensed the broken jaw, neck and spine and sent cells over to start working inside him.

A hundred yards out, Frank backhanded the sister. Tammy spun twice in air and landed hard on her front.

Daniel screamed, made an adjustment to his blaster and fired a yellow-white beam that burned a massive hole in Frank's right shoulder. A pause to look at the wound, to watch bone and muscle reform and heal over, then Frank closed the distance between them in a single step.

He tore the tech off Daniel, with the forearm still attached, and tossed it aside. Daniel's next scream was one of horrible pain, as blood sprouted from his mangled limb. His eyes rolled back in his head, and he passed out.

Lee stopped two dozen paces away, and Tinker reined in beside him. Flux and Flare had arrived at the same time on the other side. Fire rose up from Flare's hands and engulfed Frank's upper body. Flux had both palms out toward Flare, and from what Lee could see and sense, she seemed to be amplifying the fire.

Tinker threw both discs at Frank, as Lee set to healing the injured siblings. Electricity sparked between the two pieces of tech, thick bolts that forked and crackled. Frank dropped to his knees, every muscle tensed, as his flesh blackened and curled beneath the flames. Flux moved in close, a bare hand extended. She planned to interrupt Frank's power, but Lee knew it was too soon.

"Ember, no!" he shouted.

Shirt and hair gone, burned to ash, Frank's skin began to heal. In the span of a single breath, the flames no longer hurt him. He crushed the gadgets on either thigh, got up and grabbed Flux by the throat at the same moment her hand touched his arm. Face reddened, gasping for air, she struggled to break free but didn't loosen her own grip.

Lee focused on keeping Daniel alive, had finished healing Tammy and Aegis. He began gathering all the cells he could spare to shock Frank. More demons rushed in, as Tinker tossed another gadget. It stuck to Frank's waist, beeped twice and exploded. Frank roared and wheeled around, his right side a gory mess. He threw Flux at Tinker, and the two went tumbling past to the crunch of broken bones.

Frank was already healing, when he bent down to take hold of Daniel. A portal appeared beneath him, as his hand closed over an ankle. Frank fell into the swirling darkness, taking Daniel with him, and appeared three stories in the air between two buildings outside the park.

"Daniel!" Tammy yelled and ran after, as her brother plummeted to the ground alongside Frank.

XTU had arrived in four large black armored vehicles and were moving in on their position from behind. Lee made sure his sister and Tinker were healing before running off to intercept Frank.

"Rem, don't!" Keys called after. "Wait for Aegis!"

It only made Lee run faster. He had one chance at stopping Frank. A shock to the spine would work once, and paralysis wouldn't last. If he wanted to overcome Frank's power, he'd have to alter it—preferably, without getting killed.

Lee ran as hard as he could and caught up to Tammy, as they both found Frank getting to his feet in an alley. Daniel was limp and broken on the street beside him.

Tammy was crying, and emotions poured off her in waves. She drew on her power so strongly it warped the buildings to either side. Cracks went up the stonework, and the alley buckled from the force. With a grunt of angry grief, she loosed a sphere twice her size. She ran forward, screaming in pain and fear, both hands in front and conjuring more spheres. The first struck Frank and sent him sliding back on both feet, shredding the skin of his chest and shoulders.

Lee needed time to gather more cells. If he sent them in too few or too soon, Frank's body would adapt, and Lee's chance would be lost.

More spheres struck and jerked Frank backward with the force. He only growled at the pain, as they tore away gory bits of tendon and muscle, exposing the bone beneath.

Through it all, he pressed forward, reaching out to grab her.

There still wasn't enough time. Lee tried to warn her, yelled for her to stay back. It was too late. Aegis, Keys and Flare were running toward them. There was nothing they could do. Against his better judgment, Lee sent every cell he could into Frank's spine and shocked him. Frank screamed, shook and foamed at the mouth for a brief moment then took another step. His body fought against Lee, eradicating cells as fast as Lee could make them.

Frank shot forward without warning, caught Tammy by the neck and threw her against a building. Her body cracked in a dozen places. He walked over to a dumpster, picked it up with one hand and threw it at her like it was a toy. She was utterly crushed, killed in a grisly instant. The flood of her emotions ended and left behind an empty chasm.

The others had arrived to help, but it was more than Lee could take, seeing her die in such a horrible way. He sent everything he had into her, his body shaking with the effort. He could heal her, he was certain, if he just wanted it badly enough.

Aegis ran past, barreled straight into Frank. The world became a blur, as Lee forced his will upon her body. He made her organs mend, rebuilt bone and sinew, repaired every muscle, but the spark just wasn't there.

So he gave her his own.

"God damn it," he cried and dropped to his knees. He sent shocks through her spine, into her brain. "Get up!"

Aegis was thrown through a wall. Frank crushed demons underfoot, as he came down the alley toward them. Flare grabbed Lee by the collar, tried to pull him away, while Keys stood her ground. She tried to conjure another portal, but Frank dug his fingers into the wall and pulled away a brick. He threw it at her so fast she had no chance to react. It struck Keys in the head, crumbled to dust with the impact. She went down on her back beside Lee, blood running down her face.

Lee's entire body shook with the effort. He refused to give up, to give in. He had no offense of his own, no way to stop Frank, to save his team, his friends. No one had to die. He knew in his very core he could still save her.

Once again, he screamed at the corpse that was Tammy, a raw and guttural roar that brought to bear all his power.

"*Get up!*"

Frank was nearly upon them, each step he took a bloody promise.

"You should've left," he said, his voice as gravelly as the debris underfoot, "when you had the chance."

Tammy's eyes opened, both irises a brilliant blue.

Flare hauled Lee back and dragged him away. His sister was there, too, with Tinker and XTU. The officers fanned out, stun and foam guns in hand, in full body armor and helmets. They formed a protective line in front of Lee's team.

Tammy stood, her eyes glowing the same ghostly shade of Lee's swarm when he was stressed. She let loose a series of energy waves that struck Frank from behind and sent him sprawling through the police. Again and again, the waves struck without relent, killing XTU officers, shattering the ground, snapping Frank's bones as fast as they could heal.

Everyone scrambled to get away. Lee was in shock, both at what he'd done and from sheer exhaustion. He heard a roar and Ember's voice, saw Frank get up and force his way past them. Lee's vision started to blur.

"He's running!" a man yelled.

"Don't let him get away!"

Lee tried to focus, on the people and voices, the turmoil all around him, but the world stuttered and grew fuzzy at the edges.

Then everything went black.

# - Ember -

"Does it hurt?" Ember toyed with the container of tongue depressors while they waited for the doc to return and give Allison her release form.

"Not as much as you'd think." Allison finished dressing and tugged the hem of her white shirt down. She wadded up the used paper jacket and tossed it into the recycling chute. "Thanks for staying with me."

"I only offered because I figured they'd kick me out." Ember made a face at her friend.

Allison laughed. Her face was pinched and more pale than usual, and her dark curls were coming loose from her braid.

"Liar. It does hurt." Ember opened a cabinet to peer inside.

Allison glanced around the room and shook her head. *Shut up!* she signed, closing her fingers and thumb over her lips. "Honestly, it just kind of burns. From the inside out." She pulled her sleeve down over her freshly bandaged wrist.

*Sorry.* Ember signed back, attempting to ignore the crowd of ghosts that had gathered to hover nearby. They seemed to be attracted to Allison, yet unable—or unwilling—to get close to her. Only, Ember couldn't figure out why that would be. In her experience, ghosts rarely hung around the living, unless they had some previous attachment to the person. That is, with the exception of mediums. And some witches. Ember thought about her Great Aunt Callia and the way she'd been able to readily commune with the spirits, especially toward the end of her life. She flicked that thought aside and moved her hands rapidly. *You sure you're okay?*

*Yes.* Allison's signing was emphatic. "I think you better toss those," she said, pointing to the wad of cotton balls Ember had dumped on the counter. "It's not like they can use them now."

"Is cotton recyclable?"

Allison shrugged.

Ember swept the pile of cotton balls into the refuse chute and let the lid snick shut.

"Level One Alert." Ember jumped at Zeta's sudden interruption. "Flux, suit up and report to the helijet pad on the double."

Allison reached the door ahead of her and swung it wide just as Doctor Sellings, the team's physician, came down the hallway.

"Sorry, Doc, gotta go." Allison brushed past and was already jogging toward the exit.

"I haven't completed your release." The silver-haired man waved a paper at her. "And you need to fill this out."

Ember grabbed the paper from him as she passed. "Got it doc. She'll interoffice it back to you after the mission." She lengthened her stride to catch up with Allie.

They were suited up and ready to go in under five minutes. "I think that's a record," Ember said, as they headed out.

"Hang on," Allison called. "Where's Lee?" She stopped outside his door, still opaque for privacy, and knocked. The glass cleared and Lee became visible on the other side. He was still wearing his whites.

"We got the call," Kevin yelled when he saw Lee.

"Gimme a minute," Lee said, his attention on his laptop.

"Suit up! You're gonna make us late," Brody growled. "Again."

"Come on." Ember grabbed Allison by the arm. "Lee! Let's move!" she called over her shoulder, as she and Allie left the pod.

He shouted something back, but she couldn't make out his words.

Brody passed them on the way to the elevator. "He better get there before liftoff." He shoved his thumb onto the print scanner and the doors opened. "I'm not taking the ding for him."

They'd just settled into their seats when Lee came crashing up the ramp.

Allison looked up and patted the seat beside her. "Can you look at this?" She held out her bandaged arm.

He lifted the cotton wrap and eyed the angry sore. "You should have gone to medical about this."

"Jeez, Lee. That's where the bandage is from." Ember shook her head at him.

"How'd you even get cut?" Brody asked, surprise showing in his brown eyes.

Allison shrugged. "My power. It's like I'm burning myself when I use it."

Ember slumped in her seat, worry eating at her. What if Lee couldn't heal her? And would all of them have symptoms like Allison's as their powers grew and changed? She stared down at her hands, barely hearing the conversation going on around her.

Allison's skin flashed and Ember blinked against the brightness, fear gripping her. Allison just smiled and breathed in deep. Flare was a good handle for her. Her skin seemed to glow against the frame of dark curls that always seemed to spill out from whatever clip or tie she tried to put it in.

"Thank you." Allison gave Lee's hand a squeeze and Ember saw the tips of his ears redden. She'd have razzed him about it, but she didn't want Allie to think she had a problem with her liking her brother. Ember glanced at the pair, and a twinge of jealousy caused her to look away. The craft set down and the door opened, the ramp extending before she could decide which of them she might be more envious of.

"Boots on the ground." Aegis led the way.

Ember followed him out into the parking lot of what had once been a well-maintained apartment complex. Now, what remained of the landscaping was either overgrown with weeds or had gone brown from lack of water.

"Hey." Flare nudged her with an elbow. "Isn't the mall nearby?"

"I think you're right." Ember grinned.

"Shoppers beware!" The two said in unison, then high-fived.

Tinker rolled his eyes, but Ember saw Keys' mouth quirk up in an almost smile.

"Let's focus, girls," Aegis said, earning him a dirty look from all three of them.

"Women," Keys corrected him.

Looking distracted, Lee came down the ramp, unaware of Aegis' frown. He opened his mouth to say something but was cut off by the resounding crash, followed by the screams of people who hadn't been able evacuate the area before the fighting started.

In the park past the square, two figures stood opposite one another. One, a skinny teenager by the looks of him, was firing on the other, a much larger man, who seemed to be taking the blasts in stride. Another Super, a girl, ran toward them, lobbing balls of energy at the bigger guy.

Ember watched the fight, calculating the Supers' potential weaknesses. "Tammy and Daniel Sherwood," Zeta informed her, then launched into their bios. "The other is an unknown."

Great, Ember thought, recalling their recent encounters with unknowns. Several close calls had left their team wounded and exhausted. Without Lee...She pulled her thoughts back from the idea.

Flare bit her lower lip and rubbed at her recently healed wrist, probably thinking the same thing, as Aegis started giving orders and Lee began arguing with him. They'd disagreed before, but this time Lee was adamant.

"Not my call. We follow orders," Aegis said.

"Let me guess." Ember tried not to look bored. "Pairs?

Circle around and close in?"

"We have to surround all three," Tinker said.

"Exactly," Aegis agreed. "Soften them up and keep them contained until XTU arrives, which should be in about three minutes."

Lee looked worried, but Tinker snorted. "We don't need them."

"Usual pairs," Aegis told them. "Flux and Flare go wide and head in from the right. Rem and Tink take left. Me and Keys will head straight up the middle. Don't let any of them get away this time."

Lee frowned, his jaw clamped tight, as they headed out.

"So, why don't they just drop a truckload of foam on these jerks?" Flare asked as she and Ember moved into position, "save us some trouble."

"Maybe because they'd suffocate before the docs could get them back to base and un-encased from that nastiness?" Ember said. "I mean, we may all be super-powered, but we still have to breathe."

"Flux for the win." Zeta validated Ember's theory.

Over the past few weeks, they'd developed an easy rapport, and Ember was glad to have the AI as her guide, though she wasn't about to let on to Zeta she felt that way. "Points for me, then," she responded to her handler.

"I didn't realize we were keeping score," Zeta responded, then rattled off everything they knew about the Supers the team was closing in on.

"Shall we?" Ember asked as they reached their position.

Flare nodded her agreement and they headed for the fight.

"That unknown Super looks dangerous," Ember said to Flare as they neared their position. "There's something—I don't know—too confident about him."

"Name, Culvers, Jim," Zeta broke in. "Previous occupation, nurse. Wife and child recently killed by Xeno gang activity. No STAMS data available."

Meanwhile, Keys was already tossing portals across the way, her slobbering little monsters popping out and howling as they followed her into the fray.

They'd hardly gotten close when Aegis was flung backward, his head lolling on his shoulders and blood flying from his mouth and ears.

One by one, Culvers picked the demons up and destroyed them, leaving a ring of small bodies around him on the grass.

Tammy and Daniel kept at him, but his weapon and her powers seemed to be having no effect. Tammy dodged in too close, trying to get a better angle on him, and Culvers landed a solid hit. She went down with a thud and the resounding cracking of bones.

Her brother roared out his anger and his weapon belched out a powerful energy burst that cut right through the bigger man's shoulder.

Culvers glanced down at the hole and Ember gasped as it repaired and reformed, faster than any healing she'd ever seen her brother manage.

"Crap!" Flare shouted.

"Think you can distract him long enough to get me in there?" Ember asked.

Flare shuddered at the ear-piercing scream Daniel let out as Culvers ripped the kid's arm from his body and threw it over his shoulder, but she stood her ground and held out her hands. "Just like we practiced it?"

"Exactly," Ember gritted her teeth and turned her hands toward Flare, shunting her energy in reverse and using it to channel more power into Flare's fire as it lashed into the Super.

Culvers bowed beneath the roaring blast, his skin crackling and peeling away as he fell forward, knees buckling.

At the same time, Tinker hit him in the legs with some of his gadgets. They arced as they struck.

Ember gritted her teeth against the smell of burnt flesh and closed in, reaching for what remained of the scorched Super's bare flesh.

"No!" Lee screamed.

Ember didn't even have time to blink. He was already healing. Just as she managed to make contact, wrapping her fingers around his wrist, his other arm shot out and gripped her by the throat.

She gagged as his hand tightened on her neck, crushing her windpipe, choking off her air. She clawed at his fingers with one hand, trying to keep hold of him with the other, but he was too strong.

She felt herself losing strength, the light greying, her vision narrowing to pinpricks. Then there was an explosion close by and she was flying through the air. By the time she thudded to the ground, her throat had opened enough for her to pull in a shuddery breath, one that was knocked right back out of her as she landed. *Son of a—*

"Flux!" Flare was beside her, but Ember couldn't raise her head to look at her. Go, she managed to sign. Help them. Help Lee.

Flare nodded and stormed back toward the fight.

The shouting and screaming continued, interspersed with explosions and energy blasts.

Keys yelled something, but Ember's ears were still ringing as blood found its way back through her veins. Her body recovered quickly. Either her regenerative powers had ramped up, or Lee had hit her with some of his healing cells.

As her head cleared, a muffled shout overrode the rest of the yelling and screaming. "Goddamit! Get up!" Lee. His voice filled with anger and desperation.

Something crashed nearby and demons squealed out in pain.

"Get up!" her brother screamed again. Was he yelling at her?

Ember pushed herself into a sitting position.

Culvers was heading toward Lee, his gait filled with slow confidence. "You should've run," he growled.

Lee. Ember had to get to Lee. She stood, shaking off the dizziness that hit her. Her palms heating up as she crossed the square, picking up speed as she went.

By the time she reached him, Tinker and Flare were yanking Lee back, dragging him away from Culvers.

XTU had arrived. Officers in full gear formed a barrier between Culvers and the team.

Across from them, Tammy stood, looking dazed, yet intense. Her eyes a dazzling blue. Suddenly, she let loose with burst after burst of searing energy, indiscriminate and deadly.

The sound of Culvers' bones snapping beneath the painful barrage could be heard between the chaos of explosions and the shouts of dying XTU officers.

"Lee!" Ember screamed. "Get back!"

Culvers was running, his bones healing as fast as Tammy shattered them.

Shouts and curses rang out.

Lee wobbled and collapsed in a heap.

Ember dropped to his side, calling his name. "Lee! Oh, god, Lee!"

"We don't have time for this!" Aegis gripped her by the shoulders, careful not to make contact with her skin. "He's getting away."

Ember dropped to her knees, shielding Lee as a blast of energy slammed into the ground beside them, shattering concrete and sending debris in all directions. The smell of ozone filled the air.

"Dammit!" Ember leaped to her feet. "Stop! You're attacking the wrong people."

But Tammy continued to blast at anything that moved.

"What the hell is wrong with you?" Ember ran across the square, dodging Tammy's blasts and leaping the trenches the fighting had gouged into the concrete.

She reached out and grabbed the girl by the wrist and watched in horror as Tammy fell to the ground, dead.

"What the hell?" Ember backed away, staring at her hand.

"Not you," Zeta said. "It was Lee."

"Lee?" Ember glanced back at her unconscious brother. EMTs hovering around him.

"Saddle up!" Aegis shouted. "We've got a rogue Super on the loose."

"Flux," Flare said, tapping Ember on the arm. "We gotta go."

"Lee is being tended to." Zeta's voice was firm. "You still have a mission to complete. Lives to save."

Ember wavered for a brief moment, then stormed after the rest of the team. "Yeah," she muttered under her breath. "Lives to save. And assholes to make pay."

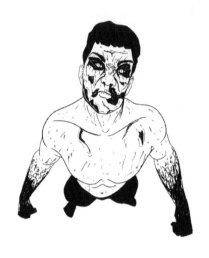

# Thirteen
Mon, Oct 3, 12:16pm

## - Lee -

Lee woke on a stretcher, still at the scene and being tended by paramedics. His team was nowhere in sight. There were bodies sprawled outside the alley, and one of them was Tammy.

"Oh, good," Anna said, relieved, "you're awake. Your vitals have been steady for two and a half minutes, but I was starting to get worried."

"What happened?" he asked and sat up. A paramedic tried to hold him back, but Lee waved him off, said he was all right.

"Culvers ran," Anna explained. "We're tracking him best we can, with satellite and traffic cameras. The rest of the team is in pursuit. You can still catch them if you hurry."

Lee pulled free of the IV and blankets, stared down at

Tammy's corpse. He didn't save her after all. He'd given everything he had, pushed his power as far as he thought it could go, and still it wasn't enough.

He wasn't enough.

"It was Ember," Anna said. It didn't surprise him she could see the scene, probably from one of the XTU body cameras or even satellite. "Tammy was already dead. Whatever you did to the body, it fell apart when your sister touched it. Will made it clear to me you're never to do that again."

Lee let out a snort. He'd almost brought someone back to life and was being chastised for it.

"Do you know where Frank is now?"

Ideas flooded his mind, from what little he knew and had observed. He was narrowing them down, the more he thought each one through.

"He's headed south on foot," Anna replied. "We have agents at his home, the hospital and the cemetery where his family is buried."

"No. He's not headed there yet," Lee said. "He'll try to lose the team first. And where's the one place we won't go?"

Spider territory.

He didn't have to say it out loud. Ten square blocks of abandoned buildings and apartments, the entire neighborhood was now home to a gang of Supers and Affected. It was also a haven for those who refused to work for Cerberus but wouldn't give up their powers. Every attempt to bring them in had ended in disaster.

"Shit." He'd never heard Anna curse before. "I'm sending agents to the other side. Unless he plans to hole up there, we'll catch him when he comes out."

"Want a lift?" an XTU officer offered.

Lee eyed the armored vehicle in the distance. It would only slow him down, but he didn't want to tell the officer that.

"I think I can get there faster on foot," he said, "stay out of traffic. Thanks for the offer, though."

He got up and began to run south, picking up speed as he went. Even the slowest Affected could hit twenty-five miles per hour. With all the training and pushing himself, it felt like he was over thirty. He wasn't sure how long he could keep it up, but as long as his team was in trouble, he'd give it everything he had.

Lee cut between buildings to avoid people and cars. Not every alley was open ended. Some were blocked by ten foot walls. He jumped them like he'd been taught, with a leap at the building on one side and a foot pushing him out and over.

"Tinker is just ahead," Anna said.

There was an overturned car in the street, no doubt left by Frank to slow the team. Tinker was there, pulling a family from the vehicle. Lee arrived just as Tinker cut free a little girl from her seatbelt with one of the tools he'd made and kept in his belt. He helped her climb out the back window.

When he looked up, he seemed relieved.

"Never thought I'd be glad to see that haircut," he said. There was blood on his uniform, but it wasn't his. Lee offered him a hand and brought him to his feet. "You okay?"

"Never better," Lee said and started to leave. "Come on, let's go."

"Hey, wait! The girl and her mother here are hurt."

Lee hadn't even noticed. Well, he noticed but didn't think it was worth tending. He was too focused on the threat getting further away. There was a middle-aged mother and three kids, a girl and two boys. None of them were seriously injured, just minor scrapes and bruises. He set cells to work in them but didn't think they'd fully heal by the time he was out of range. Still, it would be enough until they could get to a doctor.

"They'll be fine," he called back as he ran, headed down an alley between a mini-mart and dry cleaners.

"Go left up ahead," Anna said. "Follow Laurel six blocks."

Tinker caught up and glared.

"You could've waited for them to heal. We're not even going the right way. The team's that way," he said and pointed west.

"We're heading him off," Lee said and turned east. "They won't follow him into Briarwood. It's suicide." Lee leapt over a car going by as they crossed the street and into another alley. "We'll catch him as he comes out."

"Why bother?" Tinker asked and slapped the lid down on a dumpster as he ran past. It made a huge crash that sent echoes following after. "Let the Spiders deal with him."

Anna said, "Next right, up three blocks."

"Because he killed people," Lee replied angrily. "We don't let that slide." They headed south through the playground of Timber Hills elementary, hopping chain link fences and ignoring the cries of an angry teacher. "He's hunting us, you know. Supers."

"Who, Culvers?" Tinker shrugged. "I don't really care."

"Left," Anna said. They'd entered a residential area, rows of middle-class homes and apartments off in the distance. "Then south again at the next street."

"How can you not care?" Lee asked. Sometimes he felt like he was the only one who understood the choices they were making.

"I mean," Tinker said, starting to pant with the exertion, "I don't care what his motives are. He's a bad guy, I get it. I just don't give a crap why."

"There," Anna said, "the parking structure. He's headed that way."

"That's shortsighted," Lee said and shook his head. To Anna, he asked, "What about the team?"

She hesitated. "They ran into a problem. Help is on the way."

There was a gas station across the street with a sizeable

convenience store attached. With houses nearby, fast food on both sides of the street, there were lots of people who hadn't been evacuated and were in danger if a fight between Supers broke out.

"Wait," Lee said, "to us or the team? What kind of trouble?"

Screams rang out as Culvers appeared running down the sidewalk of Juniper. Shirtless and bloodied, he tossed people and cars aside as he went.

"Briarwood," Tinker guessed. "They must've gone in. Don't worry. I'm sure your girlfriend's fine."

Lee glared down the street, gathering his power. His swarm flared blue all around him.

"Alex isn't my girlfriend."

"No kidding, dumbass." Tinker activated a thick metal bracer on his left arm and pulled some kind of homemade handgun from his belt. "I was talking about Allison. You may test smart," he said and pulled back on the top of the gun, loading it, "but you're kind of stupid."

Frank stopped across the street, had recognized them and grinned.

"You don't learn," he shouted at them. He grabbed a car with both hands and threw it at the gas station. It crashed into and past the pumps, and the whole place burst into flames. Over the screaming, he happily called out, "Have fun with that!"

He took off running west down the street as a helijet arrived. The back ramp opened while it hovered twenty feet above the asphalt. One by one, eight people jumped out, landed hard and walked toward them.

"Who the shit are these guys?" Tinker asked, already moving for the gas station. He looked back, surprised, when Lee didn't follow. "Hey! Snap out of it! I know you don't give a shit about the little people, but we have to put that fire out, before it burns down the entire block. Let these guys take care of Culvers."

"Remedy!" the lead Super called, as all eight drew in close. Lee knew who it was the moment they'd landed. "You're with us," Breaker said.

"Screw that!" Tinker said. To Lee, he added, "Forget them and Culvers. People need us right here."

Lee said, "They're not the mission." He pointed east, where Frank was getting away. "He is. We don't have time to put out fires, while the guy making them gets away." He refused to argue about it and broke into a run. "Let emergency services handle it!"

The Bullet Squad followed after. Tinker cursed and ran for the gas station.

Lee couldn't even look at them, the group of killers and victims who'd had their lives stolen. At least three of them were there as a direct result of his actions.

"Get him," Breaker told one. Barely into his twenties, in the Cerberus black edged with green, the guy leapt into the air with enough force that Lee more felt than saw him leave. "Bruiser will slow him down. Everyone else? Do your thing."

Bruiser was on Frank in a single jump, landed right on top of him. The two went down into a tumble. Lee and the others were nearly there, when the two began to fight. Frank threw punches like a brawler, while his opponent was clearly trained. Frank probably hit like a freight train but didn't have the skill or speed to land one. Bruiser used Frank's own momentum against him, turned missed swings into opportunities to punch at ribs and exposed soft spots.

Lumen was first to join in, firing beams of hard light from her palms. They struck between punches with a precision born of practice and hours spent in training as a team. The moment Bruiser was turned away, light flared from her right hand with the brightness of a dozen suns. Frank cried out, his face blackened and both eyes burned away.

Lee hadn't seen Samantha since he'd undone her

paralysis. Despite the circumstances between them, he was glad she was there fighting on his side.

Frank's cry echoed in quick succession, hit a high note and exploded. Discord, Lee thought and winced at the memory of being on the receiving end of that attack. Frank's chest had been ripped open by the blast.

Breaker moved in, both hands together and pushed out. Visible vibrations filled the air between him and Frank. Bruiser quickly tumbled away. Rings rolled one into another and shook Frank violently in place. Blood quavered loose from the gaping wound, but Frank's chest began to heal regardless.

"Can you paralyze him?" Anna asked. "We need to take him alive."

Lee was fighting for control, had invaded Frank's body, but the cells were dying off. Frank's immune system had already adapted back at the alley, refused to let Lee in. It was now more a battle of wills.

A girl who looked no more than twelve flicked her wrists and moved in. Swords had appeared in her hands, as if snatched from thin air. Short and silvery, with wisps like frost rolling down each blade, they seemed to whistle with every swing. Breaker let fall his attack as she struck Frank across the thigh, middle and neck in rapid swipes.

She spun away, and another took her place. The whole team worked as one, striking in tandem, never getting in each other's way. It was as if they'd trained to take down single targets and quickly move on to the next.

"You got this," Breaker said to Lee.

His concentration lost, Lee let out a breath he'd been holding. With no way to paralyze Frank or brute force a change to his anatomy, Lee wasn't sure what he could do to help stop him.

It was probably for the best. Someone as powerful as Frank couldn't be contained or controlled, shouldn't be. He adapted to every attack, gained a limited immunity to every danger. Coupled with strength more than halfway up the chart, the man was a killing machine in the making. While Cerberus no doubt wanted him, Lee didn't think even a bullet to the brain would keep Frank down for very long.

There was a scream. The one edged in yellow had gotten caught off guard. Frank had managed to catch hold and broke both his arms. Electricity danced up and outward from his hands, up both damaged limbs, as he toppled to the pavement and squirmed in pain.

Without giving it a thought, Lee gathered cells to heal him. They flashed blue overhead, and a small swarm broke free to head his way.

"Not yet," Breaker told Lee. "Save everything for Culvers. It won't matter if we can't take him down. We may have to get creative."

*Was that already his plan?* Lee wondered. *To kill Frank if they couldn't subdue and bring him in? Could he even be killed?*

Shards of ice swept through the air in a swirl around Frank, tore away at his flesh. Blocks of asphalt rose up to throw him off balance then disappeared back into the street. He caught hold of the girl with swords by the hair as he fell. Frank drew her in closer, angling for her neck.

"You're mine!" he growled and pulled.

She reached back with a blade and cut the hair from his grasp, stabbed behind her with the other. The halo burns around his eyes were already gone, all his skin fully regenerated, but her blade pierced through an eye before she rolled away.

Frank clutched at the bloody socket.

"Now!" Breaker shouted, and one by one those who were able were on top of Frank. They took firm hold of each limb, while Bruiser locked legs around his neck. Even the road seemed to help, rose up in tendrils around the ankles and wrists. Using his entire body to hold down an arm, Breaker called out to Lee. "It's now or never, buddy."

*Buddy? Does he remember me?*

"Now, please," Bruiser said, struggling to keep his grip, with Frank writhing beneath them all.

Lee moved in close and knelt, the only idea he had left just rising to the surface.

"Do you have a knife?" he asked the girl.

Her swords were gone, so he assumed she could bring one back to her hand at will. She and the girl with ice powers were fighting to keep a leg down. A single flick of a wrist, and a thick bladed hand knife appeared. Lee took it quickly, so she wouldn't lose her grip on Frank.

As hard as he could, Lee drove the knife down into the center of Frank's stomach. It didn't pierce the skin. With both hands, his entire body, Lee pushed down onto the blade. No matter how hard he tried, he couldn't make an incision.

Frank laughed, a slow rolling of his middle.

"Lee!" Anna shouted in his ear. "You're supposed to take him in alive!"

He focused his power, brought every cell to bear on one spot, to weaken the flesh and muscle just beneath. His swarm flared blue over the skin and entered. He felt Frank's body fighting back. For every ten cells Lee sent against him, only one had any effect. It took billions to break through, all the strength he could gather, to thin and erode an area no bigger than his thumbnail. It was all he really needed.

With a grunt, Lee plunged the knife in.

He looked up at the seven others barely keeping Frank still, at the guy still writhing in pain beside them, at Breaker staring back.

"Do it," Breaker said.

There was recrimination in his voice, as if to say, *You didn't hesitate when you killed me.*

"Don't," Anna pleaded in his ear, "Don't do it."

Lee had already made up his mind, played through all the scenarios and found no other way.

"I have to," he told her.

Lee sawed at the wound to make it bigger, pulled the knife out and forced his hand into the breach. He reached all the way inside up to his elbow and, one by one, pulled free both Frank's hearts. Each still pulsed in his hand, as he tossed the bloody pieces aside.

"Lee, no." Saddened, Anna drew the sound out. They both knew what it meant. "Why?"

"I had no choice."

Frank was finally still. The others relaxed and fell back against the street in exhaustion or climbed up off him to unsteady feet. Pained cries reminded Lee that some were wounded. He sat back on his hands, did what he could to help heal, but his power was spent. It was a struggle just to stay awake.

Two helijets soon arrived, their ramps open and waiting. The Bullet Squad headed to the empty one on the left, while the other held his team. They were waiting for him to enter, some of them hurt.

Lee got to his feet and headed over. When he reached the ramps, he saw the faces of his team, his friends, his sister staring back. They knew what he'd done but didn't know what it truly meant. Not like he did. Breaker stood on the left ramp, his look an open invitation.

"You belong with us," he said.

It struck him more than any condemnation he expected back at base.

Lee snorted.

He probably did belong with them. Probably will. He gave a single nod to Breaker and walked up the ramp to join his team. He took a seat next to Ember and quietly buckled in.

"You okay?" she asked as the helijet lifted off.

She didn't reach over to touch him. He was spattered in Frank's blood, his right arm covered in it up to the elbow.

"Nope." Lee looked to the others seated across the way,

to Ember and Allison on his right. All of them were injured in one way or another, cuts and scratches, burns and bruises. "I'd heal you guys," he said, "but I just don't have it in me right now. What happened to you anyway?"

Alexandra said, "Let's just say I found out being scared out of my mind helps me focus my power." She gave a little laugh, but it came off as nervous with all the tension. "And I was *really* freaking scared."

"Three people died," Kevin said angrily to Lee, "back at that gas station, while you were playing hero. People you could've healed. I looked up their names for you, put them on your desktop. Good luck removing it."

"Back off," Ember warned him.

Allison looked over at Lee, at his arm. "He wouldn't have done it," she said in his defense, "if he didn't have to."

"Really?" Kevin asked. "Is that how it went down, Lee? Did you leave innocent people to die because you had to? Did you kill him in self-defense? Or did eight guys hold him down, while you tore his insides out?"

Allison yelled, "Culvers was a monster! He killed that brother and sister and at least seven more in Briarwood. You weren't there," she said and glared, as if blaming Kevin for what had happened to them.

"Guys," Brody said with forced calm and fatigue in his voice, "this isn't helping anyone."

"It doesn't matter," Lee said. "Once we get back, you won't have to worry about me or my choices."

"What the hell's that supposed to mean?" Ember asked pointedly. Even if she stood by him in front of the others, he could feel her disappointment.

Lee closed his eyes and tried to sleep. He was too tired for what-ifs or explanations.

Allison wouldn't let it go. "Lee?"

"It means," Brody said, "he disobeyed a direct order. And took a life. Don't be surprised if he's off the team."

Lee almost laughed. If only it was that easy.

He didn't know which was worse, feeling Alexandra's opinion of him change or realizing Allison's hadn't.

They landed in the hangar moments later. When the ramp lowered, Lee looked out.

Will was waiting at the bottom.

# - Ember -

Ember's feet barely touched ground as she ran. Her breath seared her throat and her organs were working to extremes. Her mind was filled with Lee's unconscious form, but she pushed herself to focus on catching Culvers.

Behind her, Flare's breath and pounding feet kept up a rhythm with her own. "Where?" she heard Flare ask.

"Spider turf," Ember rasped out. No need to ask Zeta to confirm. She'd been tracking their direction in her head. Though Culvers led them on a twisting maze-like route, she'd known for blocks where he was going. The one place he thought he could lose them.

"If he heads into Spider territory, we'll lose him." Flare's words matched the rhythm of her breathing.

Ember's palms itched. "He's not getting away."

"Copy that." Flare huffed out, her words as certain as Ember's. They were no longer sharing comms. Flare's handler had refused to play along after the first outing. Ember thought it was stupid, but Flare defended the decision, not wanting to get reassigned to a new AI. Ember had to grudgingly give in. She'd come to depend on Zeta's guidance. Breaking in a new handler would be more than an annoyance. It would be like losing a close family member, or a part of herself.

"Where are Aegis and Tinker?" Ember panted into her headset. The rest of the team had split off a few blocks back, trying to get ahead of Culvers and herd him back toward Flux and Flare. The team—minus Remedy and with Keys struggling to hold it together after watching so many of her demon followers crushed by Culvers—wasn't at peak, but they'd trained for such scenarios.

Ember could imagine how Keys must feel. She clamped down on her own emotions, letting the anger surge. Culvers might have lost family, but that didn't excuse what he had done to Tammy and her brother. And to Lee.

She gritted her teeth, pumping her legs and arms, knowing she was beginning to put distance between herself and Flare.

"Hey!" Flare huffed, putting on a burst of speed to come up beside her. "Won't do any good for us to catch him alone," she reminded Ember.

"Won't do much good if we don't catch him at all," Ember shot back, but she slowed enough to allow her breath to lose its ragged edge.

"But," Flare paused before continuing her thought, "what if he's adapted to you?"

"Guess we'll find out when we get there." Ember tried not to sound worried, but the same thought had been running through her mind. *Worrying isn't a solution,* she thought. *Oh, gods. When did I become my mother?*

"You've gained on him," Zeta told her. "He slowed when he crossed into Spider territory."

"Running out of steam?" Ember asked, hopefully. Her lungs burned and her legs ached. This mission had already pushed her physical abilities to their outer limit.

"It's more like he's looking for something," Zeta told her.

"Shit," Flare hissed, tapping Ember on the shoulder as they ran. "Let's not get ourselves ambushed."

Ember shrugged her off, but nodded and slowed her pace to a jog. "Zeta, how's Lee?"

"Focus on the mission," her AI replied.

"Oh, I'm focused." Ember's tone was bitter. "I just want to know as soon Lee wakes up."

"Copy that." Zeta was all business out here in the field, but there was assurance in that voice that Ember recognized and trusted. She needed that. Especially now, as they crossed what remained of Halstead Street and headed directly into Spider turf.

"You think the Spiders are smart enough to stay out of Culvers' way?" Flare asked.

"Turn left at the next intersection," Zeta continued to guide her.

They rounded the corner just in time to see a three-story high wall collapse into a grumbling avalanche of bricks and dust that poured across the sidewalk and street.

"Guess not," Ember said.

Culvers rose from beneath the rubble, his shirt torn to shreds, blood dripping from his hairline and into his face. He grinned as the jagged wound across his scalp knitted itself back together.

A gang of Spiders surrounded him. The group of rogue Supers stepped back and spread out. All of the Spiders wore black clothing, each with red bandanna tied around their upper arms.

The three nearest Flare and Flux, two guys, one pale and the other olive-skinned, and a slender girl with her bleach-blond hair pulled back into a short ponytail, stood poised and ready to strike.

"Waster and Blast," Zeta informed her. "STAMS mid-level. Waster's power is speeding up decay and rot. Blaster can lob blasts of air hard enough to dent metal plate."

"That explains the building collapsing without an explosion," Ember said under her breath.

"The blond is Phosphor," Zeta continued. "Never been tested, but projections have her rated as highly dangerous. She can ignite almost anything."

Flare grabbed Ember by the shoulder and hauled her back. "Hang on, let's let them soften him up a bit," she whispered.

Ember backed up a few steps. "Where are the rest of the team?" she asked Zeta.

"Tinker is still outside the zone. Aegis and Keys have hit a snag," came the reply.

"More Spiders?" Ember asked.

"Affirmative."

"Where?"

"Midpoint, north. But your orders are to stay with the main target. Copy?"

Ember clenched her fists. "Yeah, yeah. Copy that." She watched as Culvers strode toward the lineup of Spiders, his face split into an anticipatory grin.

"What the hell?" Flare said when Culvers strode across the boulevard, then stopped a few feet in front of the nearest gang member and slapped his hand against his own chest. "Come on," he shouted, "hit me with your best shot."

Ember watched in growing horror as Culvers stood like a statue waiting for the Super gang members to pour their powers into him.

"Is he suicidal?" Flare asked.

One by one, the Spiders attacked. And one by one, Culvers healed from their powers and then destroyed them, mowing them down as easily as he had Keys' demons. Only this involved a lot more screaming and blood. They were used to working in a pack, but they'd never had to fight as a team, didn't have the training for it. And there was no Remedy here to heal them.

"Dammit," Ember said. "He's acquiring more and more immunity. We need to stop him." She measured the distance between her and the closest Spider. She had to give them credit, they hadn't backed down, had stayed to protect their territory. "Think you can get their attention?"

"I've always had a knack for getting all eyes on me," Flare responded.

Ember resisted the urge to laugh. "Give me a three-count head start, starting now." She sprinted across the intersection. On her fourth step, light blazed, hitting the middle gang member in the chest. He fell back with a shriek. Flare's power singed clothing and skin, filling the air with the smell of burned fabric and flesh.

Culvers let out an angry howl and all eyes turned to Flare's position. Ember reached the blond girl, grabbing her hand before she could spark anything in Flare's direction.

"Tell your friends they need to let me get close enough to touch Culvers and then attack in concert. It's the only way to defeat him," she said. "If they hold back, he'll just adapt."

"Like I'm going to listen to a sellout like you." The girl tried to yank away, but Ember held tight. Phosphor's eyes widened as she realized she had lost access to her power. "Hey, what the hell are you?"

"You can call me Flux," Ember told her. "I'm your new—"

"F.U. Flux!" Phosphor cut Ember off, dropped back and side-kicked her, trying to wrench from her grip.

"Help us stop him," Ember said. "And we'll leave peacefully." She yanked Phosphor to her and wrapped an arm around her neck.

"Doesn't work like that. Not once you trespass onto Spider turf." Phosphor grabbed Ember's forearm and bent, tossing Ember over her back.

Ember flipped in midair and landed beside Phosphor, twisting the girl's arm behind her and yanking hard on it. She felt the girl's shoulder dislocate, but Phosphor only grunted.

The three men had turned toward Flare and she was now dodging bursts of power from Waster and Blast while throwing energy bolts their way. Her brows were knitted in concentration, face showing the strain of physical exertion. Culvers watched the fight as if weighing his options. Suddenly, he ran at Waster.

"So much for being allies," Ember said in Phosphor's ear. She slammed a fist into the girl's temple, knocking her unconscious, and winced at the pain in her knuckles. She dropped Phosphor on the ground. "Lucky for you, you'll heal."

She needed to help Flare. Her palms filled with heat.

"Ember," Zeta cautioned. "Orders."

"Screw that," Ember said. "This situation calls for an exception."

Energy orbs filled each of her hands and she hurled the first one at Blast, hitting him dead center in the back. He flew forward, almost taking down Flare when he tumbled to the ground at her feet, jacket smoldering.

"What the hell was that?" Flare called, eyes wide.

"A little something I've been keeping to myself," Ember said, wrinkling her nose at the burned leather.

"Nice." A smile quirked up the corners of Flare's mouth.

"Cover me." Ember ran at Culvers, but before she could connect with the big man, Waster managed to hit him with a blast of his power.

Culvers' face rotted and reformed in a rolling wave. It was like watching a horror movie then hitting the reverse button. Ember gagged at the overpowering stench of decay. She had to turn her head away to avoid retching.

In that moment Culvers struck out at her, his fist connecting with her cheek. She flew sideways, landing in a heap. He shook his hand, eyeing it curiously. Then stared at Ember. A patch of rotten flesh fell from his cheek. Then, slowly, his face finished reforming.

She stared back, vision still swimming from the blow. Maybe he can't adapt to me, after all, she thought, trying to rise.

Flare hit Blast with a bolt of energy and he went down on his hands and knees, his clothing smoking.

Then Flare paused, staring at the end of the street. Ember followed her gaze. Aegis and Keys were running toward them, but before their team members could reach them, four more Spiders appeared, blocking the way.

"Shit," Ember said, pushing herself to her feet.

Culvers grinned, gave her a one-fingered salute, then turned and ran.

Aegis disabled one of the new Spiders, locking her into an energy sphere with a wave of his hand.

"Turmoil," Zeta said.

"Not now," Ember replied.

"But you need the intel."

"Screw the intel," Ember all but yelled. "I don't care what they can do. These a-holes are going down."

Keys opened a portal and a herd of pint-sized demons poured out, snarling. The Spiders dropped back, assessing this new threat and giving Aegis and Keys enough time to skirt around them and join up with Flux and Flare.

"Four-person defensive stand!" Aegis rushed toward her, Keys on his heels. Both of her teammates looked exhausted.

"Son of a—" Ember rose to her feet, assuming her position in the back-to-back formation.

Beside her Flare groaned in frustration. "We need to get moving. He's getting away."

"First things first," Aegis replied. He trapped one of the oncoming Spiders inside an energy sphere.

"There's no way to stop Culvers. He adapts too quickly." Ember said. "The only good thing is that he doesn't seem to have adapted a resistance to my power drain." She dodged a cannon-sized ball of molten metal thrown by one of the gang members and heated by Flare. "Flare, can you try and flash those before they get close enough to cook my face?"

"Sorry," Flare said.

"Aegis," Ember said. "Guy on the left. Trap, neutralize and release?"

"Yeah," he called over his shoulder. "I'll take the one on my right. Keys keep the others off us. Now!"

Keys opened up a row of portals, keeping each one open just long enough for one or two of her impish followers to leap through, one after the other. They lunged forward in a straight line between the team and the Spiders, hissing and swiping with their long claws.

Aegis formed an energy sphere in his hand, swung his arm back, then forward again, releasing it like a bowling ball. It hit the oncoming Spider in the legs, knocking him down.

Ember leaped on the fallen soldier, grabbing him by the arm, then yanked him up just in time to use his body as a shield against a blast from Phosphor, who had regained consciousness.

"Finally," Aegis yelled, pleased with himself.

"That's new," Flare said, releasing a stream of fiery bolts at the remaining two enemy Supers, causing them to dive aside.

The man Ember held screamed and slapped at himself, trying to put out the blaze, but when he touched it, the fire transferred to his hands. His fingers curled. Skin crackled and his screams filled Ember's ears. She released him and he fell to the ground whimpering.

As soon as Ember let him go, Phosphor raised her hands to attack, but her shot flew wide as three of Keys' imps knocked her feet from under her. The blaze rocketed past Ember's head, so close she felt the heat singe her hair. Then it struck the building behind her. The brick sizzled and burned, and black smoke rose into the air.

Phosphor was on her back, striking at demons as they crawled over her, biting and scratching. One by one, they screeched and blazed out in a flash of silver fire.

The other Spiders were down.

"Should we let her up?" Keys asked.

"I have a better idea." Ember pulled a metal tube from the pocket of her suit. "I say we let her have some fun with foam."

"Good idea," Flare said, pulling out another tube. Let's pin some insects."

"Can we get an XTU team in here to mop up?" Aegis asked over his comm. "Before any others head our way." He glanced over at the exhausted team. "Yeah. Extraction would be good."

# Fourteen
Mon, Oct 3, 1:51pm

## - Lee -

Everyone was quiet, as Will pulled Lee aside. The rest of the team went on to debriefing. Ember and Allison looked back with concern as they walked. Kevin's was more one of satisfied contempt.

"What were you thinking?" Will asked, though it didn't feel like a question. "Do you have any idea the position you've put me in?"

Lee looked down at his feet. He didn't know why, but it was difficult to meet Will's gaze. It wasn't the same as getting in trouble at school and facing down a teacher or the principal. Will was a friend who neatly fit into the space where a father should be. Lee hated the knot in his stomach, the nervous flutter in his chest, that came of knowing he'd disappointed him.

"It doesn't matter," Lee managed to say. "After I found out about Discord, I began altering the density of my bones. It'll take more than a bullet to penetrate my skull."

"You think a bullet is the worst that could happen to you? Believe me, it isn't. All you've managed to do is put the people you love in danger."

Lee frowned, angry. "What's that supposed to mean?"

"I'm not the enemy, Lee." Will had yet to raise his voice, though the tightness in his jaw and shoulders betrayed emotion. "But I'm also not in charge. There's a limit to what I can do. You can gauge what I'm feeling, if what I'm saying is true. Am I threatening you?"

Lee looked him over. "No. You're worried."

"Damn right, I'm worried." Will kept his voice low, though no one in the hangar was nearby. "You ignored a direct order, neutralized a potential asset and now you're telling me you've taken away the only direct control over you the agency had. You've managed to undermine in a single day everything I've been working toward for the past five weeks."

"What the hell was I supposed to do?" Lee asked, incredulous. "Let you shoot me in the head?"

"No," Will replied, "you were supposed to trust that I would never have let it come to that. I've been doing everything I can to show the need for a separate agency, one just for Supers. Cerberus is stretched too thin with magic, monsters and artifacts. It was never equipped to handle this type of crisis." Will sighed, visibly frustrated. "We needed a win here today."

Lee said, "I gave you one. You just refuse to see it."

"That's my point," Will said. "You can't disobey direct orders because you think you know better. You don't have all the intel. That's how chain of command works. You have to trust in that command, that I know what I'm doing. You had no idea if Culvers had information we needed, if he'd stolen sensitive documents from the hospital, or if he was an asset in play. Did you consider any of that in your threat assessment, before you reasoned out a need to kill him? It's fine to look at the big picture, Lee, but not when you don't have all the information."

"You're right," Lee said. "I didn't consider any of that. But in the moment? We had no way of holding him. My power wasn't working, and the longer we fought, the less any of us could hurt him. There was no win but taking him out while we still could."

Will said, "I hope Jim and his team can corroborate. For now, I need you in confinement until I can sort this all out. I've watched you grow up, kept your family safe for years. I need you to trust me. And keep the changes you made to yourself quiet. It'll only lead to questions about why you did it. If my plans go through, you'll never have to worry about a Bullet Squad or anything like it."

Lee had nothing else to say. He nodded and turned to head for the elevator.

"One more thing," Will said. "The Sherwood girl, Tammy. Until the lab is done testing, until we know exactly what it is you did to her or whether it can spread, no more animating corpses. The last thing we need right now is a Super zombie apocalypse."

Will gave a nod to indicate the conversation was done, so Lee continued on to the elevator.

"There you are," Anna said. "I lost connection for a bit. Is everything all right?"

"Yep," Lee said as the elevator doors opened, "just headed to my jail cell."

"It's confinement," Anna said and chuckled, "not prison. Think of it as timeout for adults."

"Sure," Lee said without humor, "just like the death penalty is a really long nap."

The elevator doors closed, and it began to move. It took him further down than he'd ever been before but opened to the usual white corridor. There were no guards or agents, just rows of small cells on either side, closed off by transparent fields of blue energy.

"Yours is sixth on the right."

He'd expected the other cells to be empty, but each one he passed had someone in it. No bed, no seat, no toilet or running water, there was nothing for them to do but stand and wait or lie about on the floor.

"Who are they?" Lee asked.

It was eerily quiet. He could see a girl's mouth moving as he walked past but couldn't hear a word she said when she got up to pound against the energy field.

Anna sounded like her cheer was forced. "Like I said, they're in timeout. It's just temporary."

Lee stepped into his cell, and the field flicked on. There was a quiet buzz, like an electric hum, that he couldn't hear when he was on the other side.

He sat on the floor, waiting. There was nothing else for him to do. The imaginary clock in his mind ticked away for seventy-nine minutes.

"Hmm," Anna said. "Something's wrong. I'm being locked out of systems one by one. I'm trying to alert—"

Her voice had cut out. His energy field flickered, and the electric drone died out as well. Lee could hear footsteps clicking slowly toward him from down the hall. Whoever had gotten off the elevator was getting close and began to whistle.

"Who's there?" Lee asked and got up to look out. The people in other cells were up and banging on their fields, but no noise made it past. "What's going on?"

Jim stepped into view.

"Hey, buddy," he said and smiled. "How's it going?"

Lee almost felt relieved to see him, though surprised and a bit confused. Jim eyed the energy field with a curious look. Lee went to raise his arm to lean against the wall for dramatic flair, but when he saw the dried blood, all sense of levity left him.

"How'd you get down here?" Lee asked instead. "This is a high security area."

"There's no guards," Jim pointed out. "Tech's easy to bypass when you have the right skills."

"Or people," Lee said. "I didn't think the Bullet Squad had a tech."

"We do now. You're not a stupid guy," he said, arms crossed and smile gone. "You know what's going on. I think maybe you're just waiting for the right opportunity to do something about it."

Jim knocked on the wall.

"Let me guess," Lee said. "You're my opportunity."

The smile returned. "I wanted to get you before they do a reset. We don't have time for retraining."

"So you can get me out of here," Lee said. "Then what?"

"We burn it all down."

"But what's the plan?" Lee pressed. "You need a way to survive, to deal with the repercussions. You'll turn the entire city into a target."

"More like a Briarwood," Jim said. "Just think about it, an impenetrable city, where Supers call all the shots. Hundreds will flock to us, thousands, from towns and cities all around."

*Or maybe you'll set a bad example for them to follow.*

Lee considered it without meaning to. It was just in his nature now. Scenarios played out in his mind, details of possible futures bubbling beneath the surface.

"They'll just bomb us from the air," he said, "send in drones to spare soldiers, make us into a warning for other cities. They'll cut off power and water. Food will run out within weeks. There's no sequence of events that doesn't end with the deaths of millions."

Jim waved off his assessment. "We'll have a city full of hostages. We can use them to bargain for whatever we need. We'll take control of power and water, buy or steal everything else."

"That might work on a smaller scale," Lee said, "but you're not a criminal organization. You're less than ten guys. Even with powers, you can't take this whole complex, let alone Sungrove."

"We'll see about that." The sense of confidence coming off him, the deception and vindication, left Lee feeling that Jim had become a far more dangerous person than the one he'd met at the police station. "But you're going to have to make a choice," Jim went on, "a lot sooner than later. You can fight with us and be on top, or you can sit here and roast marshmallows."

Whatever uprising Jim had planned, Lee knew there would be no talking him out of it.

It was already happening.

Lee asked, "What would she say about all this?"

He didn't know her name but didn't have to. If Jim had remembered anything, it would be her.

"Joselyn?" Jim asked. He gave Lee an appraising look, as if further impressed. "She was more than my tutor. At least, to me. She'd probably tell me to follow orders. No matter what. Too bad she isn't here anymore. You once said you knew how to kill me. That true?"

Lee looked up at him with regret. It was a matter of semantics, but he'd been wrong at the time.

"No."

"Good." Jim let his arms drop and moved to stand directly in front of the cell. "What's it going to be? You with us, or...?"

"I have friends here," Lee said, "family. I can't attack them. If you're forcing me to choose between you, then I guess I'm against."

Jim pursed his lips in disappointment. "All right. Let it drop."

The energy field between them fell away.

Lee knew the attack was coming, had cells building in Jim since he'd arrived, but wasn't equipped to fend off the vibrations. He brought his own power to bear, sent in everything else he had, and tried to roll out of the way. Jim raised both hands, used his power to begin shaking every bit of Lee's body with waves of vibrations. Lee sent shocks down his spine, and Jim's muscles went into spasms. Waves of rolling vibrations struck the walls and ceiling, rippling the smooth metal into flakes.

There was nowhere to run. The cell was too small, and he needed more time. Jim growled with the strain and fought for control of his own body. He brought his hands back down toward Lee. The vibrations struck like a car at full speed and raced through. Lee tried to push against the force building between them, to land kicks or punches like he'd been trained. There was just no getting close enough.

He sent more shocks into the spine and brain, knew he was causing damage despite how quickly Jim was able to regenerate. Lee's skin crawled and began to tear. He dropped to his knees and screamed against the pain of every organ and muscle breaking down beneath the stress. It became difficult to concentrate on his cells within Jim, and the more his attack eased, the stronger Jim's became. Even with the alterations Lee had made to his bones, they too would shatter and turn to jelly before long.

His eyes stung with blood, and his vision blurred. The floor beneath him cracked, as both hands and every finger broke with it. Blood ran from his ears and joined the growing puddle. Lee had no choice but to relent, to draw cells from his attack and use them to heal himself. He simply wasn't strong enough, not after all he'd been through already that day. If he ignored the damage to his own body, he wouldn't survive the next few seconds, let alone put a stop to the assault.

Two voices cried out over the tumult of Lee's screams. It was Ember and Allison. Jim cursed and turned to face them, as fire filled the hallway. Twisting streamers of yellow and orange, the controlled inferno snapped out and engulfed him.

It was Jim's turn to scream.

He rolled away from the growing fires, his clothes, hair and skin scorched.

"Open them all!" Jim yelled, and Lee sensed him run in the other direction.

Ember was first inside, came running to kneel beside him. By the fear and overwhelming concern he sensed come off her, Lee imagined he looked even worse than he felt.

Allison continued to throw fire down the hall, blasts that filled the cell with waves of crackling heat. She stood just outside, as if daring Jim to come back.

The energy field to every cell went down.

"Ah shit," Allison said. "I might need a hand here."

She threw both arms wide, and walls of flame erupted to either side. The skin not covered by her outfit, her hands and face, glowed like molten glass. Veins stood out from beneath the brightness, like crimson rivers of boiling fury.

"Do yourself a favor," Allison told the girl in the opposite cell. "Stay inside until we leave, or I'll stop holding back."

The girl's eyes widened further. She was already backed up against the wall to avoid the heat. A nervous nod was all she could manage through her fear.

"Can you move?" Ember asked. She'd been careful not to touch him.

Lee only nodded. He was focused on healing, closing ruptures and mending breaks. The pain made it impossible to think about anything else. He could alter himself again, turn the pain off, but didn't want to risk making a mistake with so many lives on the line.

"We need," Lee started and coughed. His lungs had been punctured by bone fragments. When they'd healed and he could draw breath, he went on, "We need to stop them. The Bullet Squad. They're trying—"

"We know," Ember said. "Kevin knew before anyone else, had alarms hidden in every system."

"Ember!" Allison shouted. Shards of ice flew through her fire wall on the left, cutting through her uniform, as a purple field of energy began to bend the flames on her right. "I need you!"

"Be right back," Ember said to Lee. She got up and stopped, looked down at her middle and back to Lee with a sense of panic. "What the—"

Everything flared white, and she was gone.

# - Ember -

Will was waiting when the team disembarked from the aircraft. With a curt wave, he pulled Lee aside. "The rest of you get down to medical for clearance, then get cleaned up. Grab some rations," he told them before leading Lee away.

Ember looked back at them, trying to see where they were headed, but the hallways in this part of the facility were still a mystery to her.

Once the docs had cleared them, they headed back to their rooms. Ember had Zeta deliver a pile of fries and a huge chocolate protein shake.

"Carbs and protein never tasted so good," she said to Allison, who sat across from her chowing down on a bowl of brown rice and steamed veggies.

"I don't know how you eat that junk," Allison said between bites. "It's gonna do you in."

"Nothing a spare set of organs and a brother who can heal you from across the room can't take care of." Ember vacuumed up the last of her shake with a slurping sound.

"There's a problem in Omicron," Zeta said, suddenly. "Lee—improper—access—systems—communi—breaking—some—hacked—"

"What? What's going on?" Ember asked as her comm went dead.

Allison dropped her fork and stuck a finger in her ear, trying to fiddle with her earbud. "Did you get any of that?"

"We got issues," Kevin stuck his head inside the door, hands full of wires and components."

"You have comm?" Ember asked.

"Not exactly." He continued to mess with the electronic materials. "But I've got this." He slapped the mess on the wall inside the doorway.

A video feed flashed to life and Ember jumped up when she saw Lee in the picture. "Lee! That must be Omicron."

"Yeah." Allie stared at the screen. "What the hell is

Breaker doing in there?"

"I'm guessing, under the current circumstances, that it's nothing good."

"We need to get down there!" Allie shouted.

"Not without these." Kevin handed each of them a spare ear bud.

"Tinker!" Aegis roared from his cube, "stop blabbing and get this show up and running."

"He's giving the orders," Kevin said quietly, "or is about to, and as much as I think Lee screwed up out there, I don't think we should leave him to fend for himself. He's still one of us, and I have a feeling we're going to need all our allies today." He nodded at Ember and Allison. "So, if I were planning on getting to Omicron before someone sent me elsewhere, I'd be moving my ass already." He grabbed Ember's game system, then ducked out and sprinted across the hall. "Thanks for the loan," he yelled over his shoulder.

Ember and Allie glanced at one another, then rushed out the door and into the main hallway.

"Flux! Flare!" they heard Aegis call, but they were in the elevator heading down before he could order them back.

"Any idea where we're going?" Allison asked.

"Omicron," Ember said, her thoughts on Lee and what might be happening around them.

"Omicron," a voice said in her ear. The elevator slowed and lurched, stuttered, then began moving again.

"What was that?" Ember asked.

"Better question," Allison said, "Who was that?"

"You heard it too?"

"Operative Assistant Alpha," the voice said as the elevator stopped and the doors opened. "Left down the hallway, then left again."

Allison raised her eyebrows at Ember who shrugged. "Gotta love Tinker's toys." She stepped out of the elevator and jogged left.

Allison stayed on her heels as they navigated the floor,

following the directions that came from Tinker's earbuds.

Before they reached Omicron, chaos erupted. Noise and running people filled the corridors.

"Emergency stairwell to your right," Alpha said as they turned a corner and ran into three men in lab coats. The docs looked startled to see them and glanced around guiltily before running past.

Ember stared up the hallway in the direction the men had come from. Large windows opened onto what looked like a laboratory, but Ember couldn't see what the men had been running from.

"I've got a bad feel—" An explosion sent shards of glass at them. Allison's hands were up and fire flared, melting the glass before it reached them.

"Thanks," Ember told her, reaching out to press open the emergency stairwell door. "Let's go."

"Jackasses, could have at least warned us." Allison followed her into the stairwell. "Now, what?"

"One flight down," responded their virtual guide.

"I don't think those particular jackasses are on our side." Ember headed down the spiraling metal stairs, grateful for her white 'lab rat' shoes for a change, because they didn't make resounding clomping noises in the stairwell like her boots would have.

They stopped at the next landing and listened at the door.

There were sounds of fighting. "This must be the place." Ember crouched low and twisted the knob, preparing to shove open the door. "You ready, Flare?"

Allie grinned. "Ready, Flux."

Ember shoved her shoulder into the door, but it caught on something and wouldn't open. "Crap." She peeked out through the slim opening. Crumpled bodies lay just outside. "A little help? They're heavier than they look."

"Probably armed and armored. On three?" Allison braced herself against the door.

"One, two, three."

Together they shoved at the door and the bodies of the guards on the other side shifted enough to let them through.

"Remedy's cell is down the hall on the left," their virtual guide said.

"Let's go," Flare tried to push past Ember.

"Wait." Ember filled her palms with heat, as a blast of energy shook the hallway. "We need to go in shooting, but don't hit Lee."

"Duh." Allison stepped out into the corridor and flung up her hands as a tall Super shot something black and slimy at them. The gloppy mass flared and exploded midway between them and the Super who'd thrown it. He looked startled, then pulled his arm back to throw again. Before he could form up whatever it was, Ember hit him square in the chest with a bolt of heat that knocked him backward and caused him to yelp when the mass of slime he'd formed splattered all over his chest and arm.

"Damn!" Flare said. "You really were holding out on us."

"Sorry," Ember said. "Orders." She grimaced. "But I should have at least told you."

"I get it." Flare shrugged. "But there is something I need to tell you."

"Really? Now?"

"Well, yeah. It's about Lee—"

Something wet slammed into the wall beside them, causing the wall to ooze. They ducked inside the nearest room.

The unkempt Super inside looked up and grinned, waggling his tongue at them.

"Don't. Even." Flare shook her head at him.

He lurched to his feet, and lunged at her. With a flick of her wrist, Flare released a fireball that scorched the Super along with an entire side of the room. It happened so fast, he didn't even have a chance to scream.

"Damn," Ember said, grimacing at the stench of burned flesh.

"Sorry." Flare shivered. "I can't stand pervs."

"Guess that'll teach him that no means no." Ember slowly stuck her head out of the door.

The entire floor echoed with vibrating energy. Screams emanated from down the hall. "Lee!" Ember rushed toward the painful screaming, hurling magical energy spheres at anyone who got in her way. Drawing from this close to the Nexus, even with the magical dampening field in place, gave her a control she'd never had before.

Beside her, Flare kept up a steady stream of fire. Supers ducked and dodged out of their way. Those who stood to fight had no time for regret. Flux and Flare had no intention of being stopped. They struck hard and fast.

"Hang on, Lee!" Flare shouted over the din of screams and explosions, then cursed as a wound opened on her shoulder.

The vibrations shifted as they neared the end of the hallway and Breaker turned to face them. His curse died in his throat as fire engulfed him. Both Ember and Flare had struck him at the same time, and his energy emanations were no match for the blazing heat thrown at him by the two angry young women. He screamed in pain, dropped and rolled away, shouting something as he went.

Ember let him go, intent on getting to Lee. She rushed inside the cell to find him crumpled in a heap on the floor. She gasped, kneeling beside him, afraid to touch him for fear of not only slowing his self-healing, but because he was so utterly broken and bloodied. "Jeez, Lee. Are you all right?" Her voice cracked with emotion. "I'm so sorry."

He tried to wave her off but could barely move. His face contorted in a grimace of pain.

Allison stood just outside the cell, glancing now and again over her shoulder at Lee. Fire flew from her hands, singeing the ceiling and walls, keeping the other Supers at bay.

Suddenly, all the cells that had still been shut, opened.

Allison cursed. "I think I'm going to need some help." She continued to fill the hallway with fire, her flesh glowing with the effort. "Don't." Allison shook her head at the girl in the cell across the hall. "Stay inside until we leave, or you'll really be sorry."

The girl pressed herself against the back wall of her cell.

"Can you move?" Ember asked her brother.

He nodded, face intent. "We need—" a wracking cough cut off his words and blood spattered his lips and the floor in front of him.

"It's okay, Lee. Just relax and heal yourself." Ember kept her voice steady, trying to hide her fear at how hurt he was.

After a moment, he sucked in a long breath. "It's the Bullet Squad. We need to stop them—"

"We know," Ember said. "Kevin had alarms hidden in every system. And he's working on getting comms back up. Meanwhile, we have these." She tipped the Tinkered earbud out of her ear and held it up for him to see. "Not quite the AIs we're used to, but it got us here."

"Ember!" Allison shouted. Jagged ice shards flew through her firewall intact and sliced through the left sleeve of her uniform. Purple energy bent back the flames on her right. "I need you!"

"Be right back," Ember said, noting her brother's body had begun to heal. She stood, and jerked to a halt, looking down at herself, recognizing the telltale shiver of magic. "What the—"

Her vision shimmered. Lee, the cell, Allison, the fire and ice, all dimmed, the sounds of fighting muting out as she was pulled elsewhere.

She tried to fight it, but there was nothing she could do. Her blood, her oath, the tattoo that marked her as one of them, left her completely defenseless against the combined will of the coven. But she didn't have to like it.

"Dammit, mother!" she sputtered as her mother's face came into view.

"I don't have time for your tantrums, at the moment," her mother said, as Tara and Seanna rushed over to grab Ember's hands.

Ember realized suddenly where they were. The Nexus chamber. Around them, the cousins and aunties began to pull on the power of the Nexus as the members of the Cerberus coven chanted, holding the veil in place while letting a thin stream of magical energy slip through to fill the room.

"What the hell is going on?" Ember felt her cousins' fingers entwine around hers. "You're sending us back in to get Lee, right?"

Aunt Gwen shook her head, her eyes squeezed shut as if against a bright light. "No time for that."

The power rose up around Ember and she struggled to get her hands away from Tara and Seanna. "What do you mean no time? He's one of us. He's blood." She turned her pleading eyes to Seanna, hoping for help from her cousin. "He's my brother! Your betrothed!"

Seanna looked away, trying to hide the guilt she wore.

"Ember!" Her mother's voice cut across her protests. "If you and your cousins can't retrieve the artifacts, it won't matter. None of it, none of this, will matter. Do you understand?"

Ember stopped struggling. A shiver ran across her scalp. "Artifacts?"

"No time," Aunt Gwen intoned, her eyes still closed.

"We'll fill you in when we get there." Tara gave her hand a firm squeeze.

"Get where?" Ember asked, but just then, the magic hit and once more, the room and everything in it, everyone, shimmered and dissolved.

They coalesced in a dimly lit room. "Where the hell are we?" Ember peered into the darkness at the rows of shelves outlined against the pale light of security lamps.

"The Pandora reliquary," Tara said in a hushed voice, clearly impressed by their close proximity to such a huge store of powerful objects.

"What's that?" Seanna hissed, as a black shadow separated itself from the darkness and dove at them, a long arm wrapping itself around Seanna's neck. Her green eyes went wide and she choked as the demon grabbed a handful of her hair and began yanking her with it toward the dark corner.

"Rifter!" Tara jumped back, reaching toward the nearest shelf.

"Don't," Seanna gasped. "Wards," she warned, struggling to free herself from the shade that clutched her by the throat.

"Let her go," Tara growled, grasping for the shade, but her hands passed through the space she'd thought it had been.

Ember formed an orb without thinking but hesitated, the ball of energy burning bright in her hand. What if she missed?

Tara pulled a glass container from her pocket and uncorked it, murmuring something low and guttural.

"Throw...it." Seanna coughed and bent forward, trying to flip the creature off her.

It rasped out a dark laugh and said something ugly in another language.

"You...think," Seanna managed to shift her weight, spinning the creature around and putting it directly between her and Ember.

Ember's orb struck home dead-center at the same time as Tara emptied the bottle and released her spell. The creature screeched in pain and anger, slapping at itself and contorting. No longer a darker shadow against the darkness of the room, the rifter was covered in something glowing that seemed to eat away at the dark form like powerful acid. The creature grew fringy, melting where the liquid had splattered over it. With a final shriek, it finally vanished.

"You okay?" Tara asked.

"Aside from nearly being scalped and possibly eaten by a demonic spirit?" Seanna grumbled. "Sure thing." Her words sounded slow and slurry.

"How'd that thing get in here?" Ember glanced around, searching the room for signs of other spirits, suddenly realizing there weren't any ghosts in the room. She'd seen so many of them everywhere else in the facility, she'd gotten used to ignoring them. Now, the lack of them bothered her. The room was lined with rows of shelves filled with all kinds of boxes and containers.

"Most likely through the same crack in the barrier we did." Tara leaned over Seanna, checking her head. "I think it scratched her."

"It also ripped out a major chunk of hair. Can you do anything about the bleeding?" Ember peered at the blood that had dripped onto Seanna's forehead.

"Great," Seanna groaned.

"That's gonna leave a mark," Ember said. "Maybe you need to smear some of that salve on it."

Seanna pushed Tara's hands away from her head. "No way. Let's just get what we came for and get out of here before—"

The screech of the metal door being ripped open filled the room, cutting her off.

"So much for high-tech security." Seanna began chanting to set a ward between them and whatever was coming into the room.

"Cover your eyes." Tara reached inside the bag she carried and pulled out a handful of something, then flung it across the room, murmuring under her breath.

It hit the barriers layered between them and most of the

rest of the room, dropping them in a cascade of glittering particles as the door on the other side of the room was ripped off its hinges and tossed aside.

Two guys and a girl strode in through the destroyed doorway. All Supers by the look of them. The girl waved her hand and the room lit up, as if a flare had been fired up at the ceiling.

"Maybe we should have waited to drop those barriers." Ember let her hands fill with heat.

"Maybe," Tara said. "But I wouldn't want to get knocked into one by accident."

The girl said something to one of the guys. He nodded and started walking toward Ember and her cousins. He reached out one hand and the shelving units nearest him began to morph, boxes and jars sliding off, crashing and clattering to the floor, as they shifted and fell.

Seanna continued to chant, keeping her eyes on the Super striding their way, when he suddenly froze, his eyes widening in surprise. His body spasmed and he jerked like a thousand volts rolled through him.

"I guess I missed one." Tara said as he collapsed in a heap.

The girl shrieked in anger, running toward the fallen Super. "Get them!" she ordered.

The second guy glanced across the room, then back down to where his buddy still quivered, drool running out of the side of his mouth. "Screw that," he said. "I didn't sign up to fight shit I can't even see." He backed out the door, then turned and ran.

The girl stood up, raised her hands and squeezed them into fists.

Tara gasped and Seanna's chanting turned to a choking sound.

Ember watched in horror as Seanna grabbed her own throat, as if trying to remove someone's hands. "Stop it!"

The Super grinned. "I'm. Not. Finished. Yet."

"Yeah. You are." Ember threw the orb she'd been holding, sending it across the room and into the Super. It hit her in the chest, slamming her backward to crash into a shelf full of glowing bottles. She screamed as the glowing energy surrounded her. She disappeared behind the neon cloud of mist, her scream choking off into sudden silence.

Seanna coughed, heaved in a lungful of air and rubbed at her throat. "Damn," she croaked. "That's going to make spelling a lot harder. Do you think we need to tie them up?"

Ember looked across the room to where the two Supers were lying, shaping another ball of energy just in case.

"Not him," Tara said. "That barrier spell was nastier than any I've ever seen."

Ember nodded, walking slowly to where the girl Super lay. When she got close enough to see the girl's face, she turned away, letting the orb fade. There wasn't anything left of the Super's face. Ember doubted even Lee could have healed her.

Lee. She needed to get back to him and Allie. "Let's get what we came for and get the hell out of here." She eyed the rows of shelves with disdain. "Just don't tell me we have to search this whole place."

"Not exactly," Tara said. "Seanna's got a spell up her sleeve for that, but what with her head and throat..."

Seanna waved Tara over, gesturing for her to get closer. "I'm fine," she said. "Just give me a hand with the circle." She held out a piece of black chalk.

Tara made a quick circle on the floor, her lines smooth and practiced.

"Make sure you mark true north exactly."

"Duh."

Ember paced, worrying about Lee and Allie. And where was everyone else? She shivered. What if the fighting was already over? What if the facility was under rogue Super control right now? The technology they'd have, along with their own powers, would be impossible to fight.

As soon as Tara was finished marking the lines on the floor, Seanna un-stoppered a small bottle and sprinkled the contents just outside the circle. "Stand behind me." She stood facing north, held her arms out to her sides, palms up. "Oh, and don't step outside—"

"The circle." Ember and Tara finished for her.

Seanna sighed, rolled her head to loosen the tension in her shoulders, then began to chant, her words whispery soft in the gloom.

A smoky mist rose from the floor around them. Glowing tendrils writhed from within the haze. It looked like radioactive fog, only the tendrils reached out like tentacles, sensing, searching. Ember glanced at Tara.

Tara shrugged. Clearly this spell was new to her, as well.

The fingers of mist elongated, threading themselves through the room, winding over and around the shelves.

Across the room, a knot of glowing mist began to pulse, growing brighter with each oscillation. "Is that—" Ember stopped as another spot grew bright and faded in sync with the first. Then another, and another, until there were seven in all.

Seanna continued to chant, but rolled her eyes at them.

"I guess that's our cue," Tara said. "I'll take this side of the room. You go that way and—"

"We'll meet in the middle," Ember finished. Picking her way through the low-lying mist, she reached the first pulsing object, a pyramid that looked to be made of precious metals. She reached for it, snapping her hand back when an electric shock sprang from it, zapping her fingertips.

"Damn!" Tara griped from across the room. "Fricking thing is hotter than one of Seanna's burners. We need to find something to carry these in."

Ember searched the shelves nearest her. It was difficult to see clearly through the creeping fog, but she finally found a decorative wooden box that looked big enough to contain her half of the items. Nearby, she found a velvet bag full of mostly worthless crystals. Dumping the contents onto the floor, she swept the bag over the gleaming pyramid and slid the whole thing into the box. The mist that enveloped it dissipated.

She reached the second object and paused, slowly extending her hand toward it. When nothing happened, she grabbed it, an ancient wooden bowl rough-hewn on the outside, smooth and polished on the inside, and placed it in the box beside the other object. The box vibrated against her hands. "I'm not so sure we should be putting these things together," she said, eyeing the objects in suspicion.

"Just...hurry...up," Seanna said in between the lines of chanting. Her voice was strained and the misty tendrils of her spell were disintegrating. Ember moved quickly to grab the remaining objects. The first, a plain silver ring thinned by years of wear, she dropped into the box unceremoniously. The last, a lumpy cloth-wrapped bundle, pulsed rapidly even as the enshrouding fog melted away. Ember approached warily.

The sensation that hit her in the pit of her stomach startled her and she almost dropped the box. "Dammit! Not now." She grabbed for the bundle as the room began to shimmer around her and glanced anxiously at Tara and Seanna, breathing a quick sigh of relief as they, too, began to fade out.

# Fifteen
Mon, Oct 3, 4:01pm

### - Lee -

"Ember!" Lee shouted and coughed.

There was no sign of her. It was like the spell his family had used at the police station but in reverse. Was his mother trying to save them with magic? He saw Allison struggling to keep the other Supers back. What would happen to her if he was summoned as well?

Allison threw handfuls of fire through the faltering walls of flame on either side.

"Do something!" she yelled back at him.

Lee was healed but still weak, his sensory bubble no bigger than a few inches from his body. The cells would duplicate on their own over time, but he caused them to grow and spread much faster. He got up, endured the wave of dizziness that swirled his vision, then headed across to the girl in the opposite cell.

He couldn't help but be disappointed when no spell came to take him. The hollow feeling in his chest was his own fault. He should've known better than to allow even the tiniest glimmer of hope that his family cared.

"What can you do?" he asked the girl with a stern measure of authority.

"I—I'm earth," she said quickly, still afraid. "I can—I see shapes through walls. I can move rocks and dirt. Sometimes I—"

"None of that is useful here."

Lee looked out at Allison again, formulating a plan. He couldn't risk leaving any of them behind to join Jim's team. If this girl couldn't help, he'd have no choice but to paralyze her.

"Excuse me?"

She was clearly offended, but Lee didn't have time for hurt feelings. She looked him over and narrowed her eyes, held out a hand and pulled toward her every speck of dirt from his clothes and mud from his shoes. They gathered in a vortex of earthen debris that spun just above her palm.

"How's this for useless?" she asked with attitude.

The ball shot out and hit the wall to the side of her cell's entrance. It spun over and over in a furious swell, tearing away at the metal. The flecks that broke free joined the spinning ball, growing the sphere and tearing a hole in the wall. She called it back to her hand, and the ball continued to turn in air.

Lee blinked.

"That was actually pretty damn impressive. I'm sorry for what I said."

"Aww, it's okay." Her expression had softened and her fear drained away. All his energy had been focused on duplicating cells within her. "You didn't know," she said and reached a hand out to his bloodied shirt. "Are you hurt?"

As Lee had hoped, she was behaving like Emily had

while under his influence. He'd have to keep her within his sensory bubble to maintain control, but it was better than fighting every Super on their way out. He just needed more time to sway the others.

Lee wasn't entirely sure why Tammy's power had gotten stronger after she died, but he had his suspicions. It was as if her death or his cells had broken down some inner barrier or inhibitions. Whatever it was that had brought her closer to full potential, he was hoping for the same results here.

"I'm Cheryl," she said and hooked her left arm in his, while still controlling the vortex of earthen debris in her other hand. Together they started walking out of the cell. "So what do you do?"

"I'm a healer," Lee said, a bit embarrassed by her affection, especially when Allison shot him an accusing look.

"What did you to her?" Allison demanded.

The walls of fire flared to either side in time with her anger.

"It's just a side effect," Lee explained. "I'm not really doing anything. This is just how my power works."

Ice swept through from the right and caught Allison on her thigh. It cut through her uniform and left a nasty gash. She growled at the pain and used both hands to shoot a stream of flame down the corridor. A scream and panicked scurrying ensued.

Allison glared at Lee. "Did you do that us? To me?"

As much as it hurt him, Lee understood. His power was at the very least an invasion and at worst? He didn't want to think about it, would never have used it for that.

"I wouldn't," was all he said and swallowed hard. He liked Allison. Not the same way he liked Jen, but she'd become more than just one of his sister's friends. "Besides," he added, "every time your power flares, it counteracts mine. Just like Ember's cancels mine out. I couldn't if I wanted to. Not that I would. I—I just would never do that.

Not to you."

Allison let out a breath. "Okay." Her voice and sense grew apologetic. "I just—"

"No," Lee said. "You don't have to explain. I totally get it."

Cheryl leaned her head against his shoulder, with eyes closed and a happy smile.

"What do we do now?" Allison asked.

Aside from the crackle of her flames, it had gotten quiet. Lee sensed the others had calmed under his influence and drew closer.

"You can let the walls drop," Lee said. "They're on our side now."

He wasn't sure if there was a limit to how many he could influence at once, but each person he added seemed to shorten his sensory bubble. As much as he wanted their help, it would've been difficult to bring them all to face Jim's team. Instead, he took the time to find out their powers and why they were down in Omicron to begin with.

Of the twelve, six were violent. Lee had no doubts about where they would've ended up. Jim was probably counting on the chaos they'd cause. Lee couldn't risk losing control of them, so he left them paralyzed in their cells.

"Lee," Anna's voice came through his earbud. "Are you there?"

He put a hand to his ear, saw Allison do the same.

"Yes, I'm here," he said. "Anna, what's happening?"

"Everything's a mess," she replied, "but Kevin managed to regain control of a command subsystem. Now we're all working with him to take back the other systems."

Will came on the line.

"Comms are back," he said, "but Jim's team hit the armory. They've remotely set free every Super in confinement. Luckily, Abyss has safety protocols for this situation. It's on lockdown. The only way to open those cells now is with a manual override. The three he sent are probably just now realizing they need me, or pieces of me, to do it. He's got two more headed for the Reliquary. There are hundreds of dangerous artifacts stored in that section, and I can't get a hold of anyone in Pandora."

"What the hell," Lee said. "Don't you have any good news?"

Will said, "They'll be coming for me. Soon."

"That's the good news?"

"Absolutely," Will replied. "I have a plan. I need you to get to the Delta training room. We'll meet you there."

"If their tech could do all this," Lee said, "they're probably listening in."

"I'm counting on it."

Lee asked, "What about Ember? She was with me a few minutes ago, and then she vanished. Is my mother here?"

"Yes. It's difficult to tell," Will said, "with damaged sensors and the chaos around that area, but we think she's in the Nexus chamber. Both covens are most likely there trying to help."

"They need me, then," Lee said, worried for Ember, "to be a conduit or whatever. They can't use the Nexus without me. It'll kill them!"

"No," Will said, his voice steady as ever. "I need you at Delta. Remember what I said earlier?"

Lee let out a frustrated growl.

"We're on our way," he said. To Allison and the seven other Supers, he added, "Let's go."

They headed for the elevator. Once they were inside, the doors closed, and it began to move at an accelerated rate. Lee sensed frantic movement on each floor as they rose, people running or fighting, prone bodies either dead or in dire need of healing.

An explosion erupted a good distance overhead. They came to a grinding halt, as the elevator cables snapped, and safety brakes locked into place. Everyone lost their balance, but only two had fallen over. The lights changed from white to red, casting an eerie pall. Lee helped them both to their feet.

"We need to get those doors opened," he said.

Two guys pulled from either side, revealed they were between floors. With help, one by one, they each climbed out to the upper level. Lee was last to be pulled free.

Red lights flashed down the white corridor. Bodies were all about, more than a dozen toppled over and already dead. All of them were human. Encased in hardening foam, either shot or bludgeoned, none had died from powers.

"This wasn't done by Supers," Lee said. "These people were killed by XTU. Or at least XTU gear."

"It's like that all over," Anna said. "There are rogue units taking advantage of the situation. We think either Jim Armand or Alice Quinn is trying to take over the agency."

"The two from the police station?" Lee asked.

"They could be colluding," Anna continued. "Quinn has direct oversight of the Bullet Squad, while Armand is Deputy Executive Director of Abyss."

Lee sighed. "That's just great. Who the hell can we trust?"

"No one," Allison said, and her hands flared with fire.

"Take the next left," Anna said. "There's a security stairwell just ahead. I can open the panel from here, but I don't know for how long. Whoever hacked the system is still in the server room."

"Be ready," Lee said and led the group down the hall. He sensed four on the left and two on the right where the corridor ended in another hallway. "You three," he said to Cheryl and two guys roughly his age. One could generate and manipulate water, mostly ice, and the other was Body Mastery, like Lee, but focused on physical combat. "Two around the corner," he said and pointed right. To the rest, he added, "Four on the left. None of them Super."

They rounded both corners and engaged. Shards of ice whistled down the right, as the second Super closed with the officers and brought them down with a sideways kick to one and punch to the other. A whirlwind of dirt and metal flecks scoured exposed flesh. Neither officer had a chance to fire off a round.

At the same time, powers raged to the left. Fire went out in streamers, along the wall and twisting down. One officer was lifted off his feet by an ankle, sprayed foam in every direction and was thrown into another. Palm-sized discs of yellow light struck the floor, ricocheted against the right wall and sent the other two officers reeling back. Shots went off in quick succession, rose up in an arc and tore holes in the ceiling.

A second officer with a foam rifle rolled over and fired. The stream bent at the last second, as it struck a curved barrier of green energy, but foam splashed off to the sides. Two on Lee's left were caught at the shoulder and leg, held fast to the wall and floor in a struggle to get away. A third stepped in foam on accident. It bubbled out and up, spread into the pant leg and touched skin.

Allison lunged forward and scorched the officer with a blast. The rifle steamed, went wide, but a spatter caught her arm. She swung to throw it off and got her arm stuck to the wall when the foam suddenly expanded.

She cursed, and like the others, pulled in vain to break free. Short of cutting off her arm or a section of wall, the only way to break down the foam was with a chemical solution. XTU officers carried small canisters of it on their belts, but these four weren't really XTU. They didn't have tactical armor or utility gear, just weapons from the armory.

"You have to keep going," Allison said to Lee. "There's no time to find counteragent."

Lee said, "I can't just leave you here." He looked at the other three caught in foam. What would happen once he was out of range? Even if they couldn't get free, they could still attack Allison. "I won't."

"Listen to me," she said, and her expression turned

hard. "You do what it takes. That's what you do. If anyone can find a way to stop them, it's you." She grabbed hold of him by the shirt and pulled him close for an unexpected kiss. It was brief, barely a moment, but he found himself wanting more. Allison shoved him away. "Now. Go kick their asses."

Lee paralyzed the trapped Supers to be safe but didn't think there was enough time to affect the six officers. Instead he picked up the foam rifle and stuck them to the floor as well.

He led Cheryl and the remaining three of their group further down the corridor.

"Stop," Anna said. A door-shaped panel in the right wall slid open and aside. As they entered, she added, "You need to head up fourteen levels. Be careful, there's been activity in the stairwell."

The panel slid closed behind them.

By the time they hurried up past four floors, Lee sensed two Supers enter his sensory bubble from below. They were ten levels down and gaining.

"Two Supers coming up from behind," he stopped and said to the two who'd taken out the officers in the right hall. "I need you to slow them down."

They gave resolute nods and readied for a fight.

Cheryl might have paired better with the ice thrower if there was more room, but the Body Mastery fighter would do most of the slowing. Energy fields would have been a better pairing with him, but Lee wanted that power along for defense. He had no idea what else was between him and the training room.

Three more floors, and the four clashed. He didn't have to tell the two with him to ignore it and keep going. They didn't even slow at the screams and sounds of fighting. Lee was their only concern.

The security panel slid aside as they reached their goal. Another advantage of being an alien hybrid Super, as hard as they'd run, none of them were winded or even tired.

Two men were waiting with guns drawn. They wore black suits with bulletproof vests and didn't immediately fire. Lee held up both hands.

"We're the good guys," he said. "I swear."

The agents fired single shots simultaneously to either side of Lee. Each struck in the eye, Cheryl and the other Super went down.

Lee rushed forward and grabbed hold of both guns before they could take aim at him.

"They're not ours!" Anna warned. "Quick, head right! Run!"

He ignored the pain of each bullet slamming into his middle and swung the guns inward. Both agents took a slug to the leg and cried out. Lee snatched handfuls of hair, smashed their heads together and pushed them over.

"How far?" he asked and ran down the hall. He'd been to Delta before but not from the stairwell. "I don't recognize any of this."

"Left," Anna said.

He sensed two men and stopped, waited for them to pass.

"Is anyone on our side?" he asked in frustration. When the two men moved on, he rounded the corner and ran.

"It's a big complex," Anna said in way of explanation. "Cerberus is actually three separate divisions. We've had power struggles in the past but nothing like this."

Two more corridors and a similar encounter with guards, Lee finally recognized where he was. The Delta training room was just ahead.

Anna said, "I have no proof, but I think Axial is behind this."

"Discord," Lee said as he approached the steel doors. Details in his mind were clicking into place, though he'd yet to fully work them out. "He wasn't framed," Lee conjectured. "He's a mole. Maybe one of many."

The doors slid open to either side and didn't close once he'd entered.

"So it's more than just revenge," Anna said.

The training room was huge, a square the length of a football field. Will, Brody and Alexandra stood on the other side, and in the middle of the bare chamber were twelve open body bags. Realization of the plan hit Lee like a punch to the stomach. It all hinged on him.

Will said over comms, "We've been infiltrated."

Lee reached the bodies and recognized two right away. It was Tammy and Daniel Sherwood, the brother and sister from the park. He didn't know the others, but for one on the far left. That one would forever be etched in his memories.

It was Frank Culvers.

"Better hurry," Brody said to Lee. "I can't put up shields until you're done."

Alexandra started opening portals and gathering imps. She didn't have to voice her feelings. Neither of them did. Lee could feel it from across the room. They would work to face this crisis, but they were no longer a team. He walked over to join them.

Lee looked out at the corpses. "You told me not to."

"And now I'm telling you different," Will said. "You've seen Jim's power. He can bring down this entire complex on our heads if we don't stop him. We can deal with the fallout later. For now, it's one catastrophe at a time."

"I won't bring him back," Lee said and began to gather his swarm over the corpses. "You can order me all you want. I won't do it."

"That's just great," Alexandra said with a humorless laugh. "Where was this conscience when you killed him?"

The air above the bodies swirled with the blue glow of a trillion motes, a cloud growing denser with every breath.

"I killed him," Lee said and gritted his teeth with the effort, "for the same reason I won't bring him back."

Brody said, "I don't think you get what's coming. It's

not just a few dudes. It's a freaking army."

Lee directed the swarm of cells down into each body. All but Frank's. It had taken nearly everything he had to bring Tammy's body back to life in the alley that day. He was afraid he didn't have what it would take for ten more. Not unless he had time—

Jim and nine other Supers stepped through the doors.

"Ah shit, man," Brody said and took hold of Lee's arm. Lee wasn't even aware he was about to collapse. "Come on, come on."

"Now," Will said. The steel doors closed, and thick bars fell into place, locking it down. He came over to help Lee stand. "Can you work through Brody's shields?"

Sweat rolled off Lee's nose as he gave a nod.

"Go get 'em," Alexandra said, and twenty demons scrabbled off.

Jim threw his arms wide and laughed, welcoming the tiny demons that rushed toward him. The others laughed as well and spread out, powers coming to life in a variety of colors.

Lee knew there wasn't enough time, even with forced replication. The only way he saw left was to use his own body. He watched with a sort of numb fascination as the skin of his hands darkened and began to crack. Cells left him in a trail of motes, passed through Brody's layered shields and joined with the eleven bodies.

"So cute!" Jim called out and vibrated a demon into paste. "I hope you brought more!"

The other nine stopped to deal with the imps, as Alexandra growled and summoned more. Jim kept walking past, showering the floor with the blood and exploded bits of any demon that got too close.

Alexandra had always said she was afraid to open too many portals, that she might not be able to control or keep tabs on more than a dozen. In the enclosed room, with their lives in danger, she'd lost all concern. Over a hundred demons rushed headlong to their death in an attempt to keep her from harm.

Will said, "Now would be a good time."

"I'm trying," Lee rasped.

Brody had broken off to focus on the shields. Will kept Lee on his feet, shouldering his weight.

Jim reached the body bags. "What do we have here? I didn't know you were a collector!" He laughed and kicked Tammy's foot. "Maybe I should start one of my own."

Eleven pairs of ghostly blue eyes opened at once. The corpses sat up. Startled, Jim took a step back. They each turned their heads his way and began climbing to their feet.

"Huh," Jim said. "That's not good."

Lee started to heal.

Will practically hugged him as he set Lee down against the wall. "I knew you could do it," he said. "Just rest now. We got this."

Lee looked out at the ensuing fight, but his attention was drawn to Will's hand, where he had a thumb and forefinger to a button on either side of his watch. Another contingency, he assumed, either ready to blow the complex or maybe just this room. Is that why he had it sealed?

Powers had raged in the sea of demons before the Super corpses joined the fray. Streams of fire scorched flesh, ice scoured it in shards and left behind brittle patches, while darkness erupted in dense clouds that blotted out all sight and sound. Sections of floor broke away into long daggers that pierced, tendrils that gripped or rectangles that struck and shoved. The steel whisper of blades rang out in the throng, accompanied by the tonal rise that ended in explosions.

Jim ran past the undead. "Kill Lee," he told the others, "and these things die with him." He stood before the shields and sent vibrations at the first layer. "Isn't that right, buddy?"

Brody fell back against the wall, as if the assault on his shields had affected his body. Alexandra faltered as well. Her nose had started to bleed, and she wobbled on unsteady legs. Will hurried to catch her as she dropped to her knees.

Lee had regained some of his strength. He stood to face Jim, ignored the chaos in the background.

"Why?" he asked. "What do you get out of all this?"

The first layer broke apart, like flames dying in the wind. Brody cried out. He struggled to strengthen the others but looked on the verge of passing out.

"What do I get?" Jim laughed. "I get to kill you. First off, you're still a dick. And second, I *remember*."

Lee looked away.

"Yeah," Jim said. "This is all on you, buddy. Big man with a gun." He growled and shattered another layer of shield. "See, I owe you. If it wasn't for you, none of this would have happened. There wouldn't be a Bullet Squad. And Joselyn would still be alive."

The animated corpses were strong, much stronger than they'd been alive, but they hadn't been trained to fight in unison. They weren't a team. Four of Jim's were down, beaten and bloody, but five of the corpses had been torn apart.

No more demons joined the fight. Alexandra tried to open a portal beneath Samantha, to send her somewhere else, but ended up catching one of the corpses. It reappeared halfway in the ceiling, its legs no longer dangling.

"Shit," she called out. "Sorry! My bad."

"I'll make you a deal," Jim said congenially, though he kept at the shields. "Let me kill you, and I'll leave. No one else has to die."

"How about I make you a deal," Lee said in a steely tone.

He recalled every cell. The corpses stopped fighting and collapsed as one. No matter the risk, whether his body would adapt, Lee saw no other choice. He sent the entire swarm into Frank.

"Never mind." Lee looked over at Frank, watched the glow of his eyes open. "It's too late. You lose."

*We all lose.*

Jim followed his gaze. Frank climbed to his feet, and the remaining five rushed to face him.

"Either way," Jim said and redoubled his effort against the shields, "you don't get to walk away from this."

"We'll see about that," Lee said, mirroring Jim from earlier.

Fire enveloped Frank, curled and blackened his skin, but he healed within seconds. He grinned when the fire no longer affected him. The same happened when ice struck and an explosion rocked his chest. Blades passed over him without leaving a trace.

Bruiser stepped up, tried to take him with skill and brawn. Frank doubled at the first punch, but subsequent hits had no effect. He lunged with unexpected speed and took hold of Bruiser's wrist, pulled him into an extended bicep that knocked him out cold. Frank slammed his foot down on the exposed neck. The crackle of bones filled the room, and Lee felt Bruiser die.

The other four quickly followed.

Their powers were useless against him. There was nowhere to run, and he ignored their every plea. Frank even took time to kill the unconscious Supers, the ones who posed him no threat, before turning to face Jim.

The last shield had held. Jim vented his frustration and whirled, started walking toward Frank. He screamed with each attack, as if it bolstered his power. Vibrations rippled the air between them, warped and stretched the floor. The entire training room began to shake.

When they met, Frank grabbed him by the neck and threw Jim with such force that he struck a wall upside down. He crumpled to the floor but crawled to his feet.

Again and again, he tried to no avail to shatter Frank, to tear his body apart piece by piece. He attacked the floor beneath Frank, but the corpse was more agile than when it'd been alive. Frank sidestepped the attacks and closed the distance, leveled a kick to Jim's head that sent him sprawling.

Frank leapt and straddled Jim's chest, began to pummel his head over and over. Two strikes, and Jim stopped moving. Another two, and his leg no longer twitched. Frank stood, fists and arms bloodied to the elbow. He looked up straight at Lee and walked toward them.

"It's over," Lee said and tried to recall all his cells. "You can stop now."

Frank laughed, like when Lee had tried and failed to stab him in the middle.

"You never learn," he said in that gravelly voice.

"Lee?" Will asked, eyes wide as Frank struck and broke through the final shield. "Lee!"

His fear had come to pass. Frank's body had adapted to the cells, made them his own. Lee had made him stronger than ever and then lost all control.

Frank took a single step, raised his fist to end Lee, but Will pushed Lee aside. He took a glancing blow to the head and collapsed at Lee's feet.

"Will!" Lee reached down to heal him.

He didn't even have time to sense if Will was still alive when the world flared to white. Lee felt the rush of magic overwhelm his breath before he could see they were in the Nexus chamber. His mother and aunts, his sister and cousins, both covens in a circle were chanting into the turmoil.

They'd summoned him and Frank.

Ember grabbed Frank with both hands and looked in shock when he didn't crumble. He slapped her with the back of his hand, sent her down to crash hard beside Lee.

The roar in Lee's ears made it difficult to think. There

were bodies outside the circle, blurry shapes he couldn't make out through the noise of chanting and thrumming air. Pressure pushed at him from all sides, until his body felt like it was burning from within.

Frank snarled and swatted at the air, as if attacked on all sides by something he couldn't see. He took a step and plunged his fist into one of the girls. It was Tara. Blood spilled from her mouth. She looked down at his wrist, looked him in the eye and took hold with both hands. Thick branches with thorns sprouted from her wound and wrapped around his arm. More rose up from the stone floor at her bare feet, through cracks that erupted with green flame. Her head fell forward, her life gone, but her body held fast. Frank tried to pull away but couldn't break free.

Lee's power burned inside, as if liquid fire coursed through his veins. It kept turning over, doubling, even though he fought against it. The world was brightening to white again, a storm in his mind and body that sought to blind him, to drown out all other sounds but the frantic beat of hearts and words.

He needed a way to be free of it, all the emotion and voices overwhelming his senses. Ember groaned, pushed herself up onto her hands.

*Her power,* Lee thought and reached out a hand.

The last thing he remembered hearing before darkness rose up to claim him was the outward rush of sound and pressure leaving his body...

And Ember screaming.

## - Ember -

The Nexus chamber shimmered into existence. "Geez, Mom!" Ember shouted before the transport chanting even ceased. "I hope you're happy. We didn't get everything." She held out her empty hand in frustration.

"In case you hadn't noticed, we have a situation here," Aunt Gwen growled.

Ember opened her mouth and closed it again, cutting off the smart-ass remark she'd readied for her aunt.

It wasn't just the strained look on her mother's face, but the surging vibrations that came and went in almost painful waves. Dark energy was being forced into the marble chamber, then sucked out again. It rose in layers like echoes, building and subsiding, trying to sync up, but instead falling just short each time. It was like listening to a symphony where the musicians were each playing just a little bit behind or ahead of all the others. It grated on her nerves. "What's happening?"

"Something is trying to get through, banging on the door like a battering ram. If it manages to break through..."

She didn't have to finish. They all knew what would be coming through. They'd been fighting against this potentiality their entire lives. Demons and dark things slipping through the cracks was bad enough. If the Nexus was ripped open, it would be like blowing up the Hoover Dam. Only, instead of water, they'd be drowning in demons. And worse.

"Crap," Tara held up the sack of magical items she had retrieved. "Is there anything in here that can help?"

"I'm not sure," Ember's mother said. "And we don't have time to sort things out. The other coven has been holding the Nexus shut, but we need to help them now, and we wouldn't...we couldn't start without bringing you back first."

Aunt Gwen had already taken up the chant, and now

the rest of Ember's extended family formed a crescent and joined in. The voices of the two covens rose and ebbed in a call and response pattern, a rising and falling point and counterpoint that pushed and pulled against the dark energy that was attempting to break through.

Smoke suddenly poured from the box in Ember's hands. The fabric holding the metal pyramid blackened and turned to ash.

"Ember, set the box on the floor and back away." Her mother's voice was calm, but her face was pinched in fear.

The pyramid's engravings glowed, sending off so much heat, the box in Ember's hands had begun to burn.

"Put it down. Now." Her mother's control seemed forced.

Ember set the box down in the middle of the room and backed away. "What's happening?"

"We didn't lay claim in time." Her mother gripped her by the wrist and pulled her to stand with the rest of their coven.

The dark energy pulsed and grew, pushing back against the covens' magic. The pain in Ember's head grew.

An elongated ghostly image slowly appeared, pulled through the wall as if it were being dragged against its will into the chamber. The ghost struggled, its mouth open in a silent scream of horror. It was drawn inexorably to the center of the room above the pyramid, then sucked downward, disappearing into the swirling vortex that formed over the glowing object.

One by one, other ghosts followed. Each had fear etched into its visage as it was pulled into the center of the room and added to the cone of power that was forming. More and more of the spirits were dragged through the walls and absorbed as if being vacuumed up; their horror so palpable it was nauseating.

"That doesn't look good," Tara said.

"It's not," Ember's mother said. She grabbed the bag from Tara and sorted through it. "Tara, take this." She handed Tara a silver bracelet blackened around the edges with age.

Tara slipped the bracelet onto her wrist, gasping as leafy vines extended from the cusp and wrapped about her forearm.

"Dammit!" Ember's mother cursed, dumping the rest of the bag's contents onto the floor. "It's not here."

Ember shook her head, surprised at her mother's language. "I told you, we didn't get everything before you pulled us out."

"Did you get the ring?" her mother demanded.

"There's one in the box." Ember pointed to the center of the room.

Her mother's face fell and she started for the box.

Aunt Gwen stopped chanting and dove across the space between them. "No," she said. "You can't go near it."

"It's all we have." Ember's mother waved her arm, gesturing around the room at the circle of witches. "Look around you. We don't have a chance without a way to harness this power."

The rest of the coven stared in fascination at the exchange taking place before them, but continued to chant. Years of training and discipline kept them from allowing the spell to fall apart even as their leaders argued. Only their faces showed the strain of fighting the dark energies that pushed and pulled against their magic.

Anguished spirits continued to appear, forced against their will into the growing cyclone.

Ember gulped back her sickness.

"It's all we have."

"No." Aunt Gwen said again. "We have to—"

"It's too late." Ember's mother tried to push past her sister, but Aunt Gwen shoved her aside.

"It's not for you to do," she said and lunged forward, reaching through the swirling energy and into the box. Screaming in pain, she pulled out the ring and shoved it onto her finger. Blue flames curled around her hands, blistering her skin.

"Gwen!" Ember's mother reached out toward her sibling.

Gwen's face twisted in torment. "It's...too much...I can't..."

"We need Lee," Seanna shouted. "We need a conduit."

"Hold on, Gwen." Ember's mother surveyed the room, her tense movements betraying the desperation she tried to hide. "Ember. Seanna. Tara." She motioned to the girls. "I need you to form an inverse power trine around Gwen."

"What?" Ember was aghast. "It'll kill her!"

Ember's mother angrily pushed her into position. "She'll die if we don't bring Lee here. Now. And, as you can see if you open your eyes, I can't spare anyone who is helping to hold back the Nexus."

Ember stared wildly around the room. Both covens were straining to maintain the balance of power as it was. If they let up now, the dark energy would win and the chamber would become an open portal. One through which a slew of demons could emerge and destroy them all. Fighting Supers was one thing, but fighting a hoard of demons? Ember shuddered.

Tara and Seanna were already in position, standing with their backs to Aunt Gwen, who had fallen to her knees. Her body was stiff, every muscle trying to contract at once. Her skin had turned sallow, sweat poured down her face, and her nose dripped crimson. The blue flames licked at her wrists and a fierce growl of pain emanated from her as she fought to control the power.

The two cousins held out their hands and Ember wrapped her fingers around their wrists as they gripped hers. They locked hands and pulled on the rampant power within the room. Ember's mother stepped forward, corralled the gathered energy and shifted it outward. The wave of power rose over them, whipping their hair up and out in a great gale. Then, with an inward rush, the power slammed back into them and with it came Lee.

And Frank Culvers.

Ember's mother cried out.

The air in the room grew dense.

Everything seemed to move in slow motion, as if they were all underwater. Culvers slammed Lee to the floor. Ember released her grip on Tara and Seanna and grabbed for Culvers, realizing too late that he was no longer susceptible to her drain.

He clubbed her with a meaty paw, dropping her to the floor beside Lee.

Then, he lunged for Seanna, but Tara leaped between them. He punched her so hard, his fist went through her chest with a sickening sound, but instead of crumpling, Tara grabbed his arm with both hands and, with her last breath, invoked the twining bracelet on her forearm. Powerful earth magic took form and grew from her and through her. Thick vines sprouted, twining around Culvers, trapping him as her body slumped forward, lifeless.

Aunt Gwen screamed at the sight of her only daughter hanging lifeless before her. With deadly ire glaring from her eyes, she rose from the floor and pointed at Culvers. "Sorefni da te metrom!" she screamed. Green flames rose up and engulfed both Tara and Culvers.

The Super tried to escape, screaming as his body tried to repair itself and become the fire at the same time. His huge hands burned away and reformed as he tried to extricate himself from the magical greenery that twisted around him as the fire slowly won out, burning away flesh and bone and blood, until there was nothing left of him to repair.

With Lee in the room, the balance of power shifted. The chanting of the witches grew more confident and harmonious, the energy it drew on lightened. Their words rose and fell, sounding more like the music of a choir. The pain and fear fell away from them and their faces grew rapturous.

The cyclone above the pyramid pulsed, then reversed direction, pulling Culver's ashes out of the flames and into the swirling mass. With a thunderous clap, the cyclone was sucked into the pyramid.

The chanting of the combined covens rose to a crescendo while the Nexus portal shuddered.

Aunt Gwen collapsed in a heap. A visible arc of power leaped from her to Lee.

Lee writhed on the floor.

Ember got to her hands and knees and crawled toward him.

He reached for her, and she stretched forward to grasp his shaking hand, screaming as the magic shunted through her and slammed back into the Nexus below.

# Sixteen
Mon, Nov 14, 12:13am

## - Lee -

Lee stepped out onto the balcony to join Jen. Her room, as usual, was a mess.

"I still can't see it," she said, peering through a telescope mounted on a tripod.

He was exhausted. After two solid days spent healing others, all he'd wanted to do was sleep. It had been Will's idea to pay Jen a short visit. The newly appointed Director of Supernal had insisted.

"I can." Lee looked up at the midnight sky, where sparse clouds were edged in the brightness of a full moon. "It's there," he said and pointed, "just to the right."

To Lee's naked eye it was barely more than a blurry wave. Digital pictures from space showed it in much better detail. It had a clear blue core, within ripples of silver, and a gold nimbus around it like a thick lazy halo. It was a massive energy cloud roughly the same size as the moon and headed straight for it, as if intelligently guided.

"What do you think it is?" She gave up looking and took a seat in one of the plastic lawn chairs. "Aliens?"

Lee sat in the other chair. "I don't know. The Pillars are alien. So, why not?"

"Yeah," Jen said and glanced down at her phone before quickly putting it away, "but is it the same aliens or new ones? Whatever language was on the Pillars, they should have never used it to send messages into space. It's like putting a big target on our backs. 'Hey, we're a backwater planet with lots of resources you can take!'"

Lee laughed. "Whoever left the Pillars didn't try to take us over."

It felt good to be with her again, even if it was only for a little bit. He'd have to get back to base before long to help with the transition to a new facility. What had happened at Cerberus was a wakeup call for those in charge. They'd finally agreed with Will's plan for a new agency dedicated to Supers, but it also meant a lot of work to be done.

"Verdict's still out on that one," Jen said. "One thing's for sure, all the changes the Pillars made, nothing good's come of it. Well," she added with a smile and glanced down toward the kitchen, where her mother was making dinner, "maybe one thing. But any scientist worth listening to will tell you contact with aliens won't end well for us."

"We *were* contacted," Lee pointed out.

Jen shook her head. "They left a message here long before we were around. That's not contact. It's more like finding a note in a bottle. Sure, we can write a reply and throw the bottle back, but that doesn't mean the same person will find it. Contact is face to face."

"That," she said and pointed up at the approaching energy cloud, "is contact."

# - Ember -

Ember sat on the edge of the bed, staring at the branches of the maple tree silhoueted by the moon outside the round attic window. Tara had chosen this room for the view of the tree and the sound the evening breeze made as it fluttered its tri-tipped leaves. She said it reminded her of them.

The three of them.

A sharp rap at the door startled her.

Ember wiped her eyes on the hem of her shirt. *Crap!* Her mascara was running. Again. "What?"

The door swung open a few inches and Seanna peeked in. "Hey."

"Hey," Ember said.

Seanna stood poised on the threshold. "How's your mom?" Seanna's voice was raw.

"Hell," Ember gestured for her to enter. "How are any of us?"

"Aunt Gwen's still critical?"

"Yeah, but she's a stubborn old witch. Right?" Ember gave her cousin a weak smile.

"I still can't...fire...it's just—"

"Don't." Ember cut her off. "Just don't."

"Sorry." Seanna crossed the room and sat beside her on the bed, shoulders slumping. "Your mom's...reassigning me. Again."

"I know." Ember put a hand on Seanna's arm. "I'm sorry."

"It's not your fault. What happened to you. To Tara..." Seanna shook her head, unable to finish.

"Doesn't mean I'm not sorry," Ember told her.

"What's it like?" Seanna asked.

"What?" Ember said. "Connecting with a magical conduit when all hell is trying to break loose?" She shivered. "You were there. It's like sticking a fork in a wall socket while

standing in a puddle of salt water when lightning strikes."
"Not that. I meant after. What happened with you and
Lee. One instant, we have a conduit. It was amazing, beyond
anything we'd ever tapped into. Then, it was suddenly
gone...like a switch was turned off." Seanna shuddered.

Ember stood up, then sat back down again, struggling
with the restless energy that washed over her in waves
every time she recalled the Nexus chamber. "Honestly,
before all of this other stuff happened—with the pillars and
Supers and now that thing hovering in the sky—I would
have called it weird. But now..." Her fingers strayed to
the pendant at her throat, worrying at the heart-shaped
apatite Tara had polished and strung for her on her twelfth
birthday. "Whatever happened to Lee and me in the Nexus
chamber, I don't think it's over."

Seanna sat up. "What do you mean?"

Ember clutched at the pendant "I mean, it feels like
the Rumbling has started again. Only this time it's coming
from inside us."

## Acknowledgements

Thank you so much to Melissa Clazie for all her time and effort in reading my work. Her students at La Sierra High School in California should consider themselves lucky.

--J.A. Giunta

A huge shout out to my amazing beta readers, Dawn VonEpp and Linda Johnson James. Thanks for catching my inconsistencies and pointing out my areas of opportunity and doing so in such a kind and generous manner! Any errors that slipped through are all on me.

--S.A. Skinner

## ABOUT THE AUTHORS

SHARON SKINNER grew up in a small town in northern California where she spent her time reading books, making up plays and choreographing her own musicals (when she wasn't busy climbing trees and playing baseball.) She's been writing stories since the fourth grade, filling page after page with fantastical creatures, aliens, monsters and, of course, heroes.

She spent four years in the Navy, where she served aboard the first US ship to carry women to sea. She has also repaired laboratory and hospital equipment, worked as a warehouse production manager, telephone sales representative, professional trainer, visual information systems coordinator, grants professional and consultant. Somewhere along the way, she managed to obtain a B.A. in English and a Masters in Creative Writing from PRescott Collge.Her Young Adult and Middle-Grade novels tend to explore complex relationships, particularly those between mothers and daughters.

Still a voracious and eclectic reader, Sharon also loves drawing, arts and crafts, sewing, and costume-making (especially steampunk). Her guiltiest pleasure is online gaming, and her biggest weakness is home-made, double-dark chocolate fudge. She lives in Arizona with her husband and three annoying but lovable cats.

You can find her online at sharonskinner.com

JOE GIUNTA has been writing for most of his adult life, in between bouts of serious online gaming. He continues to write fantasy novels, in both adult and young adult genres, in his selfish need to create worlds that amuse him. That others enjoy the work is a happy coincidence but one that he fully appreciates.

With a Bachelor of Arts in English from the Arizona State University, he is both an avid reader and addicted gamer. He writes novels full-time and longs for the day when those efforts pay some bills—seriously, even just one bill would be nice. For those of you who purchased copies of any of his books, he is eternally in your debt. Note: this is not a legally binding contract.

He lives with his wife, Lori—who is not only a doctor of both internal medicine and psychiatry, she's also an avid gamer! His daughter, Ada Rose, is fourteen at the time of this writing. She has yet to read a single one of his books, but at least she reads others. They all live happily ever after in the perpetual summer that is central Arizona (technically there is a winter, for about three weeks in January).

Joe attributes much of his success in life to good looks, incredible talent, luck, modesty, air conditioning, friends & family and his DVR—though not necessarily all in that order. Oh, and his computer.

He hopes you enjoyed this book immensely and will share it with a friend.

Visit him online at jagiunta.com

95334444R00165

Made in the USA
Columbia, SC
14 May 2018